THE PI...

OPEN FOR BUSINESS

The Waldo Wise Series

Book 1

ISAAC FRENCH

Copyright © Isaac French 2021
This book is sold subject to the condition that it shall not, by way of trade or otherwise, be lent, resold, hired out, or otherwise circulated without the publisher's prior consent in any form of binding or cover other than that in which it is published and without a similar condition including this condition being imposed on the subsequent publisher.
The moral right of Isaac French has been asserted.
ISBN-13: 9798491706907

This is a work of fiction. Names, characters, businesses, organizations, places, events and incidents either are the product of the author's imagination or are used fictitiously. Any resemblance to actual persons, living or dead, events, or locales is entirely coincidental.

To Liz and her late sister Roni.

CONTENTS

ACKNOWLEDGEMENTS i
Chapter 1 .... *1*
Chapter 2 .... *10*
Chapter 3 .... *20*
Chapter 4 .... *26*
Chapter 5 .... *32*
Chapter 6 .... *40*
Chapter 7 .... *67*
Chapter 8 .... *86*
Chapter 9 .... *97*
Chapter 10 .... *120*
Chapter 11 .... *137*
Chapter 12 .... *159*
Chapter 13 .... *163*
Chapter 14 .... *177*
Chapter 15 .... *203*
Chapter 16 .... *211*
Chapter 17 .... *227*
Chapter 18 .... *244*
Chapter 19 .... *251*
Chapter 20 .... *253*
ABOUT THE AUTHOR 260

ACKNOWLEDGEMENTS

Thanks to my friend Vicky Dunnicliffe. She texted me whilst I was on holiday to say that she was bored with her job and asked if we could start a private detective agency. I didn't think she was serious, so I wrote about it instead. Any resemblance between Vicky and the character Jac in the novels is fortuitous.

My thanks to Judith Saville for the wine guard she gave me and the card that went with it. I have reproduced the story and the card in this novel. I hasten to add, there is no resemblance between Jude and Harriett.

Vicky
You are to blame for all this rape & pillage.
Love
Nigel or Isaac [french],
xxx   (This needs practice)

CHAPTER 1

Jac Beauley's spirits were low, mostly self-inflicted. She sat in the front office in the hope of greeting their first client. They had been open a week and there had been no interest.

Jac was staring at the floor and reflecting on their evening. She and Waldo had gone out for a bite to eat. A few drinks led to a few more drinks and then to a few more drinks. The journey from the restaurant to Waldo's flat was no more than five hundred yards but there were many pubs in between and it took them four and a half hours. By the time they reached home, they had drowned their sorrows.

Jac was pondering as to the wisdom of calling themselves 'The PI Shop' and was expecting people to ask for steak and kidney pies. 'No, no, you have misunderstood, we are PIs, you know, Private Investigators. Like on the tele.' She didn't know quite what she would say.

Suddenly, the office door opened, and the Victorian shop bell announced the arrival of a visitor. Jac came to her senses very quickly. Before her stood a tall, gaunt man staring wildly at her, his eyes betrayed fear.

She went straight into work mode, stood, and in a confident tone announced, "Hello, my name is Jac Beauley, how can I help you?"

"How do you do, Robert Harmsworth," he responded quite formally.

Jac worked on instinct and invited him straight into the interview room, which would give them privacy. She thought this man needed privacy.

"Please take a seat."

They sat opposite each other. Jac thought about starting with their planned opening remarks about the agency but abandoned these and went for the direct question, "What's the problem Mr Harmsworth?"

There was a long pause, but this did not faze her; she had learnt long ago just to let people reflect and prepare themselves, they speak when they are ready.

"Ms Beauley, I have thought long and hard about this and whether or not to involve you and your partner. I have concluded that you are the right people for me, but it doesn't make the task of telling you the problem any easier."

There was another long pause before Robert Harmsworth blurted out, "I sexually abused my daughter."

He looked up at Jac to see if there was any reaction, but he detected none. Inside, however, Jac's heart was beating fast and was thinking, 'Oh my God, what have we here!' They both sat in silence. Jac waited to see what else might emerge.

"It was a long time ago, but the guilt has never left me, and I don't want to end my days without having owned up to my guilty secret and having been properly punished."

"I understand, that is very natural," Jac said in a supportive tone. "I am not sure how we can help you, however, why do you not just go to the police and tell them your story?"

"The problem is I fear the police will not only investigate me, that is fine, but they will go in with their big boots and stir up a hornet's nest with my daughters, including the two not affected by my behaviour. I'm not sure my daughter who was involved will be any too pleased either. This calls for the upmost sensitivity, Ms Beauley, at least, in the early stages."

At this point Waldo knocked and poked his head round the interview room door. In subdued tones he enquired, "Can I get either of you a tea or a coffee?"

"Waldo, can I introduce Mr Robert Harmsworth. Mr Harmsworth, Mr Waldo Wise, my partner."

"Yes, I know. Good morning Mr Wise. I am pleased to meet you."

He had clearly done his homework carefully. Perhaps, he had even been keeping the office under surveillance, Jac thought.

Waldo and Robert Harmsworth shook hands and Waldo was impressed by the firmness of his grip and the steadiness of his gaze. He felt that he was being assessed.

"Would you like a coffee?" Waldo thought that he was the sort of man who would prefer a coffee. He took a stab at strong, black, no sugar.

"I'd love a coffee please, black, no sugar."

Ooh, spot on, I'm a natural for this business, he thought smugly.

"If you have no objection, Mr Harmsworth, I would like Waldo to join us; I would find it very helpful."

"I have no objection at all," he responded firmly, clearly growing in confidence.

Waldo returned with coffees and, to make it less confrontational, he sat on one of the unoccupied sides of the square and not beside Jac. For Waldo's sake, Jac decided to summarise the present position.

"Mr Harmsworth has explained that he sexually abused his

daughter many years ago," she began, in a very matter-of-fact tone, "and he wants to face up to his guilt and to take the punishment he believes he deserves. He prefers to involve us at this stage, as opposed to the police, as we will be more sensitive in handling the investigation and, in particular, in dealing with the two daughters not involved in the issue. He thinks that even the younger one, who was the victim of the abuse, will not be best pleased by his decision to go public. Is that a fair summary, Mr Harmsworth?"

"Yes, very fair. Shall I continue?" added Robert Harmsworth.

"Before you go any further, can we just gather a few facts, so that we have a fuller context in which to understand your story? Oh, and do you mind if we switch on the recorder? It will save us making too many notes during the discussion and will allow us to concentrate on what you have to say."

They were relieved that he had no difficulty with this. Mr Harmsworth explained that his days as a reporter on the local paper cured him of any shyness over such matters.

"Your full name and date of birth please, Mr Harmsworth. Also, when you were married? Your wife's name and age? And the names, ages of your daughters? etc. Perhaps you could just give us a potted history of all …" Jac was about to say 'the key players' and thought better of it, "… those involved."

It was clear to Waldo and Jac that Robert Harmsworth was an educated man and, despite his seventy-six years, was articulate and able to order his thoughts with absolute precision.

The details clarified, he returned to delivering the outline of his story. Waldo and Jac sat silently, and without movement, in case they distracted him.

"So, in a nutshell, after my wife's death, I brought up Lucy. The first couple of years were fine but when she reached puberty, at twelve, things got out of hand. Audrey and Linda had left home by then and we were on our own. Strangely, Lucy does not seem to bear me any ill-will, but we deliberately avoid getting too close nowadays. It seems sensible."

The story had been delivered with his head bowed and his eyes fixed on a knot in the tabletop. It appeared to help him concentrate. For the first time in five or so minutes, he raised his head and looked straight at Jac, avoiding Waldo's eyes altogether.

"So, can you help me?"

They had decided that after gathering the outline facts, their tactic would be to ask questions of clarity, hence Waldo weighed in to determine exactly what he was expecting at the end of the process.

"What I am looking for is an objective and well-researched report into the relationship between me and my daughter and then for you to accompany me to a lawyer or to the police and to lay out the case for me."

Jac chipped in.

"I understand the necessity for an objective report. But you are extremely articulate and well able to deliver your own report and all the nuances of the situation. I am confused as to what we could add at that point."

"True. Actually, I am still in two minds as to whether to involve a lawyer. I might go straight to the police and then I really would need you."

Jac, without any consultation with her partner, announced, "Well, we are sure that we can help you, Mr Harmsworth. We would be pleased to investigate the matter, but we would need you to delegate full responsibility to us to investigate the issue in the way that we judge necessary to fulfilling your requirements. This may not always please you but if the police and the courts are to be convinced by our objectivity, then we must be seen to act independently and not be subject to your control, even though you have commissioned us. Is that understood?"

"I can see how that would be necessary. I accept that," he said seriously.

In front of him, they then pieced together the number of days that each part of the investigation would take and how much time would be required for writing up the report and for supporting him during the follow-up phase. They concluded that it would take a minimum of twenty days and a maximum of twenty-five days, making the costs a little shy of fifteen thousand pounds.

"Is that within your budget, Mr Harmsworth?"

"I had allowed ten thousand for this element and a further ten thousand for the lawyer. I realised how costly it would be, but this is very important to me, and the money is the least of my worries. Fifteen thousand is fine."

"In that case," Waldo concluded, "if you will excuse me, I will go and complete a contract, so that we can both sign it before you leave. Would you like another coffee?"

"A drink of water would be very acceptable, thank you."

Waldo brought them both a drink of water. He left Jac and Robert Harmsworth chatting about North Street in a fairly relaxed but formal way, whilst he completed the contract. On returning, he talked Robert Harmsworth through the details of the contract.

"Naturally, Ms Beauley and I have not yet had an opportunity to discuss how we might handle matters, but my view is that I should do the fieldwork with your two daughters not directly involved in the case and any general matters and Ms Beauley should explore the issues with you and your daughter Lucy. Does that make sense?"

"That sounds very acceptable, and I would be very happy to work closely with you, Ms Beauley."

"And I with you, Mr Harmsworth," responded Jac.

"So, it is agreed. Let us sign the contract and we will plan our modus operandi this afternoon and begin first thing tomorrow morning."

They all signed and shook hands. Jac showed Mr Harmsworth out and they shook hands once again.

"I'll be in touch very soon," she added, still shaking his hand.

"I am pleased that we will be working together, Ms Beauley. Bye for now."

He managed a very small smile, which she reciprocated.

Once the door was closed and it was safe, she rushed to the back room and hugged Waldo.

"Well, not quite what we were expecting but we are underway. I thought we would be dealing with victims, not with perpetrators, but life leads one in strange directions sometimes," Jac mused.

"Who is to say who is the victim in these cases?" Waldo added philosophically.

π

That afternoon, Jac and Waldo sat down in the interview room to begin the planning process. Jac opened the discussion.

"My view is that if we are to remain credible with the police, we need to carry out a dawn search of his premises and seize all likely incriminating evidence. I am thinking of computers, receipts, pornographic magazines or books, DVDs, CDs, photographs, anything which is likely to indicate that his child abuse might have gone further than he has admitted. I think we have to view this not just as a case in support of the client, though it is primarily that, but a gathering of evidence, which will support his confession and support or challenge his claim that his abuse was limited to his youngest daughter."

"Gosh, is there any wonder I fancy you?" Waldo said admiringly and then added, "A dawn raid, how exciting."

"Not raid, silly, search, and I was also thinking that it might be more like my dawn, rather than yours, you know about nine thirty, ten o'clock."

"Don't ruin it for me, Jac. I was just beginning to warm to this job. Would such a raid, sorry search, just be the two of us or do we need to recruit some extra help? If I remember those houses in St. Mary Redcliffe, they are very tall houses and there will almost certainly be attics and maybe cellars."

"Good point. I think we need help. Let's keep it in the family, if we can, that'll save complications. How about my brother-in-law Max, who is a computer expert and the son of your friend who died, what was his name? Yes, of course Josh. He will add some muscle in the event that we have to do any heavy lifting. Is he allowed to work outside his contract with the rugby club?" Jac asked.

"I expect Josh will do it for free, so there would be no question of breaking his contract. We'd better see if they are available and willing to play before we go any further. Are we thinking of tomorrow morning?"

"I think it would look good in the report if we were seen to search his home the day after his visit."

Some quick phone calls won them the help they needed, and Josh said he could acquire a white van in which to carry away the evidence.

Waldo started to contemplate the difficulty of his part in proceedings and with a concerned look on his face, he asked, "How am I going to interview the two older sisters without giving the game away? Clearly, they are going to have to know sooner or later but, in the early stages of the investigation, I think it would be better to do it under the guise of something else."

Jac leant over to give Waldo a hug for no particular reason and then offered the following.

"Supposing we pretend to be carrying out a research programme into the relationship between the sexual behaviour of parents and the impact on their offspring. What I am thinking is that Harmsworth senior has volunteered to be part of the programme and is hoping his daughters will also participate. If they agree, that would give you the freedom to talk about familial matters in general and sexual behaviour in particular. Whatever we come up with, you have to be able to explore their perceptions of his sexuality."

"Nice one, Jac. I will devise the outline of a research programme and protocol, if you could then refine and tweak them for me. Perhaps you could tell Robert Harmsworth of our plan and then get him to win his daughters over to the idea."

Then, they set about making detailed plans for the next morning.

CHAPTER 2

As part of the bargain for their cooperation, Waldo had promised Max and Josh a cooked breakfast and it was well underway when the doorbell rang. They both arrived at the same time and introduced themselves. Jac opened the door to them and greeted them warmly.

"Am I OK to leave the van outside for the moment, Jac?" Josh enquired.

"Yes, it's fine, you have an hour, and I'm hoping we'll be well underway by then."

Jac peered past Josh at the vehicle he had managed to acquire. It was not quite her idea of a white van, nor did she think it had the right image for the agency. It was clearly very old and had a strange off-white hue with large patches of an interesting red-brown colour, which reminded her strongly of rust. Josh spotted her looking at the van and misinterpreted her expression.

"Don't worry, she won't break down. She's as strong as an ox and really reliable," said Josh in a jolly, boyish manner.

"She normally takes all the colts' gear to away matches. I gave her a quick brush out this morning, but she smells a bit high, I'm afraid. Perhaps you and Waldo should go by car and me and Max take the van," Josh said encouragingly.

"Yes, good thinking. Morning Max and how are you?"

She gave him a peck on the cheek and a quick hug.

"Thank you both so much for volunteering."

"We are both looking forward to it. We were just discussing it before you came to the door. Such excitement, we're not used to it."

"Come on up, breakfast is nearly ready. Waldo has been at it for a half hour."

They walked into the kitchen to be greeted by the most wonderful smells and the prospect of a cooked breakfast. Max turned down the bacon and sausage but welcomed the rest.

"I am sorry, Max, I hadn't realised you were vegetarian."

As is the wont of vegetarians these days, he corrected the non-believer with the phrase, 'I eat fish and eggs.'

Ignoring this comment, Waldo replied, "Fortunately, I cooked the meaty bits in a separate pan. Tea everyone?"

"I'd prefer decaf coffee, if I may," said Max.

"No problem, Max, I'll put on a pot right away."

Just before half eight, they made their way downstairs all geared up for the search. Over breakfast, Jac had given the lads a briefing as to their roles and how they were to deal with any awkward questions from Robert Harmsworth. Neither of the young men was told of the issue, merely the material that was being sought. It was explained that they were working for Mr Harmsworth and this search was in his interest, only he may not recognise it. A little puzzled, they both decided to let it ride in the interests of progress.

Josh and Max arrived first and parked the van directly outside Robert Harmsworth's house. Jac and Waldo arrived shortly afterwards and parked in the nearby pay and display car park. After a little kerfuffle about finding the right change – it is strange how the smaller details catch out the uninitiated – they joined the others in front of the van.

The jolly start to the day suddenly turned very serious as Jac assumed her work persona. In deep and serious tones, she made an announcement.

"I am going to explain why we are here to Mr Harmsworth and then I will signal for you to join me, as soon as I have won his approval. We must stick to our roles, unless I say otherwise."

Waldo then joined in, adopting an equally serious note, adding, "Right, the time is exactly nine o'clock on Thursday 24th June. Let the search commence and good luck everyone."

They all enjoyed this rather dramatic statement and the tension rose.

Jac rang the doorbell and waited several minutes before Robert Harmsworth opened the door in his dressing gown. A rather fetching garment for one of seventy-six, Jac thought.

"Good morning Mr Harmsworth. We are so sorry to disturb you at this time. Mr Wise and I and two associates from the agency would like to undertake a search of your property with a view to looking for any possible evidence which may support or challenge the claim you put to us yesterday."

Robert Harmsworth could not believe what he was hearing. He was silent and bemused. Jac explained in a little more detail.

"In order that our investigation is credible to the police and to the court, we have decided that it is imperative that we carry out a full search of the property and that we take away any objects which may be material to the case. It is exactly what the police would do. Also, it is important that the search happens today, as the longer we leave it, the more likely you are to dispose of items, which may further incriminate you; or that is how the police would see it. May we please come in and begin the search?"

Uncharacteristically, Robert Harmsworth laughed out loud.

"Well, you are even smarter than I thought. Of course, come in. Where are your colleagues?"

Jac turned and beckoned the others to join her. Robert Harmsworth stood on the threshold of the door and welcomed them all warmly.

"Well, what will you two think of next? Whose idea was this anyway?"

"I hate to confess, it was mine," said Jac.

"Let me introduce our colleagues, Max and Josh."

"I know you from somewhere, young man," Robert Harmsworth said, shaking Josh's hand. "Have we met before? You seem familiar, somehow."

"I don't think so, sir, I have no recollection of having met you."

Oops, their first mistake of the morning. Josh was well known in rugby circles, and it was possible that Robert Harmsworth was a rugby fan. They had never thought of that and Jac reflected on how careful they would have to be in this game, if they were going to be successful.

That hurdle over, at least for now, they began to implement the agreed plan. They systematically photographed, and then named and numbered each room and the link corridors in a search log. Max and Josh then placed bags in the rooms for the collection of small items of evidence and Jac recorded the bag numbers in the log. Jac had bought reusable bags the previous afternoon. They were all marked,

'Shop in North Street – your Quality Eco Centre'.

The task of mapping the building completed, they then split into two teams. Jac and Josh agreed to cover the hallway, cupboard under the stairs, dining room, study, kitchen, downstairs loo, garden and shed – there was no cellar – and Max and Waldo the drawing room, bedrooms, bathroom, and attic. Josh was also given the task of loading the bags and ensuring the security of the van, whist Jac controlled and recorded all of the bags and other items being loaded. She was determined that there would be no confusion over the source of evidence.

Under Jac's instructions, Josh concentrated on the sitting room, just off the hallway, inside the front door. He liked the house very much, nice proportions, tastefully though minimally furnished, a good feeling. He found nothing which might be relevant to the investigation, so he spent a little time looking out of the window and admiring the view across to the city and docks. Jac came in to find him daydreaming.

"Are you slacking, young man," she teased, and just as if it were Waldo, punched him on the arm. She was stunned by the solid muscle that her fist struck.

"My God, what are you made of?"

Without permission, she squeezed his arms and then gently punched his stomach to find another solid wall of resistance. He pretended to reel back in agony, resisting making any noise, in case Robert Harmsworth was alerted by their tomfoolery.

"Give me a hug, just to let me experience what it feels like?" she whispered, conspiratorially.

He obliged and enveloped her in his arms and gently squeezed her body, just as he did his girlfriend Abby. For the first time in her life,

Jac felt a twinge of excitement with a man. A pulse of excitement ran through her body. She kissed him gently on the cheek and escaped his grasp.

As she worked, she reflected on how she seemed to feel the same way towards Josh and his wall of muscle, as Waldo felt about camp men, loving it but not really wanting to translate it into action. She concluded that Waldo was right, however, and that she did have the vestige of hetero in her, she just hadn't realised what would trigger it. She felt slightly ashamed that it was something so mundane.

Jac asked Josh to carry out a thorough inspection of the hallway and then the cupboard under the stairs. The hallway only took seconds and again revealed nothing, so he started clearing a way into the cupboard. Tucked just inside the door, he discovered a very expensive but quite old pair of leather slippers. The right slipper appeared to be stained but it was too dark to see properly. So, he backed out of the cupboard into the hallway, in order to inspect the evidence more carefully. He came to the conclusion that the dark stain on the leather upper was blood. He wondered whether it could be human blood. He realised that they were looking for evidence of pornography, and that this was not a murder case, but he concluded that one crime could easily lead to another. He put the slippers into an evidence bag and crawled back into the cupboard to look for more incriminating evidence; he was warming to this detective business.

He was just completing the search, alas having found nothing further of interest, when he heard a discussion between Jac and Robert Harmsworth about the computer.

"I am sorry, Mr Harmsworth, if we are going to do this properly, then we have no alternative but to remove your laptop and fully investigate its contents. I promise, we will take very good care of it and will return it to you as soon as we are able, probably by Monday or Tuesday. I am sorry."

Robert Harmsworth gave way, so Josh emerged from the cupboard and took the laptop to the van.

Josh had covered the floor on the inside of the van with a grey blanket to give it a measure of respectability. Alas, its outward appearance remained challenging.

For the next two hours the search proceeded apace but only a few suspicious items were transferred to the van. At one point, to save any argument with a traffic warden, Josh drove the van around the block, returning when the coast was clear.

Max and Waldo also had sparse pickings in the drawing room and the bedrooms, just a few books and papers, which they popped into bags for later examination. There was just one possible piece of evidence, a series of exercise books, which seemed to contain Robert Harmsworth's diaries. A cursory look revealed that they were unexciting and not very revealing but Waldo decided that they should be scrutinised carefully, in case they contained hidden gems.

Max and Waldo moved to the attic and looked through a collection of items that Robert Harmsworth couldn't quite throw away or were family treasures. They were particularly taken with a number of family albums, which included photographs of the children growing up and Waldo thought some may coincide with when the abuse was alleged to have taken place. He decided to take these away for further scrutiny. Then Max found an old computer tower. It had clearly not been used for many years but, they concluded, it could be the source of valuable information. The tower was taken and loaded into the van for later analysis. They made no other finds.

Jac and Josh had completed their search of the ground floor areas. They had taken away a number of items but, in truth, Jac didn't believe they had found anything that was likely to be helpful or incriminating.

Jac told Josh to give the garden and garden shed a thorough going over, whilst she up-dated her record of the search.

Josh found Robert Harmsworth in the garden reading his book. When he saw Josh approaching, he marked his page with a bookmark, closed the book, and looked up at Josh.

"Your face is very familiar to me, young man," he repeated.

Josh was not best pleased. It was the second time that Robert Harmsworth had called him 'young man' and, to add insult to injury, Jac referred to him in the same way, when they were in the drawing room. Josh was beginning to dislike it rather. He looked down and spotted the title of the book and seized his moment to give himself a little more street cred.

"Oh, I thoroughly enjoyed that book. Not great literature but a jolly good read and inspired me to visit India. Are you enjoying it?"

"I am indeed. I spent some time in India back in the fifties, as a young reporter. A truly wonderful country but, as you know, a country of huge contrasts. The poverty and ill-health are frightening. Am I free to go into my kitchen now and make a cup of tea?" he added, as a postscript.

"I am sure you are, Mr Harmsworth, but just to be sure, I'll ask Ms Beauley for you."

He dashed off and Jac returned with him to the garden.

"You are free to come indoors now if you like, Mr Harmsworth. Would you like me to make you a cup, so that you can stay out here?" Jac volunteered.

"That would be very kind, but I will come inside if I may, it's getting rather chilly. That wind is quite vicious."

Jac and Robert Harmsworth went indoors and left Josh free to search the garden.

The garden was quite small. Most of it was given over to lawn, not very well cared for by Josh's reckoning, and a raspberry patch, which if it didn't receive attention soon, would take over the lower end of the garden completely. He found nothing of interest in the garden itself, so turned his attention to the shed. There were the usual garden implements, all rather old and rusty and clearly not in daily use; a mower that had seen better days but probably just about worked; a work bench and tools which were equally in need of care and attention; and a collection of various substances designed to kill bugs, enhance growth, and generally ease the lot of the domestic gardener – no ecologist, thought Josh. Then he spotted what appeared to be a sports bag underneath the work bench, but it was covered in muck and grime and had not been moved for many years. He yanked it out and a huge spider ran across the floor towards him. He screamed and rushed out of the shed. Fortunately, no one heard him, and his manhood remained intact. It would not do for his new fan, Jac, to realise his fear of spiders.

He opened the bag's zip, very carefully, lest there were further monsters in hiding. Strangely, the contents appeared to be in pristine order, clean and unharmed by the ravages of time. He discovered masks, handcuffs, chains and padlocks, a sparkly bra with holes at vital points, G strings and a whip. Wow, what a find, he thought. It looked like sadomasochism to him. He knew little of S & M but decided the find may be of great importance to the investigation and should be scrutinized later. He tied a tag to the bag's handle, wrote 'garden shed/under bench' on it and took it to the van. He returned to the shed to complete his search but found nothing more, so he went back indoors, declaring he had finished his task.

The search over, Jac and Waldo felt rather disappointed that it had revealed so little and yet, in another way, considered it was probably a good thing, as it seemed to support Robert Harmsworth's contention that his misdemeanours were confined to his daughter.

Josh and Max retreated to the van and left Jac and Waldo to tidy up the loose ends with Robert Harmsworth.

"Thank you so much for your patience, Mr Harmsworth. You'll be relieved to know that we have completed the search. Thank you for your cooperation and apologies once again for having disturbed your morning."

They shook hands and said their farewells.

CHAPTER 3

The next morning, Waldo was on early duty. He went through his usual routine. He unlocked the front door of the office, went outside to observe the goings-on in the street, nodded to one or two people, closed the front door after him and was just about to go through his internal office routine of lifting the receiver to make sure the phone was still working, when it rang.

He hesitated before answering it and rehearsed what he was going to say. He assumed the right posture and prepared to produce the right tone of voice, friendly but subdued.

"Good morning, Waldo Wise, The PI Shop, how can I help you?"

"Hello, my name is Cameron Mackenzie."

He stumbled over the next few words and Waldo was unable to understand what he said. He then added, "The difficulty is knowing where to start."

"Ideally we should meet and take time to discuss matters," Waldo advised. "The first hour is free, so I can assess whether we are able to help you and you can make up your mind whether we are the right people for you. So, if you would like to tell me very briefly the nub of the issue, that would do for now."

In a sharp Scottish brogue, he spat out the words, "My partner is cheating on me."

"What makes you think that, Mr Mackenzie?" Waldo was calm

and controlled.

"We have been together for twelve years and have recently been through a civil partnership. From my perspective, it is all wonderful, but I detect that all is not well with Hugo. He seems to be changing. There is nothing I can put my finger on. He is still affectionate, he has not changed his routine significantly, but I know all is not well. I can only think there is somebody else."

"OK, but he may not be being unfaithful, there may be other issues. Let's meet and discuss this further. Would you be able to come to the office or would you prefer to meet in a pub or a cafe?"

"I would prefer to meet in a cafe if that is alright with you. Is it possible for us to meet today?"

"Sure. Where do you want to meet?"

"Let's meet in The Sandwich Bar, it's a cafe in East Street, in Bedminster. I can relax more easily there. It is half way up on the left-hand side, as you are walking towards the supermarket."

"No problem."

Cameron Mackenzie asked, "How will I recognise you?"

"I'll wear my blue scarf. I'll buy a cup of tea and find a quiet table. You join me when you feel ready. Does that sound OK?"

"That sounds fine."

"Good. Look forward to meeting you in ... what shall we say, half an hour. Bye for now."

Waldo put down the phone with a sense of relief and exhilaration. He called out, "Jac, we may have another customer. Doesn't sound a very exciting case but you never know."

She came running into the front office.

"Tell me, what is it?"

"Oh, a relationship problem. It is a couple of gay guys who have been together for twelve years and have just been through a civil ceremony and are having problems. Sounds more a case of misunderstanding than philandering but if we can help clear it up for them that will be great."

"Philandering! What era do you live in? Are you sure you are cut out for this business?"

"I haven't got time to discuss my choice of vocabulary. I promised I'd meet him in half an hour."

"Anyway, I thought that we weren't going to take on relationship problems, gay or straight," Jac challenged him.

"Beggars can't be choosers," he shouted, as he put on his coat and blue scarf and grabbed a notebook.

"Don't forget the contract. I am beginning to worry where the next meal is coming from."

She kissed him and wished him good luck.

He set off at a good pace, reflecting the excitement of the moment. He then slowed when he realised that he must give himself time to think out his approach; all the plans had been about how to deal with the initial interview in the office. A cafe in Bedminster had not been how they had envisaged matters.

To get to East Street, he had to walk the whole length of North Street, before taking a dogleg into a pedestrianized area.

East Street was buzzing with activity and early morning shoppers, but it had a very dilapidated look. The shoppers were laden with heavy bags and struggling with disabilities or poverty or just with life. He passed a number of cafes, all possible candidates, before he reached the Sandwich Bar. Outside was a stand advertising full English breakfasts for three pounds fifty, served all day. 'I get the picture,' he thought to himself.

He ordered tea and a bacon bap. He didn't really want a bap, he just felt obliged to order something, as he only had a twenty-pound note.

"Oh, the toffs are in today, Mary, a twenty-pound bloody note."

"I'm sorry about that, it's all I have. Do you want me to go and change it?" Waldo asked.

"No, only joking mate, I've plenty of change really. You don't come from 'ereabouts?"

"I've just moved into North Street, down the other end."

"Blimey, its going all posh down there, is it? 'Ere you are, mate, cuppa and bacon bap. Enjoy."

He escaped the attentions of the cafe owner as quickly as he could and found a seat as far away from the counter as possible. Not exactly a discreet entrance; in this trade discreet entrances are de rigueur, he mused. He considered he should stop using phrases like de rigueur, it didn't fit with his new profession or his new surroundings. It also reminded him how much he disliked the use of the word 'enjoy', as new catering shorthand. His ponderings, however, were soon interrupted.

"Hello, I am Cam Mackenzie. Are you Mr Wise?"

"I am, Waldo Wise, very pleased to meet you, Cam."

Clutching his coffee, Cam joined Waldo.

Waldo observed that he had a good smile and the most wonderful teeth – he had always been jealous of people with wonderful teeth.

"Before we get underway, Cam, can I take a few details, such as your full name, age, address etc. and some information about Hugo too would be helpful?"

Then, Waldo sought some clarity about Cam's worries. He decided on the direct approach.

"Are you serious about Hugo's infidelity to you? Do you really believe, in your heart, that he has found someone else?"

"No, I don't. I just felt I had to say something to you, but I didn't know what to say. There is definitely something wrong, but I don't know what it is. He is normally such a good and kind and loving man and such a good communicator and yet something is worrying him or distracting him, and he can't seem to tell me. I want to help him if I can. This is not about catching him out."

"Good. Where does he work?"

"He's a lecturer in European history at the university. I have probed him on the work issue, but it didn't prompt any serious responses or apparent concerns."

"What about his family? Any issues there?"

"He has the usual baggage but nothing more than the rest of us. In fact, he and his brother have been in touch again recently and all went very well. His brother had had difficulty in coming to terms with Hugo being gay but at long last he is beginning to accept it. They've decided to trace their family-tree together, which is a good way of building bridges. No, no problems there."

"So, I presume what you would like us to do is to try and get to the bottom of this for you and then discuss with you what action might be appropriate. Does that sound about right?"

"That would be ideal."

"The problem is money, Cam. This is not likely to be a thing that we can crack in couple of hours. It is more likely to be days, even weeks. We charge five hundred pounds a day. Would you like to put a ceiling on what you want to pay, and we'll do our best to fit in with that?"

"I can afford two thousand, after that it would become problematic."

"Let's sign a contract to that effect then and I'll start thinking through how we might go about cracking the problem. Does that sound reasonable?"

Cam seemed relieved that something was going to be done. After completing and signing the contract, they shook hands and parted company.

CHAPTER 4

Over the weekend, Max went through the files and emails on Robert Harmsworth's laptop and old computer tower. He searched files, bins, hard drives, and every IT nook and cranny beyond the reach of non-geeks but found nothing. There was not a shred of evidence of Robert Harmsworth having visited a pornographic site, ordered pornographic videos or of having downloaded pornographic material and that included child pornography. Of course, Max was unaware that the case might involve child abuse, as he had only been asked to look for pornography in general. Max was very disappointed with the results, but Jac explained that this was, in fact, good news and supported the investigation.

Other materials were examined with the same vigour but also to no effect. Josh had been right about the stain on the slipper, it was blood, but it proved to be that of a cow or a bullock; a friendly scientist suggested it may be the blood from a juicy steak. Needless to say, Josh was very disappointed.

The only piece of evidence which still puzzled the investigators was the clothing and articles found in the shed.

"What do you think the implications might be of the S & M gear, have you given the matter any thought?" Jac asked Waldo.

"Well, from what Josh says, they have clearly not been touched in many years and my guess is that they are probably rather old-fashioned. I think the chances are they are something that Mr and Mrs Harmsworth used in the old days. Shall we show them to an expert in these matters and see what they say?"

"Before we do that, let's see what size they are," Jac suggested. "Who would they fit? Would they fit Lucy, for example, or her mother or someone else? Were Lucy and her mother of a similar size?"

"From the photographs, is it possible to gauge Lucy's mum's size? We can tell how tall she was from photographs at the seaside standing beside Robert. Look, she must have been five-five or five-six. What do you think, Jac?" Waldo asked.

"Yes, I guess five-five. When was this taken, do we have a date? Here it is, it's scribbled on the back, July 1971. That makes it three years before she died. She is quite busty, I would say a thirty-eight double D. What about Lucy, what size was she when she was in her teens?" Jac pondered.

"Here's a photo of father and daughter together and I would have said she looks about fifteen or so. She is much taller and slimmer than her mother. It's unlikely that they would have fitted her very well. That might not have stopped her trying, however."

"Isn't Harriet, the barmaid next door, about the same size as Mrs Harmsworth?" Waldo suggested, with an exaggerated air of innocence.

"That is very observant of you, Waldo, I didn't realise you were interested. Seriously, I think you've hit on it. Shall we get Harriet to try them on? We'll have to be careful what we tell her though, she might start to think we are into strange practices."

Waldo volunteered, with huge enthusiasm, to see if Harriet could spare the time.

"You think up a good excuse," he called over his shoulder, as he disappeared down the stairs.

Harriet was keen to oblige, and Waldo returned with her in a couple of minutes.

Jac and Harriet exchanged kisses and then Jac explained that they needed to test the size of the items in the bag.

"Oh, how exciting, is this one of your cases?"

"It is connected with a case but I'm afraid I can't tell you anymore," Jac explained.

"Neither of us is into S & M, so we know little about it."

"I have dabbled. I had a girlfriend once who was well into this sort of thing, but it isn't my bag either."

Without delay and without concern for privacy, Harriet took of her top in front of them and tried on the bra.

"A perfect fit, perhaps I could have these when you're finished with them, though …"

She tried to her fit her nipples into the holes.

"… my nipples are too big for these. Whoever it is must have big tits and very neat nipples."

She then tried on the G string, the cuffs, anklets, and was soon delving into the bag to see if there was more. It was as though the gear was made for her.

She then performed for the two of them. She paraded around the room cracking the whip, sat lewdly astride a chair, with furry bits showing, and sang, 'Hey big spender' – quite a good rendition, they thought. She then bent over the table and with legs wide apart, exposed a finely carved bum, which she wiggled expertly. She scared the pants off both Waldo and Jac, who were both a little shy about such matters.

"Shall we do this every afternoon, I like this, it's good fun, especially seeing your faces. Where have you two been hiding all these years?" Harriet cried.

They were amazed that she was not in the slightest bit inhibited. She had just exposed her body to both of them and performed like an experienced lap dancer, something that they wouldn't even try in the heat of passion. They might fantasise about doing it but would not even manage it in absolute privacy. It was clear that they both admired and envied Harriet her sense of freedom and joy in such matters.

In an attempt to bring balance to proceedings, Waldo asked a sensible question.

"Does anything strike you as odd or unusual about any of this gear, Harriet, anything at all?"

"Well, only that it is very old stuff and rather heavy. Also, nowadays it tends to be black, this is very colourful and sparkly and, of course, today it would be more revealing. This is more likely to be viewed as party-goers' fun version of S & M, rather than the real thing. I like it though."

"Thank you, Harriet, that has been really helpful," said Jac, copying Waldo's investigative tone and trying not to show her excitement at Harriet's revelations.

"Fancy a drink, Harriet?" Waldo asked, thinking of a reason to escape whilst she got dressed.

"No sorry, I have to get back."

As she said this, she managed to take everything off in seconds and stands there stark naked in front of them. They stood and stared in admiration.

"Come here," she demanded, opening her arms in welcome.

They both meekly obeyed and stepped forward. She put her hands behind their necks and pulled them on to her breasts.

"Kiss me," she commanded.

They both obliged.

"That was nice, thank you. Sorry, got to rush," and within seconds, she was fully dressed and running down the stairs.

"Oh my God, Jac, what have we done? You don't think that we have jeopardised our case in any way?"

"No, I am sure we haven't, but we have challenged the purity of our relationship, after all, we have just been cheek to cheek in a compromising way. Mind you, I thoroughly enjoyed it and so did you, by the look on your face. What hope is there for us?"

"Let's get back to the case."

With his serious voice on, Waldo tried to summarise their position, forgetting that Jac was in charge of the case.

"I think we can conclude that, at this early stage in the investigation, we have no evidence to suggest that Robert Harmsworth has had any untoward involvement with children, other than his alleged abuse of his daughter. Nor do we have any evidence to suggest that he may have had any deviant or unusual sexual relationships or inclinations with adults of either sex, in the period since his wife's death. We have secured one bag of old, though we are not sure how old, S & M gear from the garden shed of his house, which has not been disturbed for some time. The clothing would appear to have been a good fit for his deceased wife, who we estimate to have been five feet five inches tall and with a thirty-eight, double-D chest. It is unlikely to have fitted his daughter quite as well, but this does not exclude the possibility that she may have worn it."

Jac took over and turned the focus on how they might proceed.

"I believe that our next move should be to start drafting the report summarising all of this. I think I should complete the record of his visit to us last Friday, including a transcript of the conversation and the contract agreed between us. I should then outline our subsequent planning discussion and the decision to search his premises on the following day, appending the draft planning document of the overall investigation and of the search itself. I will then record the detail of the search, including photographs of the rooms and the numbering system employed during the raid. I will also explain the methodology for retaining materials taken from the house and their subsequent examination and the findings. Each entry will have a date and appropriate timings. I think I need to do all of this before I develop an interview check list for the forthcoming interviews. Does that sound right to you, Waldo?

Waldo nodded.

"I wish I had some help. This is going to be very time-consuming," Jac added with concern in her voice.

"It is probably safer at this stage, given the sensitivities involved, if you handle all of this yourself, Jac. But we must seriously think about getting extra help soon. I will try and relieve you of any other burdens. You just concentrate on this, and I'll do the rest."

Mischievously, he added, "Just leave Harriet to me."

They laughed and hugged. It occurred to them that they were underway and it felt good.

CHAPTER 5

Waldo woke early, even for him; it was just after five thirty. He could tell that he was going to get into a tizzy, his brain was firing off in all directions. So, he decided to get up, have an early breakfast, and go for a walk and explore the area. He moved around quietly, in case he disturbed Jac.

He had always had a thing about knowing his territory. He had already read a number of books about the area and had done some research on the internet. He contemplated going for a run but decided he would miss too much that way. He was after getting a feel for the place, only then would he begin to know and understand the area.

By half six he was ready. He ran downstairs and almost skipped out into the street. He took a deep breath and the air seemed clean and sharp, pretty good for a city. The traffic was already beginning to build, and the early morning runners were out in force, and dodging both, he crossed the road and turned to admire the office.

The shop front of The PI Shop, North Street, Southville, Bristol, had been deliberately designed to give it an air of quiet modesty, on the basis that its work would involve serious business.

It was on the Ashton side of the street – not strictly Southville – and only saw sunlight in the early mornings. There was no sun on this particular morning but at least the rain was holding off.

It was clear that the terrace used to be a row of houses and, over the years, the ground floors had been converted into shops. Only one house remained unconverted and that looked as though someone might be starting a conversion.

Most of the upper floors were in flats of varying degrees of sophistication or, more accurately, varying degrees of humbleness. Waldo's view was that the state of the curtains gave a clue as to the prosperity of the shop owners and the quality of tenants they were able to attract. He had deliberately curtained his flat plainly but neatly, so as not to be conspicuous, but he couldn't resist having them lined to keep out the cold; he hated the cold.

Before leaving home, Waldo studied the local map. He could see that North Street, with a little help from Dean Lane, described an arc around an island of houses, which made up Southville, and separated it from its less prosperous neighbours of Ashton and Bedminster. The island was bounded on its other side by Coronation Road, which ran alongside the River Avon. Over the next few weeks, he would realise that when the tide was in, the river provided a rather fine border, even if it was a strange, sludge-brown in colour, not unlike a strong coffee with a dash of milk, but not quite the middle-class River Avon, one associated with Stratford on Avon. When the tide was out, however, it was a very different story. Sad, depressing, unseemly were the words that came into his mind.

He headed down to Raleigh Road and the Tobacco Factory Theatre. The theatre had been one of the main reasons for them choosing the area; not good business sense but business isn't everything, was their thinking. The theatre had earned itself a national reputation and he had visited on a number of occasions in the past, but only during the Shakespeare season. He looked forward to seeing its more normal fare, though more in optimism than expectation. His experience had been that, out of season, small theatres usually relied on youngsters, fresh out of drama school, showing off their new skills. He was more hopeful of the cafe on the ground floor, however, and peering through the window, he could see that it retained the industrial nature of the original building. He had read that the building had once been part of a huge complex of buildings making up the great Raleigh Road Imperial Tobacco site. The theatre building was one of the few survivors of the war and was saved from demolition by the Bristol architect, George Ferguson, as part of his regeneration of the area.

Waldo gazed up at the imposing red brick building. He didn't like the brick. It was not the soft pink of Georgian country houses but a hard red, quite unforgiving, like its original owners.

He took the next turning right and headed towards Coronation Road and Vauxhall Bridge – a modest bridge but wide enough to cater for pedestrians, cyclists, and the double buggies of the modern mother – which crosses the River Avon and provides a quick way to the docks and Bristol's Floating Harbour.

The phrase Floating Harbour exasperated him. 'Floating harbour, it's a dock for Christ's sake with locks at both ends to keep the water in. It's the boats that float not the bloody harbour', Jac had heard him state on a number of occasions. She had a certain sympathy with his point of view.

He exchanged nods with a workman. Waldo assumed he was on his way to one of the many houses being renovated in the area. Almost every street running off North Street seemed to have at least two houses undergoing renovation and transformation. The middle-classes were moving in and despite the austerity, they were tarting-up the area.

He soon reached the bridge and stopped at its mid-point, and leaned into its hefty, leaf green, Victorian iron trellis and stared down at the mud and water below. His heart sank. He wasn't sure what inspired the thought, perhaps his medical background, but he concluded it looked like a longitudinal section of the lower gut. He had no doubt that it had great appeal to the rectal surgeon, or those obsessed with their bowel movements, or to those for whom the anus was a constant source of fascination and pleasure, but he did not think that most people would find it attractive.

His reflections were interrupted by a strong, female, middle-class voice.

"Are you alright? Do you need help?"

He turned to find a woman, jogging on the spot, with a concerned look on her face, though clearly not sufficiently concerned to stop running. He decided that she thought he must be contemplating jumping. It seemed an odd conclusion. He reckoned that any suicide attempt would only result in an embarrassing splurge in the mud and a few broken bones.

"No, I'm fine. I am so sorry to have caused you concern. I am new to the area and was just looking at the river and deciding whether it would attract bird life," he fibbed.

Wisely, he decided not to share his seedier thoughts about the lower intestine.

"Oh, how interesting. I'm a member of 'FrANC', Friends of the River Avon New Cut. I know it is not the Danube, but it is our own," she added, apologetically.

How often had his little fibs, done with the best of intentions not to upset people, resulted in him being drawn into discussions he did not want to pursue?

"Oh, I thought you were the 'Frogs'?" he commented, using his little bit of knowledge to best advantage.

"No, no, they are the Friends of Greville Smythe Park, the park just back there."

She pointed to the west, away from the city and further along Coronation Road.

"I am a Frog, as well, but I take a keener interest in the river and have just been appointed Chair of FrANC. By the way, we have spotted at least thirty birds on the Cut, including kingfishers and egrets, not bad for an urban site, eh?"

"Very good. I look forward to doing a spot of bird watching myself, when things settle down."

All of this time, he had been struggling not to look at her breasts, as they bounced up and down in time with her jogging. They seemed very full and welcoming. He kept his eyes firmly fixed on hers, however, for fear of being taken as some kind of pervert.

"Where are you living?" she asked in more relaxed tones.

Phew, I seemed to have passed the eye test, he thought.

"We have just opened up The PI Shop in North Street and I am living above it."

"Oh, how fascinating," she added with enthusiasm. "You must be the GP then?"

"Ex-GP," he corrected her. "How do you know that?" realising as he said it, that all the locals would have accessed the website by now and, no doubt, had been discussing the pros and cons of the new enterprise.

"On the website, of course. Good luck with everything and welcome to Southville. I live in Exeter Road, by the way. I'll pop in and see you soon. I'm going for my usual morning run along the Chocolate Path," she shouted over her shoulder, already resuming her run.

And with that, she bounced off across the bridge and down the steps. He watched her running beside the river and heading towards town. She looked back and they waved to one another.

Chocolate Path, now there's an interesting puzzle. As an investigator, he wondered whether he could work out why it had attracted such a name. He thought it was probably to do with Joseph Fry, but it turned out it was because it was constructed of small, black, square tiles that resembled a chocolate bar; he had failed the test.

As for his first contact with the locals, not bad, was his judgement. He then realised he had forgotten to ask her name. It was all that jogging nonsense, very off-putting.

Waldo crossed the bridge and the linked modern extension over the road and decided to head for the docks and away from the river, in case she should think he was following her – he pictured his CV with three entries; potentially suicidal, sexually perverted and a stalker, not bad for an early morning walk.

He wound his way through the cobbled back streets, which he thought particularly uninspiring, until he came out at the dockside, where the SS Great Britain is moored. He stood and admired it for a while and then watched the small, passenger ferry cross to and fro the dock, providing a shortcut to the city centre.

Waldo made his way along the dockside, being careful not to trip over the mooring bollards. He liked the haphazard nature of the granite cobbles, but they were quite tiring on the feet and kept him from lifting his eyes, for fear of ending up in the water. The water looked particularly unsavoury to the clinical eye.

He passed barges with smoke spiralling out of their chimneys; old tugs and cargo vessels being renovated by enthusiasts; a steam train already restored and ready to give tourists the short trip to the Create Centre; and a variety of ramshackle sheds, all of which looked fascinating but a million miles from their original uses. 'It is strange', he thought, 'how a once busy, grimy, clanking, corroding dock, had been transformed into a modern entertainment arena and a desirable residential area. How decadent and soft we have become'.

On reaching the M Shed, Bristol's dockland museum, he turned away from the docks and passed the remains of the old gaol. He then made his way to 'Gaol Ferry Bridge', which allowed him to cross back to Coronation Road, about a half mile up-stream from his earlier crossing.

He decided to take a quick look at the river at the central point of the bridge, though he did not wish to attract attention for the second time that morning. The view was much more interesting, as it was possible to see the remains of the original Victorian slipways and quaysides at the water's edge and imagine the ferry, prior to the bridge's construction, transporting its cargo of farm produce and animals across the river to market.

He reached the Bedminster-end of North Street and started making his way back to the office. Some of the shops were boarded up and those that were still open were mainly fast-food takeaways, double glazing outfits, and second-hand dealers of various kinds. Even here, however, he detected outposts of the middle classes and the occasional really good-looking cafe or bar.

As he reached the theatre end of North Street, the contrast was stark. The shops were thriving and the street smart and, for the most part, free of litter. There was a particularly fine frontage which caught his eye, a detective agency by the name of The PI Shop. He smiled to himself.

CHAPTER 6

"Cam, it's Waldo Wise here, can you talk?"

"Yes, no problem."

"Good, have you had a chance to look through Hugo's laptop yet and check his mobile?"

"Yes, but I couldn't see anything untoward. Most of it was work stuff and some matters relating to his brother and their investigations into the family tree; all very bland and innocent. And the same goes for the phone calls and emails. A blank I'm afraid."

"OK, let's meet and formulate a plan together, if you can spare the time. There is really no option but for me to monitor his movements and see if anything unusual emerges. Any chance we could meet today?"

They arranged to meet for lunch and Waldo persuaded him that Quayside, a sophisticated restaurant on the dock, would be more conducive to their discussions, rather than the singular charms of the Bedminster Cafe.

They met at half twelve, which gave Waldo a chance to make a few notes and work out a draft plan of campaign. Waldo was not exactly excited by the case, especially with the challenges posed by Robert Harmsworth, but he decided to give it his best shot. In any event, he liked Cam; he was a good, sensitive sort and he clearly loved his partner dearly.

"Good to see you, Cam. Shall we sit where we can see the river, or would you prefer somewhere more discreet?"

"No, I am happy with the window. I decided to tell Hugo about you, not the real you, of course, but that I had met this guy at the chess club, who was very nice and very cultured. Hugo doesn't like chess, so I knew I was on safe ground. I must have over-played it though, because he suggested I invite you to supper one evening. I hope I haven't done the wrong thing."

"Not at all, though I will turn down the invitation at this stage, if you don't mind."

Cam dug deeply into his shoulder bag and produced an envelope.

"I thought these might be helpful to you. I printed them off this morning. I even managed to find one of Hugo in his work suit."

Cam produced a number of photographs, which he handed to Waldo.

"These are really good, thanks Cam. Gosh, I didn't expect Hugo to have a beard; a nice strong face."

Waldo was struggling to find the right words, because Hugo seemed very plain and unexciting. Not quite what he had imagined.

As they sipped their glasses of wine, Waldo spent the next half an hour grilling Cam as to the fine detail of Hugo's working life and his movements: where his office was; which entrance he used; what he did for lunch and how long he normally took for lunch; what time he left the office in the evening; his normal route to and from home; and so on. At the end of the questioning, Cam was quite exhausted and ravenous, and they both settled down to enjoying a good meal.

In breaks during the meal, Cam told Waldo about his love of chess and how he hoped to play for the county soon. Waldo, however, never let go of his purpose in being with Cam and, from time to time, threw in the odd question about Cam and Hugo's relationship. After two glasses of wine and whilst waiting for coffees, Waldo risked asking about their sexual habits and whether Hugo had any particular inclinations.

"You must understand, Waldo, that we have been together a goodly number of years now, so you explore all sorts during that time and eliminate some practices and keep others. I suppose his favourite," he hesitated, "is that what you mean?"

"It could be. I don't have any particular thing in mind in asking the question, just to understand Hugo a little more."

"He likes me to be rough with him."

Waldo struggled to imagine Cam being rough. Indeed, he had great difficulty imagining him having sex, never mind about being rough. It was like that with some people, he thought, they just don't have a sexual bone in their bodies.

"You don't strike me as being naturally rough, Cam. Have I got that wrong?"

"No, you are right, Waldo. It is not my scene really, but you do these things for the one you love, don't you?"

"What about your needs, do you have anything which might help shed a little light?"

"Oh Waldo, this is difficult."

Waldo sat quietly and waited patiently for him to build his courage and then, suddenly, Cam blurted out, "I like to dress up."

In a very matter-of-fact way, Waldo nodded and said, in hushed tones, "Tell me a little more. What is your favourite? By the way, do you both dress up, does Hugo like it too?"

"I like to dress up as a little boy or girl and for Hugo to be daddy or teacher and to chastise me, by telling me off and give me gentle smacks on my bottom."

"Does Hugo enjoy it?"

"I think so. No, I am sure he does, he gets very excited when he smacks me. He does it a little hard sometimes and I am left with welts on my bottom. Oh, Waldo, I have never told anyone, I feel such a fool."

"Please don't, Cam, it is all very normal and natural. Does Hugo like to dress up as anything in particular?"

They paused as coffee was served and smiled sweetly at the waitress.

"No, but he is very fond of latex. He has a suit which covers him completely, head to toe. It has little holes for him to breathe through the nose and his mouth. There is also one other strategically placed hole. He says that his latex suit helps him focus completely on his orgasm to the exclusion of everything else. I dread it. I know when the suit comes out that he is feeling particularly rough."

"By rough, do you mean violent?"

"I suppose, on occasion, he does overstep the mark a bit. I get frightened then."

"How often does it happen?"

"Not often, I suppose once every six weeks or so. Can we stop talking about it now please, Waldo? I find it painful even to think about it. I am beginning to sweat at the thought of it."

"Just one more question, if I may, Cam, and then we'll stop. Is this tendency towards being a bit rough a recent thing or has it been around since your partnership began?"

"He's always been that way inclined, but I suppose it has become much harder-edged of late."

Waldo then changed the subject and they talked about boats, books, and everyday issues, much to Cam's relief. When the waitress came over to ask if they would like the bill, they realised that it was nearly half three and that they had been talking almost non-stop for three hours.

"Shall we go halves," Cam suggested.

"Yes, that would be good."

Waldo was relieved, because the business couldn't afford to wine and dine people at this stage of the game. They handed over their debit cards to the waitress. Waldo agreed to leave the tip.

Whilst they waited for the money to be sorted, Waldo outlined his intentions for the week, namely, that he was going to monitor Hugo at lunch times and follow him on his homeward journey for the rest of the week and see what emerged, if anything. Cam thought it a good idea.

They shook hands warmly and took different routes back to their respective homes.

π

"Good morning Mr Harmsworth, good to see you again. Are you ready for me?"

"Good morning Ms Beauley. I am ready. I've just put on some coffee; would you like one?"

"I would love one, yes please. Which room are we going to use, I'll set up, whilst you organise the coffee? You don't mind if I tape our conversation, do you?"

"Not at all. I thought we would go into the sitting room, more pleasant, don't you think? You know your way around. Help yourself."

Jac made her way into the sitting room and recalled her hug from Josh but put these thoughts to the back of her mind and prepared for the interview.

"I noticed that you like a drop of cold milk in your coffee, is that right?" he asked.

"How very observant of you, and you like yours black," she responded.

"Touché, Ms Beauley."

"I'd like to start by confirming what I am sure you know already and, that is, that the house search revealed nothing of concern. I have already written-up the results of the report and finished by concluding that there was no evidence of any contact through the internet or any other means of child pornography or, indeed, of any interest in pornography of any kind. I have brought a draft of this section of the report, so that you can look through it at your leisure. I would appreciate any comments you may like to make. The only exception to this picture of good behaviour is the bag of S & M gear we found in the garden shed. Admittedly, it is rather old-fashioned and mild by today's standards but, nevertheless, it was quite revealing and erotic for its day. We'll come back to that at the appropriate point in the discussion, if we may."

"Good Lord, I had forgotten all about those clothes. They belonged to my wife. That must have been forty years ago. Were they in the garden shed? It just goes to show my level of interest in gardening and in eroticism for that matter. Well, I never …"

"I'd like to start today by re-examining the nature of the problem and to explore it in a little more depth. I also want to try and understand why you consider what you did with your daughter a problem after all these years. You are now seventy-six and your daughter is forty-six and the two of you enjoy a loving relationship. If you proceed with your intention, you may cause difficulties for your daughter and her husband, and you may put enormous strain on relationships with your other daughters and the grandchildren. You understand the point I am making?"

"I understand what you are saying. I have carefully considered the implications of my actions. But it is my view that one should not go through life living a lie and imposing that lie on others. It is morally wrong and, though it may prove challenging to my daughters, in the short term, I think they will come to appreciate the importance of it, as their lives progress. Lucy, in particular, needs to be released from the burden of what I did. On a very selfish level, I too need to be released and to be able to die knowing that I faced up to my wrong-doing and tried to make amends for it, though I stress, I am not looking for forgiveness. I do not think I should be forgiven. I hope that explains my position and convinces you of the importance of my doing this."

"It is part of our philosophy that we explore the nature and meaning of the problems being investigated with our clients. I don't know if you are aware of Karl Popper and his work, but our research and investigation approach is based largely on his philosophy."

"I know the name, but I have never come across his work, I've just seen the occasional reference to him. I'd be interested in having a read if you have anything of his you can lend me."

"I have the very thing that you might like, 'The Logic of Scientific Discovery'. It is a strange book but fascinating. I'll bring it with me next time. So, I think we can safely conclude that you have a full understanding of the problem and why it is a problem. You have also explored the implications to yourself and to others. Of course, one of the obvious outcomes of the process is that you will be placed on the sex offender's register, and you will have to agree to special arrangements, in order to see your grandchildren, if your daughters agree that you can still see them. You are aware of this?"

"I am indeed."

"Good, then let us proceed. May I have a top-up before we get stuck in?"

"Of course, please forgive me. It is the result of living alone for too long."

"I would like you to go right back to when you were a young man and when you first met your wife. I know this has no particular relevance, but it helps me to understand how things developed. I suppose a Freudian psychiatrist would want to go back to your childhood but unless you feel there is something relevant, I suggest we give Freud and your early years a miss."

"I have never been a fan of Freud and to be honest I can think of nothing in my childhood that should have adversely affected my behaviour later in life. So, if I pick it up from when I left university and started as a cub reporter on the local paper that would seem most appropriate."

He looked for confirmation from Jac, who nodded.

"I was not particularly out-going as a young man, but I had a number of girlfriends and I did have sex, of a sort, with two other girls before I met Susie.

"Susie and I met at the local newspaper; she designed and sold display advertising. She was known to be a really good catch among the reporters, and I never really thought I stood any chance. Only a few ever succeeded in going out with her. She enjoyed a reputation as being a very good girl, no hanky-panky, you understand. She was, however, extremely out-going, very good-looking, and very sexy. All the men stopped to admire her when she walked through the office. I thought she was way beyond my reach. Then one day, we went up in the lift together. It was one of those with concertina steel gates. It creaked and clattered its way up and down the floors, I recall. We were on our way up to level three, when she turned and asked me why I had never asked her out. I was amazed and, of course, seized my moment. She seemed to think I was good looking and intelligent and a real catch. I could not believe my luck. It wasn't long before we were in a serious relationship. Is this the sort of thing you want to know?"

"This is ideal for starters, but I want as much detail as you can manage. There will be times, as we progress, that you may find it harder going, I'm sure."

"I will do my best. Well, our relationship flourished. Susie was still a virgin and we both wanted to have fuller sex, if you get my drift. So, we decided that the easiest way to secure the necessary privacy and to escape the prying eyes of our parents or, at least, to make it more acceptable to them, was to go camping or, as we termed it, hiking. We decided to walk the Cotswold Way. We took two single tents, just to reinforce the innocence of our venture."

Robert Harmsworth paused and sat very still for a few moments.

"We had walked no more than three miles from the road and couldn't wait any longer. I helped Susie pitch her tent and, as soon as it was up, she grabbed me and dragged me inside. Not that I was a reluctant partner, you understand, but I suppose I didn't want to be seen to rush things. We were very excited, as you can imagine. We virtually ripped each other's clothes off. I was worried that I might not be able to control myself, so I tried to think of things to distract me. I needn't have worried. Susie seemed to have inherited all the knowledge and skills that were needed to see us through those early days. I have always thought how remarkable it is that some people know exactly what is required and others remain quite unaware throughout their lives. You can almost tell them just by looking at them."

"My goodness, that is a frightening thought, but I think I know what you mean," was Jac's rather uninspired contribution.

Robert was warming to the challenge.

"It wasn't long before all hell let loose, and we made love for several hours before coming up for air. You know how it is, when you first discover the delights of sex. We thought that no one before us could ever have experienced such wonders.

"I remember we remained at base camp, appropriately named in this case," he jested, "for the next three days. I never got around to putting up my tent. To be honest, it never saw the light of day during the whole of our venture. There, I managed it. Was that the sort of detail you were requiring?"

"It was indeed. Well done. Did you find that difficult?"

"No, it was surprisingly easy. I don't think I would have found it as easy to talk in front of Waldo and I realise that that says more about me than it does about Waldo. To give me a chance to catch my breath for a minute, can I ask you a question?"

Jac nodded.

"Am I right in assuming that you and Waldo are only business partners?"

Jac reflected on how to answer this. Did she tell the truth about her sexuality and risk upsetting her client or did she just answer the question asked? Tell the truth, that is part of the way we do things, she mused.

"I suppose the first thing to say is that I am a lesbian and have been with my partner for the past two years. Having said that, I love Waldo, we are best friends, as well business partners. Our relationship is very precious to me. Intellectually, culturally, emotionally, I suppose even spiritually, we are very alike. People often think we are brother and sister, but I suspect that such a relationship is far more fraught. To borrow a modern phrase, we are soul mates."

"I had no idea you were a lesbian. I am not sure I have ever known one before or, at least, not been aware that I have known one. Thank you for sharing that with me. Now, where do we go from here?"

Jac admired his matter-of-fact way of dealing with the situation and moved on swiftly.

"I assume that your relationship went well from here and then you decided to marry. Was there any difficulty with that? Did either set of parents object?"

"No, everyone seemed jolly pleased. All went swimmingly. We were married in St Mary Redcliffe, across the way, and lived in a flat in town for the first six months before buying our first home. We were very happy. Within a short time, Susie became pregnant with Audrey and life couldn't have been better. My career as a journalist also proceeded apace and there seemed little to get in our way, indeed, nothing did. Susie had few problems carrying Audrey and the birth was text-book as well."

"Before you go further, was your sex life adversely affected by the pregnancy or the birth of Audrey?"

"Not at all. I think it would be fair to say that Susie was highly sexed throughout her life and being pregnant did not affect matters. If anything, as Susie got older, her appetite for sex increased and her needs became somewhat more extreme."

"You better elaborate on that for me."

"You must understand that anything I say is not a criticism of Susie. I loved her very much and I was delighted with our sex life. My friends at work did nothing but moan about how their wives went off sex after the children were born and this turned them into bitter, grumpy old men before their time. Susie always wanted sex. I had a job to keep up with her. It was great. I thought she was a bit open in front of the girls though. She had no inhibitions in talking to them about sex and believed that being naked in front of them was healthy and good for their development. I wasn't so sure. I would have preferred us to be more discreet, especially as they grew older. I think they began to find it as embarrassing as I did."

"Did you ever feel sexually interested in any of the girls? Did you help with bathing them? Did they get into the bath with you?"

"I never felt any inclination in that way, not until later, of course. I changed them, when they were babies, bathed them, dressed and undressed them, nursed and cuddled them, but there was no inkling of what was to come. In fact, I often pondered how men could do such things to children. I could never understand what possible interest men could have in children and certainly not in their own offspring. One's instinct is to love and protect, not love and abuse. It made no sense to me at all."

"As they grew older, did they share a bath with you?"

"Audrey never did. She was always more prudish than the other two. But Linda and Lucy never gave it a second thought. And to be honest, neither did I, why would I?"

"OK, let's stop there. I don't want us to rush this. I suggest we take it a step at a time. But before we finish, perhaps you could just tell me when the S & M gear came onto the scene. How old were the children? Whose idea was it to buy it? Where did you get it from?"

"Well, it was clearly Susie's idea. She fancied the idea of dressing up and exhibiting herself in an erotic way, she described it as 'a bit of fun'. To start with, I was really embarrassed by the whole idea and buying it was a complete humiliation. I insisted that we went to London to get it, so that I could get lost in the anonymity of the big city. To make matters worse, we had to ask my parents to look after the children. I seem to remember Lucy was about three years old."

"I suggest next time we start from that point and examine how your sex life developed from there. Thank you for being so open and honest about your private life, it can't have been easy for you. I know that I would find it very difficult."

"You made it easy for me. Thank you. When shall we meet again?" he asked, politely.

"Tomorrow, Waldo has an appointment with Audrey and the following day with Linda. I haven't managed to get hold of Lucy yet. Perhaps we could meet on Friday. That would give me time to write up my notes and to have discussed matters with Waldo following his interviews with the girls. Does that suit you?"

"Indeed, it does, so I'll see you on Friday at the same time then."

"In terms of Audrey and Linda, we have decided to adopt the stance that we are carrying out a research project into the sex lives of parents and its impact on their offspring and that you have volunteered. Could you contact them and persuade them to collaborate with the project?"

He agreed and was amused by the thought of how his daughters may react.

$$\pi$$

It was shortly after five p.m. Waldo parked close to Cam and Hugo's flat so that he could observe Hugo in the flesh, as he came home from work. Photographs were all very well, he considered, but they could not convey the gait or the way people hold their bodies or their mannerisms.

As he parked, he realised his first mistake.

Waldo was the proud owner of a small, two-seater Smart car, which he bought as part of becoming greener. It measured up to the first criterion for covert investigation, in that he was able to park discreetly between two cars, though parking sideways was still not a common feature and, therefore, probably not as discreet as he imagined. It fell seriously short of the mark in terms of the second criterion, however, in that it was bright yellow. He bought it before they decided to embark on their new careers. So, the covert operation was turning rapidly into a bloke sitting in a yellow car, in an area in which he was not known, parked the wrong way, and clearly waiting for someone with whom he could carry out a transaction of a dubious nature. A sore thumb came to mind. All Waldo could do was to sit it out and hope.

His embarrassment was short-lived. Within a few minutes, Hugo turned the corner and walked straight past Waldo's car without giving it a second glance. Waldo watched him closely. He had a very upright stance, perhaps even a suggestion of a backward tilt. He was taller than Waldo imagined, he thought he must be six feet, if not a little more, and quite well-built, not a frail soul like Cam. He had a long but slow stride, with a tendency to bob. He gave the impression of not being in a hurry to get home.

The next day, the weather cleared by mid-afternoon, and so Waldo set off on foot for the university. This was his first surveillance exercise, so, despite his confidence and his bluster in front of Jac, he was unsure how to play it. He concluded that the art of surveillance must be about being insignificant and remaining anonymous. He was pretty sure he could manage it whilst sitting in a car or a café, but he was less sure about how to do it hanging about on street corners. He decided against taking a paper or a book, nowadays people were always looking at their phones, which he refused to do. He had been brought up never to eat in the street and he considered being on the phone and talking loudly was equally rude. No, he would just stand there.

He arrived at four o'clock. He stood just below the exit. Then he changed his mind, as he worked out that Hugo was most likely to walk down the hill towards his home and would, therefore, pass close to him, if he stayed on the lower side of the exit. He moved further up the hill and above the university gate, where he still had a clear view. He adopted an attitude of mind that he was waiting for his partner, Jac, and that she was due to come out in about ten minutes or so. He was hoping that such thoughts would enable him to assume the right physical stance. Waldo relaxed and watched the world go by.

Hugo came out earlier than expected, perhaps by a quarter of an hour. It was only just quarter past four. At a fairly brisk pace, he made his way down the hill. He followed much the same route as Waldo had expected and headed down Park Street towards the city centre. When he reached the bridge at the bottom of the road, however, he unexpectedly turned left and went down the steep steps to the road below. Waldo increased his pace to catch up and stood on the bridge and watched Hugo from there. The road below was narrow and virtually deserted and Waldo assessed it too risky to follow directly. To Waldo's surprise, he went into the King's Head, just fifty yards along the road. It was a long time since Waldo had been into the pub but he remembered it as a bit of a dive.

What to do next? He stood on the bridge looking towards the pub, trying to decide on his next move. After hesitating for some time, he decided that he had to risk it and go in and order a drink, after all, Hugo could be having a secret assignation.

Waldo went in the main door and was faced with a choice of going left into the lounge or right into the public bar. He opted for the lounge, for he couldn't imagine that Hugo would want to mix with the all-day drinkers.

It was apparent that little money had been spent on the pub in the last few years, for it still had the same grubby appearance. The main change was that it was no longer smoky, but it didn't look as though they had refreshed the paint. It still had that wonderful, tobacco-stained hue, so typical of the old-fashioned British pub.

Waldo went straight up to the bar and ordered a lager-shandy. He always struggled to know what to order in pubs, as he was not a beer drinker. He loved wine but had never managed to find a beer that he could drink, hence the shandy; it looked butch but wasn't.

Waldo had a quick look round for a seat and also to assess where Hugo might be but could see no sign of him. 'Bugger', he muttered under his breath, and sat down in a window seat, facing down the road that he judged Hugo might take. Then he spotted a pint, standing on the bar. It was unaccompanied. He reasoned that the beer could be Hugo's and, sure enough, after a few minutes, Hugo emerged from the direction of the 'gents' and propped up the bar. Waldo envied him the ease with which he assumed his stance. It was as though he assumed that position every day of his life. Hugo passed the time of day with the barman, who was clearly gay. He enjoyed watching him and it took away the pressure of trying not to be noticed. After five minutes, Hugo left his pint and his brief case and went out through the main door. He went immediately to a house opposite the pub and rang the doorbell. He then held a brief conversation with someone over the intercom and came back into the lounge bar to finish his pint, which he did in just two gulps. He said goodbye to the barman and went off down the road towards his home.

Waldo decided not to follow. Instead, he sat and waited and slowly sipped his pint, thinking through what he had just seen. Slowly but surely, it dawned on him that the King's Head had become a gay bar and that Cam and Hugo were probably frequent visitors. He was still nonplussed by what happened when Hugo went opposite. It looked as though it was the entrance to flats, one of which was probably occupied by friends of Hugo and Cam. If that was the case, who did Hugo speak to and why didn't he get invited in? By leaving his pint and briefcase, he clearly was not expecting an invitation. So, what was it all about?

π

Robert had cleared the way with his daughters for Waldo to question them about the family and their sex lives, though not without some difficulty.

Waldo began with Audrey.

"As you know, the aim of this research is to help shed light on the extent to which the sexual inclinations and behaviours of parents, during the child-rearing years, influence and shape their offspring's sexual inclinations and behaviours. Is there anything you would like to ask me about the project, before we get underway?

"Not really, though I must say I am not looking forward to this one bit. What was daddy thinking of, the twit?"

"I have been your father's friend for a number of years, so you can probably blame me for persuading him."

Waldo had agreed with Robert Harmsworth that he could use this line if his daughters challenged him.

"Most people feel the same way and then end up quite enjoying the experience. The sooner we start, I suspect the better it will be for you. Perhaps you could begin by telling me about your perception of your mother and father as parents. Were they good, kind, loving parents? Were they strict, did they believe in corporal punishment? Did they favour one daughter over another?"

This gentle start put Audrey at her ease but was not particularly revealing in terms of Waldo's hidden agenda. So, he sharpened the questioning.

"Did your parents walk around naked at home, if so, did you find it disturbing?"

"They did and I didn't like it, especially by the time I was about eleven or twelve. My father wasn't keen either; he took every opportunity to cover up. It was mummy who was behind all of that."

"Did you ever feel any kind of unease with your father, say, when he was bathing you or looking after you, when your mother wasn't there?"

"Oh, good Lord no. He was a perfect father. Mummy was the troublesome one. She used to say things like, 'Daddy has a very big penis and he is very good in bed', which I found embarrassing. Linda and Lucy were fascinated and kept asking me questions, as though I understood any better than them. I didn't have a clue but, of course, could not confess it to my younger sisters. I hadn't seen any other man's penis, at the time, so I assumed they all looked like daddy's. And I never had a clue what was meant by 'good in bed', only some strange instinct that men and women, when they were married, made love and were able to make babies. But it was all very vague.

"The most embarrassing thing of all was mummy's noise. By the time I was twelve or thirteen, I began to realise that mummy wasn't just laughing or crying but making a noise that went with this lovemaking business, though I didn't understand exactly why she needed to do it. At first, I thought they must be fighting and that daddy was hurting mummy but mummy said that that wasn't true, daddy would never hurt her. She said that she was just enjoying herself and not to worry. I would understand when I grew up. I now know that they must have made love pretty often, as she was always crying out. To make matters worse, she always insisted that all bedroom doors were left open and that included theirs. In the end, I used to stuff my ears with tissue paper and stick my head under the pillow."

"Your mother died when you were still relatively young."

"Yes, it was tragic. I was eighteen at the time and had just taken my 'A' levels. It all happened so quickly. She was diagnosed with breast cancer and was dead within six months. We were all in a state of shock. Daddy coped well during her illness. I suppose he had us to look after, and he never had a chance to think, but once mummy died, he fell apart for a while. I had to cope as best I could with the other two girls. Linda was easy, she's a very practical girl, but Lucy was a nightmare. In many ways, Lucy was just like mummy, impetuous and hare-brained. I thought of cancelling my place at university, but daddy insisted I go, and I think my absence helped him to come out of it."

"Did you meet your husband at university?"

"Yes, but we didn't get together until our final year; we were too studious, and even then, there was no serious sexual relationship. We both believed in waiting until we were married, though I must confess that once we were engaged, we did indulge. We were both twenty-two when we married, we could see no point in waiting longer."

"Did you both enjoy sex or was it irksome for you? Do you enjoy sex today?"

"We have always enjoyed sex, but the bedroom door is firmly closed, and we never make any untoward noises."

"Would you say you are conventional in your love-making or are you adventurous?"

"We are very conventional."

"You have highlighted two particular issues which concerned you. I refer to your mother's habit of leaving the bedroom door open and the noise she made when making love. Were there any other matters which worried you as a child or a young person?"

"Not worried me as such but there were Tuesday nights, mummy's dance nights. Daddy used to get in a bit of a lather on Tuesdays. He didn't seem to mind her going out, in fact, he encouraged her, but he was never sure in what state she would come back. I never got to the bottom of it because we were confined to our rooms on Tuesdays after nine o'clock, even though I normally didn't go until ten. Linda might be able to tell you more, because one night, when there was a real upset at the door, Linda sneaked a look. All I know is that mummy was confined to bed for the next few days. Daddy said she was unwell and we weren't allowed to disturb her. It was the only time I remember their bedroom door being closed."

Waldo completed the discussion and grabbed a few words with her husband to try and justify the rationale of the research protocol. He reassured himself that Robert Harmsworth was well-loved and well-respected and that there was no danger of him having done anything unseemly. Waldo thanked Audrey and her husband profusely for their time and left. He thanked his lucky stars that no one asked to see a copy of the research on completion – he was dreading having to lie any further.

Waldo's visit to Linda followed similar lines and with no new insights into the Harmsworth household. Again, Robert Harmsworth emerged as an exemplary father, whom Linda, her husband, and the three children adored. He was perceived as kind, caring, helpful, and loving and there was no suggestion of anything amiss.

Tuesday nights remained a puzzle. Linda had seen her mother return and, on one occasion, she seemed to have been mugged. One of the dance group brought her home in his car and apologised to Mr Harmsworth for her state. She didn't hear any more, because her father had spotted her and sent her to bed. He was not willing to talk about it in the morning.

Waldo concluded from his two visits that there was little to say in terms of the report, other than positive and supportive statements about his exemplary behaviour as a father, grandfather, and father-in-law; he was well-loved by all concerned. This was excellent news and would help Robert Harmsworth's case when it came to the formal confession and the legal case.

$$\pi$$

By twelve noon on the following day, Waldo was again in place to observe Hugo's movements. The sun was shining and there was a lot of activity around the faculty entrance. At about twelve thirty, a group of six people emerged chatting and laughing and Hugo was amongst them. They were deeply involved in their conversations and did not notice anyone else. They crossed the road and entered the grounds of another university site and occupied a couple of benches. The gardens were a delight, but the group didn't take the slightest bit of notice of their surroundings. Waldo noticed a large family of long-tailed tits fly into the tree above the group, noisily flitting from branch to branch but the academics showed no sign of recognition or interest in what was happening above or about them. Hugo was in conversation with an attractive young woman in her thirties, who was intent on explaining something. By their serious expressions, it was clearly work related. Waldo walked by them, just to check that his assumption was correct. He caught the phrases 'statistical evidence' and 'empirical evidence'. When Waldo was just a few feet passed them, he heard Hugo go into full voice, countering the theories just expressed. The woman listened intently but got out her sandwich and started to eat. Hugo unwrapped his sandwich but waited until he had completed his argument before starting to eat. Within a half hour, the group made its way back to the department and Waldo set off home.

For Hugo's homeward journey, Waldo decided to take the risk and wait for Hugo at the bottom of Park Street. He went into a cafe, which was a favourite of his, and had a coffee. He was able to see the road and observe people as they passed and was only a short distance from the bridge and the steps, which Hugo had taken the day before.

By quarter to five, Waldo began to think that he had made a mistake, for the previous day Hugo would already have been in the pub and well into his pint. Waldo had no alternative but to wait. At five minutes past five, Hugo walked past, and Waldo immediately rose to follow him. He thanked the waitress, who was clearing the tables in a relaxed, unhurried way. Waldo was just about to stop and look over the bridge, only to see Hugo head straight down Park Street for the centre of town. A lucky break, for he had thought of going straight to the pub and waiting for him there.

Within ten minutes, Hugo turned the corner of his street and was back home at roughly the same time as he would have arrived home the day before.

Waldo reflected on this timing, trying to assess its implications in terms of his observations. Yesterday, Hugo left fifteen minutes earlier than Cam had estimated he left, namely at four fifteen, giving him sufficient time to have a pint. Today, Waldo estimated that he left at approximately four thirty, unless he went somewhere else between the university and the bottom of Park Street, thus arriving about ten minutes later than before but, by not bothering with a pint, he arrived home at roughly the same time. Waldo was puzzled. A half an hour here or there was not sufficient time to get up to mischief. He concluded, therefore, that if he was misbehaving, then on those occasions he must leave much earlier, unless, of course, the mischief was occurring on site. Waldo decided that for the next two days, he would resume his observations at the university and not further down the route, and he would monitor from lunch time right through to Hugo's going-home time, in case he was missing something vital.

Waldo realised that almost two full days of observation would mean that he increased the likelihood of being spotted by someone and being reported to the police as acting suspiciously. He discussed the matter with Jac, and she offered Waldo the use of her old van. For several years now, Waldo had ribbed Jac about her 'old wreck', its age, its lack of distinction, and the environmental damage it caused every time she took it out. But now, he had to admit, that it was almost certainly the perfect observation vehicle. She claimed victory and foresight and thumped him to celebrate.

The biggest problem facing Waldo was how to deal with the parking meter, for there was a maximum of two hours parking and the meters were checked regularly. He decided on two ploys. The first was that he would not put any money into the meter until he had to, that way he might get away with up to three hours of parking. After that, he would pull the breakdown trick. He would move to the other side of the road, where there were double yellow lines but no meters, put up the bonnet and put a red triangle behind the vehicle. He would explain to the parking meter attendant that the breakdown company was due in forty minutes and point to the organisation's sticker in Jac's front window. After an hour, he would then move back into a parking bay, for it would then be legal to return. Problem sorted, he thought.

Yesterday's group of people, including the young woman with whom Hugo had been talking, came out chatting and crossed the road and went into the garden opposite. There was, however, no sign of Hugo. Waldo waited, expecting him to appear but the group returned after lunch, and there was still no sign of him.

Waldo had already worked the breakdown trick and was just in the process of parking legally, when Hugo appeared. He was virtually running down the hill. Waldo shuffled the car backwards and forwards to waste a few moments and then drove down the hill after Hugo. They reached the road junction at the same time. He lingered as long as he could, before a vehicle came up behind him and he was obliged to move off. He drove past Hugo, who was following his usual route, first right, first left and then down Park Street. Waldo decided to park further down the road, spotted a number of spaces and moved into one and quickly paid the maximum meter charge. Hugo had slowed a little now but was taking full advantage of his long stride and was moving at a fast pace. Waldo checked his watch, it was five-past three.

Waldo locked the van and then walked after Hugo. He watched as Hugo went down the steps at the bottom of Park Street. Waldo reached the bridge, as Hugo entered the door opposite the pub.

"Christ, what now?" he said aloud, much to the surprise of a passer-by.

Waldo lingered on the bridge, trying to decide on his best approach. In the absence of any good ideas, he decided to have a drink in the pub and observe any movements in and out of the door.

It was the same barman on duty and he recognised Waldo and greeted him warmly. Waldo considered that the barman had reached the conclusion that he was a closet gay and sooner or later he would become bolder. If that were the case, Waldo thought this may work in his favour. He ordered his usual pint of shandy and settled into the window seat. He picked up a paper lying on a nearby table and started to read.

Three quarters of an hour went by and there was no sign of Hugo or anyone else for that matter. He was struggling to pass the time without drawing attention to himself, when he was saved by the arrival of a big camp guy, who filled the place with laughter and bonhomie. He was well over six feet tall, full-bodied and, though he clearly worked out, he was not one of those gays seeking the Adonis look; he had it naturally. After ten minutes banter with the barman, he came over and introduced himself to Waldo.

"Hi, I'm Jean Pierre, you're new around here."

"Hi, Waldo, pleased to meet you."

They shook hands.

"Gosh that's some grip," Waldo said, reeling from the natural strength of the guy. "You have cheered up the pub no end," he added.

"Yes dear, you'd never know I am a depressive. So, what brings you to these parts?"

"I live in Southville but I am doing some work at the university, so I've started to call in for the occasional pint on my way home."

"Oh, I like brains, it's a real turn on. You know this is a gay bar. You don't look gay to me, dearie."

"No, I'm not. You don't mind me being here, do you?"

"Of course not, love, you are welcome. If ever you want to experiment or you just feel like a massage, I work across the way. Just ask for Jean Pierre."

"I may well do that, perhaps see you soon."

"That would be good. Got to go, I start work in five. Bye-si-bye."

So, it was a massage parlour for gays. Things were working out very nicely. He liked this surveillance lark. He thought that if he booked in with Jean Pierre for a massage, he could then pick his brains. He considered whether or not he was brave enough to risk it or whether it was above and beyond the call of duty. He reflected further as he supped on his second pint. Clearly Hugo was not seeing Jean Pierre, because he was already in there, so he wondered who else might work there. Whilst he was still contemplating matters, Hugo emerged and came straight into the pub and ordered a pint. Waldo got up and left, before Hugo had time to look around and spot him. He thought that too many sightings might lead to him being recognised.

Waldo got back into the van and saw that he had just a half an hour left on the meter. That meant that Hugo must have had a good hour with whoever it was. That's a long massage. Waldo drove to

Hugo and Cam's flat and waited outside to see what time Hugo returned. As expected, he strolled around the corner, just after five. Everything appeared normal.

CHAPTER 7

Jac was used to Waldo returning from his prison visits feeling rather jolly. Waldo liked Ian and he enjoyed their conversations. He had been visiting him now for nearly two years and he had grown very fond of him, even though he had been a notorious abductor and rapist of young women.

On this occasion, on Waldo's return, he was clearly upset. Jac thought he may have been crying.

It was an area of Waldo's life that Jac had never managed to penetrate. She had probed from, time to time, but generally he kept it to himself. She decided to ask what was troubling him. Waldo handed her a letter, which she read in silence.

'Dearest Waldo,

This morning, I expect you have been directed into the Governor's office and he has told you the news of my 'tragic' death. He will have handed you the sealed envelope containing this note and, when you have finished reading it, he will probably ask if he can take a photocopy to help with his enquiry into my death. Seems fair enough to me but I will leave it to your discretion.

I am sorry that I did not share with you my intention to die. I thought you might feel obliged to let the authorities know. I didn't want to put that responsibility on to you.

I think it right and proper that I should die and a lot of people in society would agree with me. After all, I have abducted, raped, frightened witless and, I am sure in some cases, permanently damaged the mental health and well-being of a large number of women.

There were times when I detected that you thought I was being flippant in describing my experiences but let me reassure you that I know how horrific my actions have been. Whatever my circumstances and whatever my problem, there can be no excuse for what I did. I acknowledge that absolutely and to mark this I shall bring my life to an end.

I think it unfair of society, however, to deny me the right to take my own life and instead condemn me to a life of imprisonment and isolation. I know that most people, who care about prisoners, believe it to be immoral and inhumane that society should support capital punishment. I put it to you that it would be much fairer, once the court has determined the verdict, to leave it to the convicted person to choose from a range of suitable punishments, so that they can decide their own fates. In my case, I would undoubtedly have chosen to be executed by injection. I am far too cowardly to have chosen being shot or any of the other more dramatic solutions. On the other hand, I feel it very cruel to be imprisoned for life.

If society had chosen life imprisonment on the grounds that it was the cruellest form of revenge that it could inflict, that would seem fair enough to me. But to choose it on the grounds that it is more humane than capital punishment is totally without recognition of the needs of the convicted person. It is worth thinking about, Waldo. You may like to take up the cause for those who come after me.

My main purpose in writing is to thank you for your visits and your friendship. I hope I am not over-stepping the mark, when I say that, towards the end, I thought that we had developed a close relationship and that we were very fond of each other. I was certainly very fond of you. I confess that when we first met and during those early months, I thought you were just another do-gooder, who wanted to feel better about themselves by visiting a pathetic character in prison. Of course, there must have been something of that in you to attract you into the visitor service in the first place, but you were different, very different.

Do you remember those early months when, other than the odd grunt, I wouldn't respond to your questions? But you persisted in coming to see me. I liked it when after a few attempts at conversation, you would then settle back and we would both sit there in absolute silence. It didn't seem to worry you and I found it restful and helpful to share silence with someone. Then, after about thirty or forty minutes you would quietly rise from your chair, shake my hand, and say, 'See you next week, Ian, same time, same place,' and call to be let out into the big wide world.

I think it was very special that yesterday, as though you realised it was going to be our final time together, you suggested that we spend a half an hour in silence, like the old times. It was really very beautiful, and it was during that time that I managed to gather the strength and resolve for the ordeal that lay ahead. I knew that within a few hours I would be dead. I am so grateful to you for that special time together.

As you know, I often reflect on what separates you and me, apart from the fact that I am a rapist and convicted criminal; minor differences I am sure you will agree. I have come to believe that the difference is that you genuinely like and respect other people and I don't. Generally, I have nothing but, I was going to say hatred for people, but it is not that, it is disdain. In many ways that is far more destructive, because it means that I have no feelings for them. Hatred invokes the same emotions as love, just the negative side, whereas disdain produces no emotional reaction other than boredom and that is truly worrying. I start off by liking them and things go downhill from there. For me, the whole process of building friendships, so beloved of 'normal' people, ends in my being let down, disappointed, disenchanted. I am of the view that people, deep down, are inadequate and worthless and they disguise this by looking good or being highly qualified or doing important jobs or, dare I say it, helping others. I thought you were of the same ilk, but time has proved otherwise. You were one of the few people I have grown to respect and like and time did not destroy that. Between you and Carol, you have transformed my life and enabled me to die in peace. Thank you so much. Would you give Carol my love? Also, if you are able to help her in any way or protect her from the hardships of the world, that would be really good.

I must go now. I have to prepare for the big event.

Goodbye friend and thank you once again.

Ian.'

"Gosh, Waldo, I am very sorry. I know you liked him a lot."

Jac put her arm around him, they cuddled and she kissed his cheeks and his eyes tenderly.

After several minutes of silence, she asked about Carol.

"Who's Carol, Waldo? In his letter, Ian says, 'give her my love'. Is that his ex?"

"No, his ex won't have anything to do with him. She emigrated to Australia. No, Carol was his final victim. After Carol he did not abduct or rape again and gave himself up to the police. In Carol, he met someone whom he believed responded to him sexually and emotionally. The first woman in his life ever to do so. Evidently, she testified against him in the trial, but she refused to say anything hateful against him, as the others had done. He also maintained that they exchanged glances at the trial that confirmed their feelings for one another.

"Jac, he was a man with real humanity, quite sensitive in many ways. Oh, I know he did some terrible things but, in many ways, he shared our values. I know it is hard to believe.

"I remember him telling me of his first victim, Yvonne, I think she was called. She was a librarian in the central library. She had a shrivelled hand. All his victims had some kind of disability, you know. One of his strange quirks. Anyway, he told me that he delayed abducting Yvonne because she was attending line-dancing lessons and she had so little in her life that he only abducted her after the lessons were over. It even came out in the trial."

Without the need for further prompting, he then went on to talk about Carol.

"Carol is deaf, you know. For Ian that was her disability. Apart from that she was a stunner. I thought I might go around to Carol's place and see if she wants to attend the funeral. What do you think?"

Jac thought it worth a try. Waldo fell asleep in her arms.

$$\pi$$

Waldo approached the door with trepidation. He was very uncertain as to whether he was doing the right thing. He pressed the doorbell and waited for a long while, before trying a second time. As he had anticipated, there was a small security camera pointing straight at him, so the occupant was able to judge whether or not to answer the door. Waldo considered that, as she was neither expecting him nor knew him, it was unlikely that she would respond. He decided to change tack and to write a letter first, so that she would know to expect him. He was about to leave, when all of a sudden, a high-pitched voice asked what he wanted.

Now he had prepared for this moment, so he held up to the camera a card with large print.

I AM WALDO WISE, IAN WEBB'S PRISON VISITOR

MAY I SPEAK WITH YOU PLEASE?

He also showed his prison visitor pass, though he realised that she couldn't possibly read it.

There was a long break before the door opened and Carol stood before him. Ian was right, she was stunningly beautiful. He held up another card.

SORRY MY SIGN LANGUAGE IS RUSTY

I WANT TO TALK TO YOU ABOUT IAN'S FUNERAL

She opened the door fully and beckoned him in. Her flat was sparsely furnished and had few frills but was tasteful and welcoming.

"Would you like a cup of tea?" she asked.

Even without the intercom, her voice was still rather disturbing, but he tried not to show it.

Waldo looked straight at her and said that he would love a cup, exaggerating his lip movements and raising his voice, as though he were talking to a foreigner.

By the time she returned, Waldo had had time to gather his thoughts and produced a notebook and pen, ready for their conversation; he judged that an exchange of notes might be the best approach.

"Don't worry about the notepad," she said, "If you look directly at me whilst you talk, I should be able to understand you perfectly well. If you feel uncomfortable with me staring at you, we could use the laptop?"

She pointed to a laptop on a desk behind her, where she had clearly been working prior to Waldo's arrival.

"Not at all," Waldo said, risking a smile for the first time. She smiled back and Waldo was overwhelmed by her wonderful smile, and thought, no wonder Ian fell for her.

Waldo decided that Carol was sufficiently robust for him not to pussyfoot around. So, he told her firstly about his prison visits and the affection that had grown between him and Ian and then ventured a summary of Ian's story of his abductions and rapes. He also spent a good deal of time explaining Ian's reaction to his meeting with Carol and his gratitude and feelings for her. He left out the juicier bits; Ian had spared nothing in his reports.

On a number of occasions during his tale, he offered Carol the opportunity to comment but she shook her head and asked him to continue.

He finished by telling her of the forthcoming funeral arrangements and asked if she would like to join him. He doubted there would be many attending. Waldo explained that he was going to say a few words, in his memory.

Throughout his explanation, Carol showed no sign of emotion. She sat, carefully observing his lips, and absorbing every detail of his story. Then she simply said, "Yes, I would like to come to the funeral with you."

They finished by making detailed plans for the following Wednesday, the day of the funeral, shook hands, and said their farewells.

$$\pi$$

Waldo was expecting just three people to attend the funeral, a representative of the prison service, who may or may not have known Ian, Carol, and himself. The newspapers had lost interest in the case some time ago and his parents had disowned him.

Waldo agreed with Carol that he would drive. He had cleaned the car in her honour. He arrived at Carol's at the appointed hour, and she was peering out of the window awaiting his arrival.

She was beautifully dressed for the occasion in a very simple black dress, which came just above the knee and, with her high heels, she stood just a little taller than Waldo. He thought how elegant she looked, like a model but with a fuller and more appealing figure.

She slid into the passenger seat, and they exchanged subdued smiles. He drove sedately, as befitted the occasion. She was unsure whether this was how he drove normally or whether he was getting in the mood for the service. She didn't like to ask.

They arrived at the crematorium with ten minutes to spare and walked slowly around the grounds, waiting for the hearse to arrive. They felt relaxed in each other's company. He pointed to a song thrush, singing its heart out perched high on an oak tree. Carol acknowledged his sighting with a nod and a smile. Then he realised how foolish he had been and that she had probably never had the delight of listening to a song thrush. His hand covered his mouth to acknowledge his stupidity, as he looked across to Carol. She laughed and gave him a nudge with her elbow.

The hearse crunched up the driveway and they entered the chapel ready for the service. As Waldo had predicted, there were just the three of them. Carol and Waldo nodded soberly towards the prison officer and to the prison chaplain, who had agreed to lead the service. They reciprocated.

The chaplain looked rather nervous and unsure of himself. Waldo thought it was probably because he knew the crimes that Ian had committed and he felt uncomfortable about giving him his blessing.

At the appropriate point in proceedings, the chaplain nodded to Waldo to come to the front and deliver his eulogy. As he left the pew, he gave Carol a copy of his words, so that she might follow what he was saying.

"I became Ian's prison visitor shortly after he began his life sentence. I was not looking forward to it, given Ian's reputation and the nature of his crimes, but if you are a visitor you have to take the rough with the smooth. In the same way, Ian tolerated me in the early days but, for whatever reason, we both decided to give it a go and see if anything would come of the visits.

"After eighteen months of visiting him once a fortnight and latterly every week, I learned to respect and like Ian very much and, from what I understand, he felt the same way about me. This does not mean that I condone what he did but I came to know 'another' Ian; the one beneath the surface and beyond his troubles.

"Ian never made any excuses for his behaviour. He looked for explanations as to why he behaved in such a manner, but he never once tried to excuse himself or seek forgiveness. I think it was typical of the man that he never blamed his parents, his brothers, his partners, his teachers, his friends, his enemies or, indeed, anyone or anything else for what he did. He put it down to his personality, his circumstances, his weaknesses, and his obsessive drives but, in truth, he had no more idea than you or I, why he became a notorious abductor and rapist.

"I do not want to go through the detail of his life or to praise him unduly; this would not be fair to his victims, his relatives, or to Ian. I would just like to say that the man I came to know was a sensitive and lovely man and I was very fond of him. I learnt something very special from Ian and that was that even the most outrageous and perhaps dangerous individuals can also be kindly and caring and loving.

"Society does not have a good or effective way of dealing with its very serious offenders. There is no rehabilitation or prospect of release or hope of any kind, just four walls and the most boring of daily routines. I believe he did the right thing in taking his life. He chose to die, and he did not die in misery. He chose the only intelligent option open to him and died whilst he still had the ability to think and feel in the same way as you or I.

"You did wrong and you hurt a lot of people, Ian. But I learnt a lot from you, and I was very fond of you. I will miss you."

On returning to his seat, he could see that Carol was staring at the piece of paper he had given her and that her eyes and cheeks were wet with tears.

They left the crematorium without saying a word. Without asking her permission, he drove her to the Ship, a boat that had been converted into a pub and moored on the well-known floating harbour. They had a drink.

The activity on the river and wind blowing up the gorge helped to take their minds off matters and relieved them of the necessity of talking. On their second drink, he asked Carol what she did for a living.

"I'm unemployed, silly. Who wants someone who is deaf and when she speaks sounds like a strangulated monkey?"

Waldo turned to face her before speaking.

"When I first met you, you had been doing something on the computer. It looked as though you were working."

"I occasionally do research for the Head of Psychology at the university, we studied at Durham together. He feels sorry for me. Though I must say, what I am doing now is a particularly interesting study. Alas, I only ever get to do desk research and that is not my style."

"Your degree and your research skills could be very useful. If Jac agrees, would you be interested in working for us?"

"What do you do? Who's Jac?"

"Sorry, I assumed you knew. I feel as though we've known each other for a long time. It's all Ian's fault. Let's have something to eat and then come back to the office with me and I'll explain what we do. Would you like that?"

"I'd love it."

Surprisingly, they both chose substantial main courses, Carol fish and chips and Waldo his favourite roast duck. They cleared their plates. Carol wondered what Ian would have chosen.

"I suspect he was a roast beef and Yorkshire pud man, something robust to go with his other appetites. Oh, forgive me, I shouldn't have said that," she said.

They looked at each other and burst out laughing. Waldo thought that Ian would have appreciated the sentiment.

"He would not want us to be sad for long and would encourage us to celebrate his death."

Waldo raised his glass and clinked glasses with Carol.

"Here's to Ian."

"To Ian," she cried, raising her glass.

"And here's to you and the possibility of you ..." Waldo proclaimed, getting ahead of himself.

Carol interrupted him before he promised too much. She was cautious about hoping for too much, in the light of her previous experience in life.

$$\pi$$

Jac was out when the two of them got back to the office; she was doing a follow-up visit to Robert Harmsworth.

"Come in and welcome to our new world," Waldo said, facing Carol and trying to mouth the words clearly.

Like most people, he also instinctively still raised his voice in the hope that it might just get through but, realising his mistake, he deliberately softened his voice. He gave Carol a copy of their publicity bumph to read. The phone rang and Waldo picked it up. Carol wandered through the offices reading and nosing around, whilst he answered it. Waldo was thinking, now there's a problem, of course, Carol wouldn't be able to answer the phone.

As soon as he replaced the phone, Carol re-appeared and said, "What lovely offices but where are all your computers?"

Waldo laughed.

"Jac and I just have a laptop each and we email anything we need to share."

"As your caseloads build, surely that won't be sufficient?"

"No, you are right."

Waldo threw her a question.

"What will we need then?"

"I would have to understand your business before I could make a judgement like that, but I would be happy to work it through for you. Perhaps, it could be part of a trial to see if I could be useful to you and we like each other."

At that moment, Jac walked through the door and slumped into the sofa with a big sigh, without saying a word and having failed to notice Carol.

Jac was just about to say something untoward, when she noticed Carol.

"Oh, I'm sorry, we haven't met, I'm Jac Beauley."

The two women shook hands.

"Hi, I'm Carol Grigg."

"Welcome Carol. Of course, you have been to the funeral with

Waldo. You two clearly got on well then?"

Forgetting Carol's deafness, Jac turned away as she finished her sentence.

Carol lost the meaning and cast a look towards Waldo. He mouthed her comment clearly and simplified what she had said. "Jac thinks we must like each other, as you came back here with me."

Waldo then turned to Jac.

"Jac, Carol has a hearing problem, so it would be helpful if you turned toward her when you speak; she lip-reads brilliantly. Carol took a degree in psychology and does part-time research for the university. Do you think she might be useful to us?"

Jac looked at Carol.

"That sounds promising," correcting her previous mistake and turning towards Carol as she spoke.

"If you would excuse us just for minute, Carol, Waldo and I need to talk."

Carol nodded and smiled. Jac beckoned Waldo to join her in the interview room. As Waldo made his way across the office, he was thinking that he had over-stepped the mark and that he was going to be chastised. Jac took a very measured stance.

"As you know, Waldo, I am desperate for help but is Carol the right person? I have here a tape with two hours of discussion with Robert Harmsworth and I have notes in support. What would be wonderful is to have someone translate them into text for me, whilst I think through the next moves. But an audio tape isn't much good to her, is it?"

"No, I suspect not, though there may be some 'app' we could use to transfer it to computer."

"Anyway, this is highly confidential stuff. We don't know her from Adam."

"True. Let me follow up with references and talk to Carol about technological aids, which might enable her to work more effectively with us. I think she is very bright and very able and could be really valuable to us. Are you happy for me to follow it through?"

"Yes, of course, let's go for it. What have we got to lose?" Jac said and, in an encouraging way, added, "Shall we offer her a trial?"

"I suggest I talk to her about what we do and discuss what contribution she could make to our work. I will then draft a role description and see if you are happy with it. Meanwhile, I will check out references and assistive technology. If all is well, I think we then offer her a position as a self-employed Associate and get her to sign a contract and a statement of confidentiality; I could adapt one that we used in the GP practice. How does that sound?"

"That sounds brilliant. It's the advantage of having been around for so long," said Jac, teasing him about his longevity. "She has a lovely face; so open, so clear. We'd better keep her well away from Harriet. Let's go back in now and tell her what we are thinking. She might not be interested, of course."

Carol's reaction was one of delight at the news. She couldn't wait to prove herself. She rejected Waldo's offer of a lift and waved goodbye, holding open the door as she left for an older woman wanting to come in. They smiled as they passed each other.

"Hello, you won't know me, I'm Margaret, a friend of Robert Harmsworth, you're doing some work for him, I believe."

Aware of the danger of breaking confidences, Jac ignored the question but politely introduced herself and Waldo.

"I'm glad to see things are taking off, I was a bit worried to start with," Margaret stated boldly.

Jac couldn't imagine Robert Harmsworth talking about his problem. To divert attention away from him, Jac changed tack.

"How do you know about us?" she asked rather puzzled.

"I sit in the cafe opposite having a cup of tea, doing my crossword and monitoring what's happening in the street. At my age that's about as exciting as it gets. That's where I met Robert. We haven't known each other long. I met him when he was eyeing you up and trying to decide whether to employ you; we got talking. He must be your first customer? Robert and I went to see the Tempest at the Tobacco Factory. We saw the two of you there. Wasn't it wonderful?"

"Yes, it was really good. Are you a regular at the Tobacco Factory, Margaret?"

"No, it was my first time but try stopping me from now on. Now, I mustn't keep you, I know how busy you have become in the last few weeks. There are a couple of things I would like to tell you, which may be of interest."

Waldo and Jac both reached the same conclusion at the same time, namely that Margaret was not just an idle gossip but an intelligent and observant individual.

"Would you like a cuppa?" Waldo asked. "I was just going to put the kettle on."

"I'd love one," Jac and Margaret said in harmony and giggled conspiratorially.

Waldo went off to make tea and Jac and Margaret found out a little more about each other.

"I know that Waldo lives above the shop, but do you live locally?"

Margaret inquired gently.

"No, I live on the Somerset Levels, in Langport. My partner and I have a house overlooking the river Parrot. Do you know Langport?"

"I have been there but not for many years. To say I know it would be an exaggeration. I live above the charity shop opposite. I have lived in Southville for the past forty years. My husband and I brought up the boys here. It's my home. I love it. I like the fact that Waldo lives and works here, that's rather nice."

Jac did not take it as a rebuke but as a hint that she needed to live closer. She thought Margaret was probably right about that. She noticed Margaret's paper folded open at the cryptic crossword and saw that she had completed most of it.

"Have you done one across, I haven't managed it yet?" Jac asked.

"Alas, that top left corner is a brute today. No, I'm hoping my boy will help."

At that point, Waldo came back into the front office with three cups of tea and three slices of Victoria sponge cake.

"I thought we should all relax and have a treat. I bought the cake from the bakers down the road. It's a very good baker's, isn't it?"

"Their carrot cake is also rather good, should you fancy a change," Margaret advised. "Now, let me get down to business. You eat and I'll talk.

"A woman, I would think in her late forties, early fifties perhaps, well-dressed but looking pretty distraught and hence somewhat dishevelled, has stood outside your shop on three occasions now. The first time was at the end of last week, she didn't stop, just read the blurb on the window and walked on. On Monday, she was back, this time she lingered but neither of you were in. She waited for about five or so minutes and then walked on. Again, she looked anxious. She was back again this lunch time, and this time waited half an hour but, obviously, you have only just returned. I am concerned that she needs your help and is failing to make contact."

"She hasn't left a message on the telephone or emailed us," Waldo observed.

"Perhaps she doesn't like to. Some people prefer face-to-face, especially when it's something very personal," Margaret advised.

"Yes, you are right, Margaret, we need someone in the office all of the time, who can field calls and act as the first point of contact with visitors, but we thought we'd better leave appointing a receptionist until things get going. Have you ever seen her before, Margaret? You know the area well."

"I must say she does look familiar but for the life of me I can't remember where I have seen her. I'll ask Jeremy, my boy, he might know her. Jem still lives with me, he's autistic and suffers from depression, but he's as sharp as a needle, he might remember her. He monitors what's going on in the street too, when he hasn't got his head down in the computer."

"How old is your boy, Margaret?"

"He's forty this year. It's a terrible shame. He's a nice lad and really clever."

Waldo slipped back into his old role.

"I suppose he sees his doctor regularly and is on medication?"

"Oh yes, he's very assiduous about taking his medicine and it does help. He's going through a very good patch at the moment. He's taking an Open University degree; I think it's in criminology. Unfortunately, he just cannot relate to people. Even he and I have our troubles.

"Anyway, enough about Jem, poor lad. What I'll do is get him to keep an eye out from his eerie and see if he recognises her. He went to school in the area and knows most of the kids and their mums and dads, far better than I do."

"That would be very kind, Margaret. We will also keep an eye open and hopefully spot our visitor."

Margaret drank the last of her tea and stood up ready to go.

"I see you're fairly friendly with Harriet from the pub?" she threw out as a farewell remark. "She's a jolly soul, isn't she, and a good one."

"You know Harriet too? Gosh, she gets around," Jac said, a little disparagingly.

"She does, indeed, and I suppose it was that which worried me. If I understand your position correctly, you are setting yourselves up as an agency to help people who have problems of a social nature, who can't or don't want to use social workers, the police, unions, lawyers, and so on. You are a kind of last resort, but which is highly skilled and above corruption. Robert told me that you are even setting up a fund for those who can't afford to pay, so that they too can access your services. That's right, isn't it?"

Waldo nodded without making any comment. Jac explained that whilst they aspired to achieve the goals Margaret had just outlined, they were still a distant hope and there was still no money in the reserve fund.

Both correctly suspected that Margaret had not yet finished her remarks.

"Don't get me wrong, I like Harriet and she's really good fun, but she does have a reputation as a bit of a wild one, which would not exactly help your cause and may taint your image. Please forgive me if I am over-stepping the mark. I come from a family who fought for the rights of individuals and helped them solve problems. I feel strongly about these matters, and I believe in your cause. I know you are commercial, but you are different. I would hate it to fail, because of some silly thing like this. You know what people are."

"Well, that gives us plenty to think about, Margaret. Thank you ever so much for everything and please keep in contact. Do call in from time to time, we'd love to see you," Jac said enthusiastically.

They all shook hands and there was plenty of joking and jesting as they parted company.

CHAPTER 8

Cam and Waldo met for lunch the next day. They met at The Quayside Restaurant again and they were pleased to see each other, though Waldo maintained a subdued tone at the start, knowing that he had some unfavourable news to convey. They ordered drinks and passed the time of day. Cam couldn't hold back any longer.

"Well, how's it going Waldo? Any news?"

"Well, I have observed what may be unusual behaviour but, you understand, I have nothing positive to report yet. Are you aware that, occasionally, Hugo visits a pub on the way home?"

"No, I am not. I'm surprised but now you come to mention it, he sometimes has a faint smell of beer on his breath. We both use a mouth freshener."

"Do you and Hugo ever visit the King's Head just off the bottom of Park Street? Is it a pub you know?"

"No, I don't know it, why is that where he goes?"

"Yes, it is. I am less certain of this but are you aware that he may stop off on his way home and have a massage?"

"Massage! No, I am not."

Waldo was concerned, because Cam began to look very flustered and to raise his voice.

"Now keep calm, Cam. I am not absolutely sure of my facts yet. I just need to sound you out, so that I know if this is a line of enquiry worth pursuing. On Tuesday afternoon, he left work a quarter of an hour early and called in for a pint. Just that, nothing more. On Thursday, however, he left work much earlier and he called in for a pint but only after he had been opposite, I think, for a massage."

"I am dumb-founded."

"Well, as I say, these are only preliminary findings and in terms of the massage, it is only speculation on my part; I have no direct evidence at this time. In the light of your lack of knowledge about his visits, however, over the next week, I intend to pursue them in more detail, so that when we meet next week, I can confirm or deny them. Is that alright with you?"

"I don't know what to say, I feel pretty shattered."

"Would you rather I stopped the investigation now? Would you rather not know any more?"

"No, please carry on. Perhaps, during this lunch hour you can help me to gather my thoughts, so that I can behave normally when Hugo comes home tonight. After all, we don't know anything for sure, do we?"

"Absolutely. All I know for certain is that he sometimes grabs a pint on the way home and that, on one occasion, he went into the building opposite for an hour, prior to having a pint and coming home. That is all I know."

"It could be quite significant though, couldn't it?"

"It could be but let us not jump to any conclusions at this stage. Let's talk about something else now and enjoy our lunch together.

π

After Waldo's positive report on the outcomes of his visits to the daughters, Jac was keen for Robert Harmsworth to pick up where he left off and explain about the S & M outfit.

"The problem is," he began, "when you have been married to someone for a number of years and you have brought three children into the world and you know each other extremely well, it is very difficult to appreciate the delights of seeing them dressed in revealing gear and acting erotically. Susie had no problem, she seemed to have no embarrassment, whatsoever, but I just couldn't get used to it. I suppose if we had been new, it would have been different. She called me a spoil-sport. So, the outfit didn't get used for a year or more."

He hesitated and was clearly struggling to know whether he should say anymore. Jac let him struggle.

"I suppose I am going to have to tell you the full story," he confessed.

Jac sat very still and did not say a word.

"Susie and I became very friendly with a couple down the road. Our children played together, and we all got on really well. One evening, when we all had a little too much wine and the atmosphere became rather raucous, Katy and Jim confessed that they were swingers. You know what I mean by swingers, the word is probably old-fashioned and out of use by now?"

Jac signalled that she understood but said nothing.

"Jim got up and went around the table behind Susie and started massaging her shoulders and Katy did the same to me. It wasn't long before Jim and Susie disappeared upstairs and left Katy and me to get on with it. I made love to her but very reluctantly and I was determined to sort things as soon as we got home. I was furious. Susie, however, thoroughly enjoyed herself and thought I was over-reacting.

"It was a difficult moment in our marriage. In some respects, Susie gave me an ultimatum; either I went along with the shenanigans, or we would have to part. I am not sure she would have gone her own way, but she left me in no doubt that she needed excitement outside of the marriage. It took me a very long time to come to terms with it, but I didn't want to lose her. Not to bore you with the finer detail, the relationship with the couple resumed and after a few more months they invited us to a party, which turned out to be for their swinger, or is it swinging, friends. I hardly saw Susie all night. I had a number of entanglements during the evening, all of which seemed particularly unsavoury and unfulfilling. It was not for me. Needless to say, Susie loved every minute of it. It became clear during the evening that the group, or as many of them as they could muster, met every other Tuesday evening, taking it in turns to host the event. Swinging did not appeal to me, nor did the idea that I was to be turned-on to people who I did not particularly like or fancy, on alternate Tuesdays. It seemed absurd. Susie and I talked it over and we agreed that she could attend the events on her own and I would babysit, though we would not host the event; we agreed to pay Katy and Jim to host it for us. I remained friends with Katy and Jim, but we ceased to swing, if that is the right expression, and I never attended the swingers gathering again. In the family, it became known as mummy's Tuesday dance night. Needless to say, the S & M gear came into regular use."

The confession took a lot out of Robert, but Jac was determined to keep the confessional going.

"According to Waldo, both the girls mentioned mummy's dance night but were unable to throw any light on the subject. Linda was aware that on at least one occasion she returned home after having been mugged. Can you throw any light on that?"

There was a long silence, when Robert Harmsworth considered what to say. Jac offered to make a coffee and he gratefully accepted; he needed time to think. When Jac returned with the coffees and resumed her seat, Robert Harmsworth was ready.

"As time went on, and Tuesdays became a regular feature of Susie's life, her needs became more and more extreme. I noticed it in our sex life. I should point out that our love for one another and our enjoyment of sex never waned during this time. There were times, however, when I wanted to end it all, but I never shared that with Susie.

"Things came to a head one evening when she came back very late and was delivered by one of the group. She had been quite severely beaten. Her face was bloody, her body covered in bruises, and she had a strange-looking welt around her neck. I asked the guy whether she had been mugged or something. He looked at me quizzically, shook his head, and shrugged his shoulders. I guessed this must have been part of some sexual act. I thanked him for bringing her home. I spotted Linda at the top of the stairs and, in my authoritative, father voice, told her to go back to bed. I spent the next hour cleaning up Susie and then put her to bed. She was not fit to leave her bed for three days. I never asked her about the details of what happened; I couldn't face it. We agreed not to say anything to the children. It happened on two further occasions.

"Shortly after the third time, Susie went to see the doctor with a lump in her breast. He sent her for a scan, and she was diagnosed with breast cancer. She had an operation to remove her left breast and was informed afterwards that the cancer had spread and she would require intensive radiotherapy and chemotherapy. As you know, within six months she was dead. The whole family was devastated. I was bereft. For all her flaws, Susie was a marvellous and wonderful person, whom I loved dearly. She was the life and soul of the family and everything and everybody she touched."

Robert Harmsworth's face betrayed his pain and his loss and Jac could see that there was little point in taking the conversation any further.

"Let's stop there. Thank you for being so candid. Can I leave my next visit until I have had a chance to talk to Lucy? By the way, I'm having difficulty getting hold of her."

"Oh, how foolish I am. I am so sorry. In all the excitement, it had slipped my mind that she and John and their friends have all gone to Italy. They're away for most of August. One of their friends has a huge villa in Tuscany. What are we to do?"

"I am not sure she would welcome a visit from me on her hols. Let's reflect on things over the weekend and meet next week to determine our best approach. Whatever we decide, I think it is important that we don't lose momentum."

Robert Harmsworth agreed, and they decided to speak on the phone very soon. They parted company with a handshake and a kindly exchange of looks.

$$\pi$$

Waldo was pretty nervous but there was also something in him that was looking forward to the experience. He'd chosen to visit the massage parlour on the same day as Hugo, so that he could maximise the benefit of his personal 'sacrifice'. He thought the risk of being recognised by Hugo was no longer significant, for all would be revealed very shortly – many a true word, he thought to himself and chuckled.

Waldo went into the pub first and had a G & T to give himself courage. No sign of Hugo yet but he should already be there, if he had done his calculations correctly.

The barman greeted Waldo. "I hear you've booked in with Jean Pierre today? He's a lovely chap and you've nothing to fear, he won't push it too far or too fast, as it were," and burst into laughter.

Waldo was surprised he knew of his appointment, clearly confidentiality was not part of their professional practice. Waldo tried to join in with the repartee, but his efforts fell well short of the mark, partly due to his nervousness and partly due to his lack of ability; he was no great wit. They exchanged further tittle-tattle and then Waldo looked at his watch and realised his time had come.

"Well, time's up. Be kind to me, Jean Pierre," he pleaded out loud with his hands clasped in act of prayer.

The barman laughed and wished him well.

"Do come in and see me afterwards. I can't wait to hear how you get on."

Waldo rang the doorbell and heard the door lock release. He pushed the door open and made his way down a dimly lit corridor. He was not sure where to go or what to do. The lack of signage was on a par with his old health centre. His fellow GPs considered that patients in Bath were capable of working out what to do and where to go for themselves. He reached a door at the far end of the corridor and tentatively opened it.

Sitting on a leather sofa, with his legs spread-eagled, was a very muscular individual, whose biceps stretched the material of his white T shirt to breaking point and whose jeans, Waldo concluded, could only have been sprayed on. His arms were heavily tattooed, though subdued lighting precluded the possibility of discerning any detail.

"I'm here to see Jean Pierre for a massage."

Waldo emphasised the latter part of the sentence, in case there was any misunderstanding.

"Ah, yes, you're the straight guy, Jean Pierre mentioned you. Welcome, he'll be down in a minute."

As he said this, Jean Pierre came running down the stairs two at a time.

"Hello Waldo darling. I am pleased to see you. I never thought you'd have the courage."

Pointing at the receptionist, he added, "You don't want to get mixed up with this sex maniac, he'd have your knickers off soon as look at you. Come with me, sweetie."

And with that Waldo followed Jean Pierre upstairs to the pink room.

"What do you think of my little place? All my own work."

Waldo smiled and said, "Not quite my cup of tea, Jean Pierre, but very interesting."

"Bless, you intellectuals."

For the first time, Waldo had a chance to look at what Jean Pierre was wearing. His ensemble consisted of a tightly fitting pink singlet and matching shorts, which were very short indeed, and a pair of pink trainers. Waldo thought the whole outfit rather strange and unappealing; he'd had higher hopes. There was, however, no doubting that Jean Pierre had the most beautiful body, well-proportioned, well-honed and toned and that he was extremely good looking; an Adonis.

His musings, however, were brought to an abrupt end by Jean Pierre's request.

"Off with them then sweetie. We haven't all day."

"What shall I take off? Do I leave my boxer shorts on?"

"If you would feel better leaving them on, then that's OK with me, but you would be my first customer, ever, to leave them on."

Jean Pierre tapped the massage table, which was topped with a sheet in a delicate shade of pink.

"Face down to start with, sweetie, we don't want you getting over-excited right away."

Waldo decided to be bold and strip off. He lay on the table as instructed. Jean Pierre removed his singlet and his shorts to reveal a G string of astounding skimpiness and made of a material which set off his bits to best effect. It was clear to Waldo that there was much to hide.

Jean Pierre put on an Ella Fitzgerald disc to fool them both into thinking that it wasn't three o'clock in the afternoon. He rubbed his hands in massage oil and began to massage Waldo's back. Waldo had never actually had a massage before and there was no doubt in his mind that Jean Pierre was an expert. His fingers and palms exerted a delicate balance between firmness and lightness, which made his skin tingle and his muscles relax. He started to let his thoughts drift and to enjoy the experience. Jean Pierre didn't say a word. He concentrated on his job.

Waldo's thoughts were disturbed from their wanderings when Jean Pierre, standing at the head of the massage table, leant over to massage his bottom, letting his ample groin gently rub against Waldo's head. Waldo could not resist a little look-see. He was greeted by a monster peeking over the top of the G string. He'd never seen the like before; fearsome. He lay his head down quickly lest he invited trouble. He decided to distract Jean Pierre by pursuing his real goal of learning more of the 'ins and outs' of the massage parlour.

"Are you the only one working here today, Jean Pierre?"

"No, Jimmy's on today. Now there's a man you should avoid. He's into the aggressive stuff, which quite a few gay guys like. If you think I'm fit, you want to see Jimmy. He's obsessed by fitness and the body beautiful. He's also into tattoos and has a particularly challenging portrayal of violence on his tender bits. He's actually a sweetie underneath it all but his professional persona is one of S & M with the emphasis on S. Even I struggle to cope with Jimmy's approach and I've been around a bit."

As he was talking, Jean Pierre moved away from Waldo's head and stood on his right side, so that his fingers could explore Waldo's bottom and legs more easily. After a few moments, with a deft and effortless movement, no doubt born of long experience, Jean Pierre suddenly lifted Waldo and folded his legs underneath his body. Jean Pierre then stretched Waldo's arms out straight above his head, so that he assumed a cat-like, yogic position. Waldo was helpless in the grip of this herculean force. Jean Pierre resumed the massage and increased the pressure, as he bore down heavily on Waldo. Waldo's heart began to race, as he suspected matters were getting out of hand. He hated to confess it, but the experience was very pleasing.

"I think that's enough now, Jean Pierre. Brilliantly done, and very pleasurable, but not for me, really."

"Are you sure you don't want me? Look, you can have all of this."

Waldo turned to find Jean Pierre had removed his G string and was standing there in all his glory. Waldo smiled admiringly.

"You must be very proud of that," he muttered, "but I must say 'no' to your kind offer. I admire but do not want to experience."

"Before this massage is over you will have relented," Jean Pierre teased and with that resumed the massage.

π

After the massage, Waldo went back into the bar for a recuperative drink and to see if Hugo had emerged.

"Well how did it go? You look very pleased with yourself? Are you one of us now?" the barman asked.

"No, I don't think so but, I must say, Jean Pierre is very good at his job and quite persuasive."

They both laughed and the barman poured Waldo a pint of shandy to refresh him.

"On the house," he said, "I think you are to be congratulated. Not many straight guys would have done that, brilliant. I think you were right to go with Jean Pierre though; Jimmy wouldn't be your type. Nor mine, he likes pain, lots of pain and inflicting it, which is more to the point. Your good health."

They both raised their glasses and enjoyed their pints.

Waldo was feeling very proud of himself and had almost forgotten why he was there. The arrival of Hugo for his post-massage drink brought him back to reality. Hugo was looking very red-faced and washed-out and looked as though he would need more than a drink to revive him. Waldo withdrew quietly to the corner of the lounge and started an exchange of text messages with Jac, in order to avoid having a conversation with Hugo. After a brief conversation with the barman, Hugo went to the loo and Waldo seized his moment. He downed his pint quickly, a challenge for a wine drinker, and left the pub, waving and calling 'goodbye' to the barman.

"See you again soon, I hope," he shouted after Waldo.

CHAPTER 9

Waldo was strolling down North Street towards the office feeling very relaxed and carefree, if a little tired, after his exertions with Jean Pierre. In the distance, he spotted a woman peering through the office window. He then saw Margaret cross the road and tap her on the shoulder. Waldo quickened his pace and Margaret looked up and saw him hastening towards them.

"Dr Wise," Margaret announced grandly, "this is Mrs Woodry and she needs your help."

"Thank you, Margaret, you have been very kind. Hello Mrs Woodry, I am pleased to meet you and I am sorry we have been so elusive. We have only just opened, and we still need to employ a receptionist. Fortunately, Margaret has been helping by keeping an eye open for us."

They shook hands. Margaret raised a hand by way of farewell and Waldo reciprocated and then she disappeared back into the cafe opposite. Waldo unlocked the office door and invited Mrs Woodry in. She looked distraught.

"Please come through to the interview room, Mrs Woodry, where we will be undisturbed. Can I get you a tea or coffee?"

She shook her head and sat down without saying a word.

"My apologies again that no one was here to meet you. Now, all I know at the moment is that you are called Mrs Woodry and that's thanks to Margaret. Do you live locally?"

In a thin, precise, high-pitched, educated voice, she explained, "We have a small house on the docks. It is all I could afford after my husband left but it's big enough for us, that is my son and me. We manage."

Waldo decided to give her time to settle.

"My name is Waldo Wise, and my business partner is Jac Beauley. Jac should be back soon, and I can introduce you. I was a GP in Bath for ten years and Jac a psychologist."

Waldo just talked, not that she was listening, but he wanted to give her time.

"Perhaps you could start by giving me your full name and that of your son and an address and contact numbers, before outlining the nature of the problem. What we normally do then is determine how we might help you and work out the costs, so that you can decide if you want to use our services. Does that sound alright to you?"

Without responding to Waldo in any way, she proceeded to tell him their names and how they could be contacted. She was called Joanna Woodry and her son was James Woodry. Waldo knew the terrace of houses where they lived. It was part of a development on the South side of the docks. They were fortunate in having one overlooking the busy inner harbour and harbour-side restaurants, which she said pleased James a lot. "He spends many hours looking at what's going on."

This was the first hint that the problem may involve James.

"How old is your son?"

"He is twenty-six, but he first became ill whilst he was at university. I realised that all was not well when he came home early at the end of his first year. I had no idea what the problem was. He just said he was unwell but could give no further explanation. Then we were asked to go up and meet the college medical team."

She stopped and just stared at the table.

"Is it a physical or a mental illness?" Waldo asked.

"He has schizophrenia. It is a dreadful illness, Dr Wise but, of course, you would know that."

"Schizophrenia is dreadful for the patient and often just as bad for those looking after the patient. How do you cope?"

Joanna Woodry choked back the tears and it was some minutes before she was able to resume her story.

"I am afraid that I am not coping at all well at the moment. In truth, I haven't been coping for the past six months or so. I get by. It is why I am here. I am desperate for help, Dr Wise."

"You realise, Mrs Woodry, that we don't offer direct support to people. What I mean is that we do not offer a care service, but we do try and resolve problems for people, so that they are better able to cope. How do you think we might be able to help you?"

"My main problem is with the psychiatrist and the Community Mental Health Team. They will not recognise that James is a danger to himself and to the community. I have explained how threatening he can be towards me and to others. I have seen him in the street, when he suddenly, I think the expression is, 'kicks off', without any warning and he shouts and screams and he really is very aggressive towards people. They cross the street to avoid him and mothers with babies know him now and avoid him like the plague. Sooner or later, he is going to harm someone, or worse, kill them. You read about such cases in the papers and then there is an outcry from the general public, but nothing ever seems to change. I fear my son is going to be the next headline. I love my son, Dr Wise, and I do not want him to end his days locked up in an institution, but we also have to think about public safety. I am at my wits end. I do not know what to do and the Community Team won't listen."

"Have you talked to your GP about it?"

"She's been really good. She sees James and me once a fortnight and has referred James to the Community Team on three occasions now. I have seen the letters she has written, and they are very full and persuasive. But each time they re-assess him and say that, given his condition, he is doing very well. They also say that they keep his medication under review and, providing he takes his medicine, then all should be well."

"As James's carer, have your needs been assessed?" Waldo asked.

"They asked me to complete a form about my needs, which I did. As a result, James attends a day centre, once a week, which they say is more about giving me a break than meeting James's needs. I must say, he seems to quite like going, it's just a pity it isn't five days a week; now that really would be helpful. You see, Dr Wise, he just roams the streets and gets into trouble with the police, and they return him home to me. When he is at the day centre, he has transport there and back, I know where he is and that he is safe. I can relax. The rest of the time, I sit on the edge of my seat, worrying."

"Have there been any instances of violence? Have the police had cause to charge him? Have they ever detained him?"

"No actual violence as yet, but sometimes you can see it in his eyes, he is very angry or, even worse, he is scared and on the point of exploding. Police try to avoid him, because they know he is under the care of mental health services, so if there is any trouble, they just call the emergency team."

"Have you tried that?"

"Oh yes, I call them all the time. They consider me an absolute nuisance; I know they do. They are very good with James. They are hopeless with me."

"How do you think we may be able to help you, Mrs Woodry?"

"I hoped you might be able to gather evidence that would support my case and persuade that bloody psychiatrist, excuse my language, Dr Wise, that James needs more direct help than he is getting at the moment. I am sure there is more that can be done, it is just that I am no longer capable of looking after him twenty-four hours a day, seven days a week; well, six anyway. Can you help me, Dr Wise?"

"We would certainly be able to observe his behaviour, keep a detailed record of where he goes and what he does and assess to what extent he is a danger to himself and to others. I don't know enough about the treatment of schizophrenia to know what else might be offered to him and I need to talk to Jac and others in-the-know to find out. I know that mental health services, generally, are seriously under-funded, so that may be one of the problems, but there have been a number of investigations into such cases, where serious incidences have occurred, and the Government has issued strong guidance on what actions need to be taken. So, we would be happy to make an assessment in the way you suggest. Perhaps, if you would allow us, we could also make a detailed assessment of your needs, as the primary carer in this case.

"This is a very difficult set of circumstances, Mrs Woodry, and I feel sure that we can help you. The problem is that I can't see us being able to do the right thing by you without spending at least ten days of our time on the investigation, writing up our findings and arguing with the powers that be. I might be wrong about that but that is my best guess at this stage. This means that it would cost you about five thousand pounds, can you afford that?"

"His father will pay for this. He has escaped without taking any responsibility for his son's care and, occasionally, when I force the issue, he buys his way out of trouble. This is going to be one of those occasions but a bit more costly than he would like, I am sure."

"What I suggest I do then is discuss with Jac how we might help you. We'll do some homework into schizophrenia and its treatment, and we'll put together ideas about how we can observe your son, in order to make the appropriate assessments. We'll work out how many days that would take and prepare a draft contract for your consideration.

"I think we will need about a week to do the preparation properly. Perhaps, we could meet this time next week to discuss our proposals, what do you think?"

"That sounds good. James goes to the day centre on Wednesdays, so it would be ideal for us to meet then. I know I am neurotic about James and that I get myself into a terrible state, but I am genuinely concerned that he might harm someone. His behaviour is deteriorating and there are days when he really scares me. Thank you for your time, Dr Wise."

"It has been a pleasure to meet you, Mrs Woodry. I sincerely hope that we will be able to help you."

As he was showing Mrs Woodry to the door, Jac came back and he was able to introduce her.

They watched Mrs Woodry walk up the street. Jac turned to Waldo and said, "My God, Waldo, she looks dreadful. What is the problem?"

He was just about to start telling Jac the story, when Margaret popped her head around the door.

"According to my Jem, Mrs Woodry is or was Mrs Dunwoody. Mr Dunwoody was the Head of a comprehensive school in North Bristol and was convicted of paedophilia; a big scandal in Bristol five or six years ago. Jem doesn't know Mrs Dunwoody or her son. Byeeeeeeee," she cried as she shut the door and scampered back across the road.

The thought occurred to Waldo that he needed to check the authenticity of this claim, as it may prove crucial to the case. He ran after Margaret and reached the other side of the road just as she was going into the cafe.

"Margaret, sorry to bother you, but how does your boy know that what he is saying is true? He doesn't know Mrs Dunwoody and he doesn't know her son. How can he be sure?"

"I asked him the same thing, Waldo."

Margaret was growing in confidence with every exchange.

"Evidently, he had some memory of her face connected with a criminal case but could not place it immediately; he has a photographic memory about some things. So, he took a photograph of her outside the office, blew it up, and then started searching his files; don't ask me what files, I haven't a clue. As he was going through them, he recalled her face being connected with a local incident, but it took another couple of hours to pin it down, because the name was wrong. Then he came across a report in the local newspaper and there was a photograph of the family, and the name was Dunwoody not Woodry. It was a piece of cake after that. Would you like a copy of the article and any of the files he has?"

"I would, very much, if that is alright with Jem. He may not be willing to let me have them, of course, but if he could guide me to the right website that would be helpful."

"Oh, Jem won't mind. He'd be delighted to think his work was proving useful."

"Thank him for me, Margaret, and thank you too."

Margaret grinned mischievously.

"Oh, and one more thing, Waldo, we believe you are being followed. We have seen them twice now. They look like Hell's Angels or something of the sort. Yesterday morning, they started to close in on you, when you came out of your flat door. You had taken about five or six steps, you hesitated, turned back and went indoors and shut the door behind you."

"Yes, that's right, I decided to make a few phone calls."

"Well, it's a jolly good job you did. They looked as though they were going to sort you out."

"Blimey, who could they be? I haven't offended anyone to the best of my knowledge."

"When you went back in, they considered ringing your doorbell but thought better of it and retreated. They waited on the corner opposite, just down from the cafe, but gave up after half an hour. I saw them shoot around the corner on their bikes not two minutes later; definitely bikers and definitely up to no good."

"Well, thank you for the tip off, Margaret. I will keep a wary eye open. I hadn't bargained on being open to attack in this job. I thought that was for more conventional private investigators, not for those of us working in the care market. You've got me worried now, Margaret."

π

Jac and Waldo spent most of the evening discussing how they might help Mrs Woodry. Then, they turned their attention to employing Carol and a receptionist.

Waldo explained to Jac that he had done quite a lot of homework on the assistive technology side of things and that the Bristol Centre for Deaf People was happy to give them all the advice and support they needed. From what the organisation knew of Carol, they believed that she was moderately deaf and there were a number of devices which might be of help in the office, so that she could make a really valuable contribution. Waldo explained that when he talked to the Centre, and gave them examples of the tapes, they were pretty convinced there would be no problem in transposing them electronically and for Carol to work on them from there.

"It sounds exciting, Waldo. Let's get Carol to fill in an application form and then we'll all meet together with the Centre staff and explore the various devices that would be helpful. If all goes well, we can then draft a job description and employ her as an Associate."

"Alright, shall we have another drink and discuss employing a receptionist, if you're up to it?" Waldo asked cautiously, knowing that Jac was tired.

"Are you sure we can afford it at this stage of the game, Waldo? I know more work is coming our way, but it may dry up and then we would be left paying someone we could ill-afford, or worse, having to make him or her redundant."

"I think we have to take the risk," Waldo stated, quite firmly, which was unusual for him.

"If you take the case of Mrs Woodry, she has been trying to make contact with us for the past few weeks, but we have been busy and out of the office. If we employ Carol, and she works mostly in the office, that will help, but her role is likely to be connected with research and supporting us in case work. I think we should employ a part-time receptionist, to begin with, perhaps to work complementary hours to Carol, so that we have cover on most days, at most times. Relying on Margaret is unprofessional and that is no criticism of Margaret, how she handled Mrs Woodry was first class."

"We could do worse than employ Margaret, of course," Jac suggested. "She is bright, enthusiastic, energetic and local, very local."

"Well, there's a thought," Waldo said encouragingly.

They smiled at each other. The idea of recruiting Margaret was quite appealing to them both.

"There is the problem, of course, that she knows and is friendly with Robert Harmsworth and that could be quite a serious consideration."

And with that thought, they agreed to work all these ideas through and to prepare a more detailed plan when their minds were fresher. They retired to the pub for a drink and a bite to eat.

$$\pi$$

When Waldo next met Mrs Woodry, she confirmed that her name used to be Dunwoody and that her husband was, indeed, convicted of being part of a paedophile ring. She added, in his defence, that there was no evidence of untoward behaviour with the children in his school or of any of the photographs being of children in his care.

"He was released from prison about two months ago and is now living in Norfolk. Obviously, he is on the sex offenders register and is reporting daily to the police station, but he is free, after a fashion. We don't see him anymore, but I keep in contact over James and let him know how he's doing, which, as you will appreciate, is not always good news."

With this issue out of the way, they agreed a programme of work. For Waldo, still being relatively close to the medical establishment, an important part of the process involved writing to Mrs Woodry's GP and to the head of the mental health team to let them know what was happening. He decided to address the letter to the GP, Dr Karen Knightly, and copy it to the Mental Health Trust.

Jac and Waldo reached the conclusion that they should assess Mrs Woodry's needs, as a carer, at the earliest opportunity, as it might give them some insights into her concerns and her motivations.

As it turned out, this was a wise move. Jac emerged from the process extremely concerned about Mrs Woodry's mental health, detecting symptoms of severe stress and quite serious depression; they called in additional help straightaway. They disguised their concerns by informing Mrs Woodry that they would like a second opinion, in order to reinforce their case for support. She seemed to enjoy the attention and put up no resistance.

The senior psychologist, whom they brought in to assess Mrs Woodry, confirmed that there were very worrying symptoms. He was of the view that, whilst she was not mentally ill, in a clinical sense, the situation was worrying and that her health needed careful monitoring and management. He shared Jac's concern that the matter was very serious. He strongly advised that they referred her back to her GP, as soon as possible. Waldo called Dr Knightly and she agreed to see him and Jac that afternoon.

"Come in, Dr Wise, very pleased to meet you again after all this time, and you, Dr Beauley."

They all shook hands and exchanged pleasantries. They agreed to use first names in this informal setting.

Karen couldn't resist asking him about his new role.

"Your job sounds jolly interesting, Waldo, how did you manage to escape from the humdrum of medicine?"

This took up a further five minutes but Waldo thought it important to establish a rapport before getting down to the more worrying business of Mrs Woodry. Waldo could see that Jac was getting a little impatient with them and couldn't wait to get down to more serious discussion. In a break in their conversation, Jac intervened and suggested she briefed Karen about Mrs Woodry's assessment.

Karen became paler at each revelation, thinking to herself, 'Why for Christ's sake didn't I pick this up during one of my consultations.' Waldo and Jac said reassuring things about how difficult it was to spot problems of this sort during a short consultation. Nevertheless, Karen remained somewhat perturbed by the findings and her lack of insight.

"If you agree, I will give John Godber a ring right away," Karen suggested. "John heads up the community psychiatric services," she added.

They both thought it a good idea. He was in a meeting when Karen called but his secretary promised to get him to ring back in five minutes. As promised, he called back and after listening to Karen's explanation, he was very co-operative and open-minded about the issue. Evidently, they too had had concerns about Mrs Woodry and James for some time but clearly things had deteriorated in recent weeks – a clever political response, Waldo thought.

Karen agreed to arrange a case conference with John Godber, the team manager, members of the community team, Jac, Waldo, and herself. The meeting was scheduled for a Wednesday in three weeks time.

Jac and Waldo realised they had very little time in which to gather evidence in support of Mrs Woodry's claim. It called for drastic action.

They planned to set up cameras within the Woodry home, so that they could record James's behaviour in all of the main living areas. They also agreed to follow him during his daily walks and assess the degree of threat he posed to himself and to the public. They agreed to tell James of their intentions.

π

Jac and Waldo moved fast. Within two days they had recruited Carol and Margaret to the team and both assumed their seats in the front office, immediately, as they had no other commitments.

Margaret was employed as receptionist and anything else that she or they could think of. Carol was employed as an Associate with special responsibility for research, IT, managing the business, providing support to case work and, like Margaret, anything that she or they could think of.

One of Carol's and Margaret's first duties had been to secure three quotations from firms to install cameras in the Woodry household. The team stood around, whilst Margaret opened the quotations and read out the bottom line. They were taken aback by the cost.

"It is such a small house and we are only asking them to cover four rooms, the hallway and the porch area. Three thousand pounds, that's daylight bloody robbery," was Jac's contribution.

"I have a thought," Margaret suggested, positively. "My Jem is an expert on cameras. Shall I ask him to examine the floor plans and the proposed project plan and ask him to assess what a reasonable figure would be?"

"If you would, Margaret, please, that would be most helpful. They could be ripping us off," said Jac, "or more importantly, our client," she added, correcting herself.

With coffees sorted, they settled down to their first get-together as a team. They sat in the front office and Jac and Waldo briefed the others as to current cases. They agreed with Margaret that she should not have any access to the Harmsworth case and files, as she was friendly with Robert Harmsworth. Jac had also spoken to Robert about Margaret's employment and the measures they had taken to keep files confidential. He had no objections and seemed delighted that Margaret had been given the job.

Carol, with her business manager hat on, raised the subject of regular team meetings. It was agreed that Friday lunchtimes would suit everyone and Jac and Waldo said they would try to make it back by lunchtime but, of course, it would depend on work demands at the time. It was further agreed they would start each team meeting with a modest working lunch; Margaret was to arrange sandwiches and soft drinks.

There was generally a jolly atmosphere and spirits were high. Jac thought it was more akin to a family gathering than an office meeting.

After the initial meeting was over, Jac and Waldo went about their duties and Carol and Margaret set about making the office more business-like and ensuring the systems worked effectively. One or two changes irritated Jac and Waldo but they knew that if you shared with someone, you had to compromise. They exchanged glances every now and then but decided that things were better left to the experts. Time would tell if some of the changes would prove effective but, as they were so rarely in the office, it made sense for Carol and Margaret to be in charge of making the office run smoothly.

At about eleven o'clock, Margaret nipped off to talk to Jem about the cost of cameras. At half eleven she reappeared and announced that Jem could do the whole job, provide and install the cameras, for less than twelve hundred. Jac and Waldo were at a loss as to how to react. They didn't know Jem and hardly knew Margaret.

"I have asked him to put a proper quote together and he is working on that now. He says that the cameras they have suggested are far too good for what we need."

They noted the use of the word 'we', she already felt part of the team and that was good.

"And he thinks the cost of installation should be about half what they are quoting; he reckons about four hours at the most and they are quoting a full day. Now, I don't want you to feel embarrassed by my intervention or obliged to accept his quote, after all, you don't know him."

As if at a union meeting, Margaret added, "So, I declare my interest in the matter and will have nothing further to do with the process or the decision."

"Thank you, Margaret," Waldo added, "I think that is right and proper. Jac, Carol, and I will determine who gets the contract but your contribution is much appreciated."

"He'll have the quote ready by lunch time. I said I would pop back in an hour."

And with that she busied herself picking up the cups and saucers and taking them through to the back room to wash them.

Carol smiled knowingly at us. "There now, that's telling you."

After lunch, Carol opened Jem's quote. He had included a very detailed specification: the type of cameras that were appropriate and why; the placement of the cameras and a correction to our proposed siting of the hallway camera to effect greater coverage; a recommendation as to the central recording unit and where it should be sited; and details of the installation work and the time for the fitting of each unit. Each item was costed, each section sub-totalled and a grand total at the end. The total cost was less than half the lowest quote from the others and it put them to shame in terms of the quality and detail of the submission.

They discussed the options and Jac summed up the position.

"The question is, 'Can we risk going with Jem?' We know that he is autistic and has mental health issues, but Margaret says he is in good form, at the moment, so that should not be a problem. In terms of cost and the detail of his proposal, no one comes near his submission. I think we have no option but to take the risk. If he fails to deliver, then we will have to fall back on one of the other quotes."

"I agree," said Carol, "and what wins the day for me, is the fact that Jem says he can complete the installation in two days, all the others are at least a week away. The only one who can complete quickly is the highest quote, at over three thousand pounds. I don't think that we should hesitate."

So, the decision was made. It was also agreed that Waldo should accompany Jem during the installation to ensure there were no problems. Carol did a formal letter accepting the quotation, which she gave to Margaret to deliver on her way home. Needless to say, Margaret was delighted. It was the first work her boy had had in six months.

$$\pi$$

On Thursday morning, Margaret brought Jem into the office. Jac and Carol had made themselves scarce, in case he was upset by meeting too many people at once.

He had a full beard, which was trimmed precisely, in the fashion of a naval commander, and a full head of hair with natural waves to complement his nautical look. He was wearing a sports jacket, matching trousers, shirt, and tie. Margaret had clearly supervised his dressing. He felt uncomfortable, especially with the tie, and he was constantly fiddling with his collar and trying to release the pressure on his neck. He and Waldo shook hands, but he said nothing and did not look Waldo in the eye. Waldo did not embarrass him with the usual niceties, and they wasted no time in setting out for their destination. As they went out of the door, Margaret looked very anxious, but Waldo turned and gave a reassuring smile, thinking to himself that it would take more than a smile to soothe a mother's fears for her son.

Waldo and Jem loaded the car with all the gear and then drove in silence to the Woodry's, which was less than five minutes away. Waldo asked Jem to stay in the car, whilst he prepared the way. Mrs Woodry seemed pleased to see him and was delighted that they were following-up their promise so quickly. She asked Waldo if he would mind if she went shopping whilst the work was being done. Waldo was hugely relieved.

She then introduced Waldo to James, who was sitting staring out of the window. He ignored the introduction and she apologised for his behaviour. Waldo was reassuring and thought to himself that this was the second mother he had tried to reassure in the past hour. Mrs Woodry left the house almost at once and before Waldo had had a chance to introduce Jem.

Jem and Waldo started by carrying out a survey of the house together. When they went into the sitting room, despite introductions, Jem and James ignored each another. Jem laid the floor plan on the table and started to match the plan with the proposed fitting sites.

Without a word, James got up and peered at the plan. After a few moments, he picked it up and took it into the dining room. Jem and Waldo followed. Waldo was feeling rather disconcerted by this intervention, but Jem showed no signs of concern. James then pointed to the proposed fitting site on the plan and the addition of a corner unit, without saying a word. Jem nodded gravely and proposed an alternative by pointing to the opposite corner. James made no acknowledgment of the suggestion but again picked up the plan and wondered off to the front door, opened it, and pointed to a further impediment to the proposed fitting. The two of them worked out the best sites without exchanging a word. Waldo realised that two highly intelligent minds were analysing and solving problems and that words between them were an irrelevance. He withdrew into the kitchen and sat at the kitchen table and started the crossword.

For the next few hours, during the fitting process, the two men worked together, as though they had known each other for years. Waldo did not interfere or say anything to either of them. Words would have got in the way. Schizophrenia met autism in creative harmony.

With the fitting completed and the central monitor connected, they were ready to test the system. At last Jem spoke to Waldo. He asked him to go outside the house, to come in and then walk from room to room. Waldo carried out his instructions and ended up in the hallway with the two of them staring at the monitor and rubbing their hands with glee. They were really pleased with their morning's work.

Jem asked Waldo to repeat his walk through the house, so that he could test the recording facility. Waldo did so and when he returned, Jem played it back on the laptop for Waldo to see. The image was perfect, even where the light was not strong. Waldo suggested they start the recording proper. He explained to James that they were going to leave it running all of the time and that it would record his movements and those of his mother. He explained that the cupboard containing the recording device would be locked from then on and only the PI Shop team would have access to it. He also added that they would be observing his movements, outside of the house, during the following week and asked if he had problem with that. He made no response.

With the fitting completed, James lost interest, ignored Waldo, and wondered into the sitting room and sat down to watch the television. Jem joined him and they watched television together.

Mrs Woodry returned shortly afterwards, and Waldo took her through the system. She seemed very pleased.

Jem and Waldo drove back to North Street again in silence. Waldo thanked him for his work, and they shook hands.

Margaret was waiting patiently in the office for their return.

"He did a superb job, Margaret, and he and James got on really well together. Brilliant," Waldo concluded.

She looked very proud. At last, her son had proved his worth.

"Carol, could you arrange for Jem to be paid as soon as possible, please," Waldo added.

"It's already done," she said rather sharply and handed Margaret an envelope addressed to her son, which contained a cheque for the full amount.

Margaret had a tear in her eye and Carol gave her a hug.

$$\pi$$

Waldo had promised Karen Knightly to give her an update on progress with James's case. He had been invited for a light supper.

He asked Karen whether he could bring Carol as part of her induction. She welcomed the idea.

At about six thirty, Waldo and Carol set off in jolly mood, chatting amicably, Waldo remembering to turn towards her when he spoke. They decided to take the most demanding route to Clifton, up the steep hill of Clifton Vale, which rose from the docks directly to the dizzy, social heights of Clifton. As they reached the top of the Vale, they turned left, along a poorly lit road, towards the main village and Karen's house.

Waldo heard heavy footsteps behind him and looked back, a little anxiously, Margaret's warning about bikers still lurking in the back of his mind. He could see the outline of a tall, hefty figure, dressed in black, fast approaching them. Carol gave Waldo a nudge in the ribs as she observed a similar figure heading towards them. They looked at each other in alarm.

Waldo and Carol stopped, turned their backs to the railings and waited to see if the threat was real or imagined, neither of them knowing quite what to do. The two figures drew within a few feet of them and stopped. They were big, heavy men dressed in black leather. From their wide aggressive stances and what they could see of their faces, they drew the conclusion that they were not friendly.

Carol wriggled her hips and wrestled with her skirt, until she was able to pull it all the way up to her waist, exposing the full length of her lower half. All three men stood and admired the vision of loveliness before them. They were drawn to a dark, equilateral triangle, at the junction of her limbs and pondered as to whether it was natural or a piece of skimpy underwear. Alas, the poor light precluded them from drawing any firm conclusion on the matter, though they were favouring natural. Their musings were rudely interrupted by Carol's right leg being drawn up and shooting out and smashing into the face of one of the men, her stiletto piercing his cheek and stabbing him fiercely in the gum; several teeth were seen to detach themselves from the owner. In one straight movement, like a falling tree, he went to ground, where he lay unconscious and bloody.

Waldo did not wish to be found wanting in these circumstances but knew he did not have the strength or the skill to take on his opponent in a round of fisticuffs. He concluded that his only asset was his robust forehead, which, although it had never been tested in aggression, had received many serious blows over the years and had come through with flying colours. He turned, grabbed the long hair of the figure before him and, pulling his body toward him, smashed his head between the top of the nose and the base of the forehead of his opponent. It produced a nasty cracking sound and blood shot from the man's nostrils in two hot streams. Waldo noticed it went all over his new coat, which he had put on especially for his visit to Clifton. He felt somewhat dizzy but OK after his deed and waited a number of seconds to see if it had had the desired effect. His opponent sank slowly to his knees and then fell forward on to his face with a dull thud. Waldo stepped to the side to allow him to fall freely.

Waldo immediately sprang to the aid of Carol's victim, judging that his airway might become blocked by blood and teeth and bits of flesh from various parts of the mouth. He cleared the airway and shouted to Carol to phone the police. She dialled 999 and then gave Waldo her phone, pushed him out of the way in an angry fashion for having forgotten her deafness, and continued to care for the injured man. Waldo, realising his mistake, shouted 'sorry' and took over the phone call. He asked for police and ambulance, gave a very clear description of their whereabouts, gave his name and address but then refused to stay on the line, on the grounds that he was a qualified medic and had duties to perform.

On the arrival of the police, as Carol and Waldo were unharmed and admitted having caused the injuries, they were immediately arrested and taken to the nearest police station for questioning.

They were kept waiting for about thirty minutes, under the watchful eye of the duty sergeant, until a more senior figure was available to question them and, presumably, until more information had been gathered from the scene. They had some delightful and interesting company during their wait and were questioned at length by a drunk, who believed they were in for causing an affray; he would brook no other excuses or explanation.

Waldo phoned Karen to apologise for running late and explained, in embarrassed tones, that they had been arrested. She volunteered to come and rescue them, but Waldo explained that when everything was understood, they would be free to go, as they had been the ones who had been threatened.

"I admire your faith in the law, Waldo. Should your view change, however, I shall be here to help."

Whilst he was on the phone, Carol had noticed quite a lot of congealed blood on Waldo's forehead, which she judged belonged to the opposition, rather than to Waldo. She delved into her pocket and pulled out a neatly folded white handkerchief. She ruffled it and then put it to her lips to wet it and, without seeking permission, proceeded to clean Waldo's forehead. He was so taken aback at such an intimate act, he was unsure how to react and, as a result, did nothing and said nothing. He was just building himself up to utter something when they were invited into the interview room.

During the interrogation, Waldo was asked if he was gay. He said he was generally very happy and sexually straight. The follow-up question, however, proved more taxing, in that he was asked if he had ever attended the gay massage parlour at the bottom of Park Street, as the victims of his bruising encounter were into gay-bashing and were targeting members of the club. Carol and the policemen were greatly amused by his explanation.

After making statements, Carol and Waldo were released. They arrived at Karen's several hours late and told her the full story. It was received with bewilderment and amusement.

Not a word was ever said about Carol's cleaning operation on Waldo. The story of Waldo's visit to the massage parlour, however, was aired and embellished on numerous occasions. Alas, Waldo's coat remained stained with blood but, for Waldo, it became the source of many a tale of his heroics; in fact, it had been the only act of physical heroism that he had performed throughout his life.

CHAPTER 10

Polly pushed open the office door and breezed in, greeting Margaret at the same time.

"Hello Margaret, I'd heard they'd taken you on. Are they treating you properly?"

"Hello Polly, they are and I'm loving it."

To divert attention away from herself, and avoid any further interrogation, she turned to Carol.

"Can I introduce Carol, who is our office manager, researcher, coffee maker – we all have that in our title – and anything else you'd care to mention."

"Hello my dear, I'm Polly Gibbons, local historian and general busy-body."

They shook hands and Polly noticed Carol's hearing devices on her desk.

"Are you deaf? I see you have the usual technology."

"I have a moderate to severe hearing difficulty," Carol responded, desperately trying to modify her voice, so that it didn't come over too badly.

Polly ignored the strained tones. Looking straight at Carol, so that she could lip-read her without difficulty, said, "Welcome to Southville. I haven't seen you around here before."

"No, I live in Totterdown but I like this area very much."

"Best in Bristol, dear, best in Bristol."

As her time was precious, she pressed on with her reason for calling.

"I met Dr Wise on Vauxhall Bridge the other morning, when I was out for a run, and said I'd call in. That must be more than a month ago now. I'm afraid I've been jolly busy on Council matters. Is he in?"

Margaret thought it typical of Polly to use his title, he never did, though she recalled using it herself when she introduced Mrs Woodry. Waldo would say, 'I'm no longer practicing, so I haven't the right to use the title'.

"No, I'm afraid not but he'll be back later this afternoon."

"Mm, no, that's no good, I'm speaking at a Council meeting this afternoon. Never mind, give him my regards and perhaps you'd be kind enough to give him my mobile number, Margaret," assuming everyone had her mobile.

"Which is …?" Margaret added, a little cheekily.

"Oh blast, I can never remember it."

And she had to delve into her bag to find her phone. The number found and communicated, Polly wasted no further time on idle chitchat and hastened toward the door, calling out, "Must rush. Lovely to meet you, Carol. And say hello to Jem for me, Margaret. Toodle pip."

With Polly safely out of the way, Carol and Margaret burst into laughter and breathed a sigh of relief.

"She means well," Margaret explained, "and there is no one like her for getting things done, but oh dear, she wears me out. Poor old Waldo, is he up to her?"

π

Jac and Carol agreed to share the task of following James.

His routine was to leave the house at about half nine and then, well, his mother didn't know for sure, but she thought he normally headed towards the town centre via the Arnolfini and the Watershed, which are art centres on the dockside. Jac and Carol did a recce and decided to leave the car back at the office, as there were few places to park and the route he seemed likely to take involved many pedestrianized areas and bridges. They decided to do the Monday together, as it was a first time for both of them.

"Have you any advice for us, Waldo? You are the only one who has done surveillance so far."

"It's no good asking me, I had no idea what I was doing. My big mistake was making the assumption that Hugo would follow the same route every day and stick to the same times. I tried a short cut, which didn't work. I don't know that the same rules would apply to James though. I suspect that he follows exactly the same route every day and, for the most part, does exactly the same things, whatever they might be. The only thing that is likely to change his routine is if somebody interferes or challenges him in some way. But the truth is that I haven't a clue. Good luck."

"Well, thank you for that," said Jac. "Come on, Carol, we will work it out for ourselves, as the male sleuth department is bloody uncooperative."

"I'm not being uncooperative. My experience is limited to one exercise, which I got away with, just. Not exactly a convincing CV. Anyway, your circumstances are different."

With that the women sloped off to the interview room to hatch their plans.

π

They left the office at quarter to nine and headed for the docks and James's house. They stood by the old crane, which guards the entrance to the south bank of the floating harbour and a spit of land between the river and the main dock area, called Spike Island, so that they could see James' front door.

It was not a particularly warm day, so they both wore coats and scarves. Carol was sporting a hat at a jaunty angle. Jac was admiring it when James emerged and, in accordance with what his mother had predicted, walked across the bridge and turned left in front of the Arnolfini. He was walking slowly and with his head bowed. The women found it difficult to walk quite that slowly without feeling conspicuous.

"We are going to have to pretend that we are deeply involved in conversation to go this slowly," said Jac.

"Isn't it tricky? How did Waldo manage it on his own? I remember him saying that the most difficult bit was sitting in an empty pub for hours, pretending he wasn't bored and was waiting for someone."

"Neither of us are exactly chatterboxes," added Carol, "and, if I talk a lot, you'll have to listen to my horrible voice all the time. It'll drive you mad."

"You're too conscious of your voice," Jac said in a schoolmarmish way. "It isn't that bad," Jac said, being supportive but without going over the top, "I don't even notice it anymore. It is you, that's what is important."

Carol grabbed Jac's hand and for a few minutes they walked together hand-in-hand along the dockside, without saying a word, enjoying the gentle bustle of the early morning activity of the boat people.

James continued at the same, steady pace, head still bowed, apparently not seeing anyone and not wanting to be seen. To the women, his isolated walk seemed like a joyless escape from his four walls. He crossed the pedestrian bridge and turned right towards the Watershed.

The women stopped on the bridge and watched his slow progress along the water's edge. All of a sudden, he stopped and gave some money to a Big Issue seller and took the paper. There was a short conversation between the two before James moved on again.

"Let's just watch the ferry, for a moment," said Carol. "He's walking so slowly we can soon catch him up."

The ferry was full as it arrived at the slipway. The women both agreed that it was a really good idea, and very green, that commuters parked on the edge of the city and caught the ferry into the centre and to their offices. They looked up from their musings only to find James had disappeared.

"Bloody hell, we've lost him. He must have gone into the Watershed to get a drink or warm up or something."

They ran over the bridge, Carol making a huge clumping noise with her heels; Jac was more sensibly shod.

"Slow down there, girls, there's no hurry," shouted the Big Issue seller. "It may never happen."

They resorted to the usual female defence of laughter and delicious smiles and continued at a pace.

"You go into the Watershed and I'll go straight on into town and on to St Augustine's Parade, just in case. Give me a ring if you find him," shouted Jac and ran on past the Watershed entrance.

Jac checked out the fountain area opposite the Hippodrome

Theatre. Inwardly, Jac had a quick rant about the fountains, 'the most pathetic dribbles that any major city has managed in the whole history of fountain-hood.' There was no sign of him. She changed tack and rushed up towards College Green and the Civic Centre. Just as she reached the edge of the Green her phone went, it was Carol.

"Relax, he's here, having a coffee and almond croissant and reading the Big Issue. This lad knows how to live. I'll get us both a coffee. Do you want a cake?"

"No, just coffee, please." Jac then hesitated. "Are you having a cake?"

"Well, only if you are. I'll see what they have. Leave it to me."

When Jac arrived at the cafe, she was looking a little red-faced and flustered. Carol had already found a seat and had bought a Danish for them to share.

"After all that activity, you should have the lion's share," and she cut it into one third and two third portions and picked up the smaller piece and immediately bit into it, to prevent any dispute.

"This surveillance business is harder than it looks," commented Jac, as she tucked into her pastry.

"Don't tell Waldo that we nearly lost him, especially as we aren't even a quarter of a mile from his home, yet. We'd never live it down."

They were giggling about this when James slowly rose from his table and came over to them.

"Are you following me?" he asked.

Jac reacted remarkably quickly, given that she and Carol were in the midst of sharing a joke.

"Yes, if you recall, James, Waldo said that we would be following you all week. Are you OK with that?"

"Yes, I just wondered whether it was you."

And with that he wandered back to his table and continued to read his paper.

"Well, where does that leave us?" asked Carol.

"Our best efforts at secret surveillance have been spotted within the first half hour. Doesn't that undermine the validity of our findings?"

"I don't think so. I don't think it changes anything. We always said that we would seek his approval to carry out the surveillance and we never said it would be undercover. In the same way, he is aware of the camera in his home, indeed, he helped install them. Our task is to monitor his activity during the day and to see if he puts himself or others in danger. Mrs Woodry alleged that his actions or his demeanour frightens people and mothers with children know him and avoid him. So, nothing changes, in fact, it makes our task very easy, because we don't have to pretend. I know, I'll give Waldo a ring and see if he agrees.

"Waldo, it's me. Carol and I are having a coffee in the Watershed and James is here too, reading the Big Issue. Just now, he came over to ask if we were tailing him, and I said that we were. The fact that he knows we are following him doesn't invalidate the findings, does it?"

"No, I told him we would be following him, and he clearly took it in, even though he appeared not to. He must have been on the lookout for you, otherwise it would have taken him longer to suss you out, unless of course …" his voice tailed off teasingly, at this point.

"We have been discretion itself," Jac stated emphatically.

"I suppose the sceptics on the Mental Health Team might have preferred it had he not been aware of your presence, in case he modifies his behaviour. Let me think about it. Meanwhile, just press on. Are you enjoying yourselves?"

"We are, but I am not sure it would be fun on one's own. Being with Carol is nice."

And with that the call ended.

The rest of the day was relatively uneventful. James ignored the two women and continued his journey through the city, stopping for lunch at exactly twelve thirty, tea at three o'clock on the dot, and arrived home at precisely the time his mother said, namely at four thirty. He made no further acknowledgement of their presence for the rest of the day. In many ways, Jac and Carol thought his behaviour very reassuring.

On Tuesday, Carol, on her own, followed James along the same route and James did exactly the same things. James did not acknowledge her presence.

Wednesday was Jac's turn and the same happened and there was nothing untoward to report. In general, James ignored people and people ignored him. He did ordinary things, in ordinary ways.

Jac, Carol, and Waldo reviewed the situation on the evening of the third day of surveillance. They decided to use a third party, unknown to James, on the following day.

"Ideally, we don't want to have to pay anyone, so I suggest we fall back on Josh again, if he can manage it. The rugby season hasn't started yet, so he's on light duties at the club and should be able to spare the time."

That evening, Waldo and Josh ate dinner together and compared notes about life. He asked about Josh's marriage plans and received some fairly non-committal answers. They talked rugby for a while and last year's poor team performance and what was happening at the club. Then they got down to the briefing.

"Gosh, this is exciting. I'd like to work for you more often if you have jobs like this."

"The key to it, will be not giving the game away as to who you are. I suggest you go straight to the Watershed and order yourself a coffee and have a paper to read. It's a risk but I think it one worth taking. Jac will position herself in the car park adjacent to the Dock Cafe, where she can monitor his front door without being seen and will be able to cover the first bit of his journey should he change tack. She'll phone you if necessary."

Despite the new tactics, Thursday's surveillance revealed the same result. James kept his head down and followed the same routine. Josh also did the Friday but with the same result. In the team meeting, they concluded, on the evidence of one week, that Mrs Woodry had either exaggerated his behaviour or that James was going through a very good patch or he was modifying his behaviour. Whatever, without spending an extraordinary amount of money on the task, it seemed that they were unlikely to turn up the result that Mrs Woodry wanted.

π

Waldo was upstairs, relaxing with a glass of red wine after his meal and wondering whether to give Polly a ring. He decided to brave it.

"Hello, it's Waldo Wise here, we met on Vauxhall Bridge. I understand you called into the office."

"Oh, hello Waldo, thanks for ringing. Are you settling in OK?"

"Yes, thank you, and business is starting to pick up, so yes, things are looking very good."

"Nice choice in picking Margaret, salt of the earth, you know, hard-working and honest, who could ask for more."

"Yes, she's very good. Carol too, I think we've picked a winner there as well."

"Yes, and it's good to see you employing someone with a hearing difficulty, that's really good news. Anyway, why I called around was to ask if you'd like to drop in for a bit of supper some time. Have you got your diary handy?"

Waldo thought, oh no, bloody hell, that's the last thing I want. But, being English, responded, "I'd love too. Yes, here it is, when were you thinking?"

"How's about a Friday? Not next week, I can't do that but the week after. Shall we say seven thirty? I wasn't thinking of inviting anyone else, just the two of us, so that we could get to know each other a bit."

"Lovely, look forward to it."

And the call was over without further ado. Waldo concluded that he would be wise to avoid getting too close to Polly, if anyone had ever managed to get close to her that is, in case he ended up being dragged into every local campaign, including the colonic irrigation of the river Avon. He felt reassured, however, for he judged there was no chance of her trying to seduce him or anything of that sort.

$$\pi$$

At five o'clock each day, Carol called round to the Woodry's house on her way home. She took out the disc from the central control unit and replaced it with a fresh one. She also took the opportunity of checking with Mrs Woodry that all was well.

Each morning, Carol went through the previous day's recording to see if there was anything untoward, but everything remained the same each day. Carol pulled out one or two events which might be deemed to be worrying, but each time Jac and Waldo concluded there was nothing of any consequence or upon which they should act. All three, however, remained very concerned about Mrs Woodry's state of health and concluded that she may not have been diagnosed as mentally ill by the psychologist but her behaviour was far from normal.

Over the weekend, all three reflected on the findings of the week. They had agreed to put together the evidence of the internal surveillance cameras and their street surveillance of James, in time for the case conference on the following Wednesday.

On Monday morning, after a coffee and catching up with their emails, they met in the interview room to begin the work of producing the case file. Carol agreed to produce edited highlights of the camera surveillance to reinforce the points they intended to make about Mrs Woodry's health. As they were doing so, they realised that they had no observational information about Mrs Woodry, other than within the home, and this was probably a weakness in the case, given their concerns about her. However, by the time they finished, the evidence was probably as strong as one could hope in the circumstances and very much fuller than anything one could expect in normal health service work.

Dr Knightly made the Health Centre meeting room available for the conference and agreed to chair the meeting. The meeting was due to convene at twelve noon and sandwiches had been ordered.

Jac and Carol went around early to set up a video screen so that the selected camera shots could be viewed easily and to ensure that there would be no slip-ups. Unusually for the NHS, the systems all seemed to work. Before leaving and returning to the office, Carol placed copies of the file at every place around the table. Karen Knightly popped in to check that all was well, and Carol handed her a copy of the file and explained its structure and main features. Karen was impressed and, from her reaction to Carol, very impressed with her too and said so. Carol looked chuffed.

The Chair opened the meeting. "Welcome, ladies and gentlemen, to the case conference regarding James Woodry, and I suppose to be strictly accurate, we should add Mrs Woodry too. Do we all know one another, by the way?"

There was a mix of 'yeses' and 'noes' and so she asked everyone to introduce themselves and to say what their role was in relation to the Woodrys. As was usual in these instances, some people managed to complete the exercise in seconds, whilst others needed time in which to massage their egos.

"Good, thank you for that. As you will see, I have produced an outline agenda, which starts with Dr Wise and Dr Beauley informing us of their observations during last week. I suggest that we then each add our penny's worth from our observations of the case over recent weeks and months and then we discuss possible implications for James and Mrs Woodry and possible actions. It would be very helpful if we could leave this room having agreed an action plan. Are you all happy with this approach? Good, well over to you, Waldo and Jac."

It was just like old times. They were into the swing of it in no time and they could see that they had everyone's full attention. At crucial points in the presentation, Jac showed clips from the recording. In just over twenty minutes, and without one interruption, they completed their report. They resisted giving any interpretations of the emerging evidence at this stage of proceedings.

Karen then asked each person in turn to give a résumé of their observations and impressions of first James and then Mrs Woodry.

There were no surprises. It was clear from the level of consistency in the presentations that the Mental Health Team representatives had had a pre-meeting and agreed a common line. Its members welcomed the observations about James, which confirmed their own view of his behaviour. They made very few comments about Mrs Woodry, other than she was constantly hassling them to increase James's support and for him to attend the day centre at least three times a week. Their unanimous view was that James's well-being was neither enhanced nor worsened by his attendance; it was almost an irrelevance to him.

Karen concentrated her views on Mrs Woodry and expressed her grave concern at the findings.

"Other than increasing her medication," she slipped seamlessly into solutions, "I am not sure what I can do."

Addressing anyone prepared to listen, she asked if anyone had knowledge of any other help available. The Mental Health Team, as if a flock of pink flamingos, all lifted their shoulders in unison, and as they released them, uttered a sympathetic sigh. If it wasn't such a serious matter, it would have been amusing. In other words, sorry but we cannot help. The diagnosis was that she was not mentally ill and, therefore, that precluded them from intervening. Waldo and Jac's evidence must have been like manna from heaven to them.

"Surely there is something more we can do to help her?" pleaded Karen helplessly.

Jac and Waldo decided it was time for them to intervene, having experienced this scenario so often in their previous lives. Waldo paved the way.

"I think this is the classic dilemma facing all health and social services, namely, a carer is unwell and not coping, but does not fall easily into a category recognised as in need of help. There are, of course, voluntary organisations, which support carers and I suspect that she would benefit from attending such a group but, in our view, she has already passed the point where such groups could be of immediate help to her. Jac and I have discussed the matter in anticipation of this dilemma arising and believe that there is little alternative but to persuade Mrs Woodry that she should relinquish her caring role."

Jac jumped in.

"We believe that if Karen, Waldo, and I work with Mrs Woodry and James over the next few weeks, we might be able to persuade her, and James too, that it is in James's best interest to move into specialist accommodation. It would perhaps be wisest to phase it in, so that both become accustomed to the new regime. We are of the view that once Mrs Woodry experiences the relief and freedom of not having to look after her son twenty-four hours a day, she will begin to recover. Obviously, it will be important for us to help her let go of any feelings of guilt, so that she can feel at ease with James living elsewhere."

"I can see the sense in that approach," chipped in Karen, seeing a dim light at the end of the tunnel. "Of course, such a solution is dependent on the accommodation being available for James. Also, I think to put us in with an even chance of winning, it would be important for the accommodation to be of a reasonable standard. It would be no good offering him temporary or emergency accommodation. It would have to convince Mrs Woodry that there would be a good chance of him settling in and enjoying a reasonable quality of life."

Jac and Waldo kept their heads low to disguise their delight. Karen could not have done better if they had fed her the line beforehand. This placed the ball firmly back in the court of the psychiatrist and the Mental Health Trust.

The psychiatrist made the case for the defence. He delivered his coup d'état.

"Obviously, accommodation is at a premium, and it is not in our hands to make the judgement as to who is allocated rooms in the better accommodation."

"No, I appreciate that," Waldo commented, "but your support will be crucial to us even having a chance. What is the process nowadays, by the way?"

"The accommodation team meet on a monthly basis and the evidence is weighed as to who is allocated what accommodation."

"Are you a member of the team?" Waldo asked nonchalantly.

"Yes, I am, but I am only one voice amongst many, well six others, to be precise."

"There is usually a GP representative, if I am not mistaken. Do you know who that is, Karen?"

"Yes, that's Peter from our neighbouring practice in Bedminster. I can certainly have a word, that's good thinking, Waldo."

"And a Social Services representative," Waldo continued, building the pressure.

"Anyone in with social services?"

Jac said that she knew Leslie Bounds very well, and she was happy to explain the circumstances to her.

Karen then resumed her role as Chair by trying to gain commitment to the emerging solution.

"We all seem to accept that there is little or no evidence to suggest that James's behaviour is deteriorating or a danger to himself or members of the public. Are we agreed?"

There were nods all around the table.

"We all seem to agree that Mrs Woodry, whilst not mentally ill, is experiencing a serious breakdown," she emphasised the word serious, "and can no longer cope with James at home on a twenty-four-hour basis."

She looked around for any dissent, as she had stretched the evidence to its outer limit. There was none.

"In the light of these circumstances, Jac and Waldo have proposed that the most workable solution, and in the interest of both Mrs Woodry and James, is for Mrs Woodry to be persuaded that, despite her motherly instincts, she should let go of the responsibility of looking after James. The job of persuading her should fall to me, supported by Waldo and Jac. Are we agreed?"

Everyone around the table agreed.

"Finally, it will be important to persuade James of the correctness of the decision and, in order to help implement the decision, for him to be offered one of the newer, high quality residences available within the city. David to lead that case within the Accommodation Team, and for others around the table to lobby members of the team, with whom we have influence. Do you agree with that, David, and do the rest of us support that solution?"

David nodded but kept a very straight face and avoided looking directly at Karen. Everyone else agreed.

"When is the next meeting, by the way?"

"Next Tuesday," David reluctantly acknowledged.

"Excellent, that gives just under a week to do our lobbying. I will ensure that notes of the meeting, under confidential cover, are circulated to us all. It remains for me just to thank you all for your time today and for your very positive contributions."

Everyone seemed very pleased at the outcome, and they rose slowly from their seats, chatting amicably to their neighbours, with the exception of David, who tried to make a quick getaway. Karen stepped forward and blocked his path and indulged in light conversation, knowing that he would try and avoid the solution, if he possibly could – he needed to preserve his precious accommodation for more needy cases. She knew she had a lot more to do to ensure he was won over or had no alternative. She produced a trump card.

"David, you know we are looking for representatives for the Commissioning Board, would you be interested?"

Waldo decided that he liked Karen very much.

CHAPTER 11

It was six o'clock on Friday evening, and Margaret and Carol had already left the office. Jac and Waldo were tidying up, ready for the weekend.

"Can I stay tonight?" Jac asked.

"I was hoping you'd stay. Do you fancy the cinema? Shall I see what's on at the Watershed?"

"I checked earlier in the week and nothing grabbed me. Do you know what I would really fancy? I would like fish and chips and to sit and watch rubbish tele. What do you think?"

"Brilliant idea," Waldo agreed, and he gave her a hug.

The office telephone rang. They discussed whether or not to answer it.

"It's probably a wrong number. Ah well, I suppose I should answer it."

Waldo picked up the phone. "Waldo Wise, can I help?"

There was silence at the other end of the line but there was clearly someone there. He waited for the caller to say something. Eventually a rather weak, female voice said, "Dr Wise, can you call round. I am sorry to bother you."

"Is that you, Mrs Woodry?" Jac and Waldo exchanged glances.

"Yes, could you call round please, I need your help."

"Of course, Dr Beauley and I will be with you shortly. Is James alright?"

But she had already put down the phone.

"You agreed to go around on a Friday night, when we have such important matters to attend to?" Jac said, reminding Waldo of his degree of dedication, or was it foolhardiness?

"Well, what could I say? Anyway, you would have done the same. It will only take us ten minutes and we can buy fish and chips on the way home."

They set off towards the docks and were walking along hand in hand, feeling rather buoyant and jolly. It was a nice evening, and the air refreshed their tired bodies.

Waldo rang the doorbell and waited. There was no response. The curtains were closed and the house appeared to be in darkness. They waited a little longer and were just about to ring again, when the door opened, very slowly. Mrs Woodry poked her head around the half-opened door and beckoned for them to come in.

As they entered, they were greeted by a strange odour; a pungent, metallic smell, unpleasant and cloying. Waldo was very familiar with it, but he couldn't place it. Mrs Woodry led them into the sitting room, in which there was just one small table light on in the corner of the room. The television was switched off and there was no sign of James. Mrs Woodry sat forward on the edge of the armchair seat. She was wearing a mackintosh, which seemed rather strange, unless she had just come back indoors. She looked dreadful, even in the low light.

Waldo went towards her and, as he did so, the smell became overwhelming. He remembered what it was.

"What is the matter, Mrs Woodry? You look very unwell. Are you in pain?"

She shook her head. Her face was grey and her hair very dishevelled. This was a woman who would not normally appear in public without her clothes being immaculate and every hair in place. Waldo felt her forehead and it was clammy and as cold as death.

"I think we should call the emergency doctor, Mrs Woodry?"

"No, there is no need," she said with sudden confidence and strength. "I am not ill."

Waldo asked Jac to fetch Mrs Woodry a glass of water. He was buying time whilst he tried to fathom what to do.

Jac returned seconds later, without the glass of water, but looking very pale and shocked.

"I think you should go into the kitchen, Waldo."

Waldo rose from his kneeling position beside Mrs Woodry and did as Jac advised. The kitchen door was open now and Jac had put on the light. The kitchen was long and thin, like a galley on a yacht. At the far end, slumped against the kitchen units, was the body of James, or he supposed it to be James. It was difficult to tell. His face had been badly mutilated, and his throat cut. His shirt and trousers were drenched in blood, and it looked as though he had also been stabbed in the abdomen. The knife lay beside him in a pool of blood. It was a fish filleting knife. Waldo had always thought that such a knife had a particularly lethal look but had never imagined he would see evidence of its capability. Then the smell hit him again. It was the unmistakable smell of blood and guts. It was the smell of operations and operating theatres.

Waldo became strangely serene. He tried to find James's pulse but to no effect. James was dead. He thought he must have died almost immediately after the attack. He pulled out his phone and dialled 999 and asked for an ambulance and the police. He explained that there had been a stabbing and he thought the victim was dead but, you can never be absolutely sure, he added cautiously. The emergency service took him through the usual procedure and asked a lot of inane questions, which if he were the murderer, he would have lied about or just put down the phone. Still, they have a job to do, he thought. They asked him to stay on the phone until the emergency services arrived.

He returned to the sitting room. Jac was sitting with her arm around Mrs Woodry. They were sitting in silence. Mrs Woodry looked up at Waldo when he entered the room.

"I stabbed him, Dr Wise. I stabbed him until he was dead. I thought he was going to attack me. He is dead, isn't he?" she asked, almost pleading the case for death.

"He is dead," Waldo echoed.

"How long ago did the incident happen, Mrs Woodry?"

"About ten minutes before I rang you. I didn't know what to do. Thank you for coming over."

The serenity seemed to have also overtaken Mrs Woodry. Jac sat unmoved, also wrapped in the same air of calmness.

"The emergency services are on their way," Waldo said reassuringly but no one seemed concerned.

The police were the first to arrive. They heard the siren blaring and the squeal of tyres. Waldo opened the door and they rushed past him, as if speed would help bring back James.

"Fuck me," said the lead cop, on seeing the kitchen and James's body.

"Fucking hell," said his mate. They turned to Waldo.

"Who did this?"

"I cannot be absolutely sure, but I expect his mother, who is in the sitting room with my colleague, Dr Beauley," he thought titles might be useful on this occasion.

"Is she a mental case, then?" one of the officers enquired with great delicacy.

"Not to my knowledge, though her son suffered from schizophrenia. I believe she stabbed him in self-defence."

"Self-defence, who are you kidding, mate? Looks like a frenzied attack to me. Look at his fucking face, for Christ's sake."

Waldo found it difficult to counter this logic but refrained from saying anything.

The ambulance arrived and the ambulance team joined in with the chorus of 'fuck me's' and 'Christ almighties.' They ignored any thought of disturbing the evidence and ploughed straight into the kitchen. It took them only a short time to declare that the person was, indeed, dead.

"I haven't seen one like this in a long time. Fuck me, why did they have to do all this? They must be mad," and with that, they declared there was nothing more that they could do and wished their police colleagues, "All the best mates, rather you than me."

Before long, three more police cars arrived and flashing blue lights drew attention to the incident. A crowd gathered to watch the spectacle. Shortly afterwards, the television cameras arrived, and lights were set up to facilitate filming.

The police inspector took charge of the scene and asked Mrs Woodry the direct question, "Did you kill your son?"

Mrs Woodry, in a calm and confident voice, confessed that she did. He then arrested her and gabbled something which resembled her rights.

The two young policemen, who were first on the scene, were told by the inspector to accompany her to the police station for further questioning. This was their big moment and, one suspects, the reason why they had joined the force. They acted out their roles to perfection. Instinctively, or perhaps because of training, or perhaps from watching too much television, they assumed a new importance and demeanour. The taller of the two officers, braving the smell, grabbed Mrs Woodry by the arm and said in a deep serious voice – all the effing and blinding having been left far behind – "Come with me, madam."

The other officer found a cloth to drape over Mrs Woodry's head to prevent her from being recognised, though by whom or for what purpose, it was difficult to decide. They left the house. The two men shaded their eyes from the glare of the lights and led Mrs Woodry to the car. They opened the back door of the car, and in accordance with TV regulations, guided her head downward, so that it did not bang against the door surround; a rare and touching moment in a brutal process.

After brief questioning by the inspector, Jac and Waldo were also asked to go directly to the police station but, unlike Mrs Woodry, they were not offered a lift. They were asked to make no comment to the press before they had been formally interviewed. They left the house to the flash of cameras and were immediately assaulted by reporters, asking if they were relatives of the victim or the murderer; it would appear that poor Mrs Woodry had already been convicted.

Suddenly the attention shifted away from them, as the pathologist and her team arrived, and they were able to escape. They ignored the inspector's request to go directly to the station and walked back home in silence. As they reached North Street, Waldo suggested that they bought fish and chips and ate them before making their way to the station.

"We could be hours waiting to be questioned and all they are likely to offer us is a cup of tea."

"I'm not sure I can eat anything, Waldo, my hands and clothes stink."

"Let's go back and have a shower and change and then see how we feel. Perhaps, I should shower first and then I can go and get the chips, if we fancy them," Waldo suggested.

The idea pleased Jac.

When Waldo returned with the fish and chips, Jac was sitting in her dressing gown, sipping a glass of wine, revealing rather more leg than was befitting the seriousness of the occasion.

"Gosh, they smell good," she said, "perhaps I can eat after all."

"It was very strange what happened back there, and I don't mean the incident," Waldo commented, using his academic voice. "A few moments after viewing the scene, I suddenly became very calm and time slowed. It seemed to me that, once we arrived, something similar overcame Mrs Woodry. Did you notice?"

"I did, I'm afraid it took me over too. I suppose the incident was so horrific and so beyond anything we normally have to cope with, that adrenalin kicked in and helped us keep calm."

"Perhaps it's something we should study at some point. Anyway, let's eat, I'm starving."

And with that they tucked into the fish and chips.

Within the hour, they were at the police station and no questions were asked as to why it had taken them so long to get there. Presumably they were assessed as being unimportant, given that the police already had the perpetrator of the crime. Jac and Waldo were bit-players. They made and signed statements and by three o'clock in the morning were free to go. They strolled back home through the centre of Bristol, arm in arm, like a married couple. Jac leant her head on Waldo's shoulder.

Bristol was quiet now.

"Not quite the peaceful night we had planned," Jac said dreamily. "Do you mind if we sleep together tonight, Waldo?"

"Mind, I mind very much. Do you mind if we have sex tonight, Jac?" he teased.

"Mind, I would be devastated if you didn't ask. There is the remote possibility, of course, that I might fall asleep during it, but you won't be offended, will you?" Jac said, casually.

"Isn't shagging someone who's asleep an offence?" Waldo queried.

"Not if they have agreed to be shagged but are so bored with the process that they drop off."

"Oh, that's alright then."

"It seems unreal to be bantering like this, when an important client of ours has just killed her son and has been arrested for murder," Waldo considered.

"True, but we'll face that in the morning, if you don't mind," was all Jac could muster by way of a comment.

The whole evening had taken on a surreal air.

π

In the morning, after carrying out their own postmortem of events, Jac and Waldo concluded that there was nothing more they could do; matters were outside of their control. Jac decided to stay for the weekend and volunteered to get the evening meal. She also agreed to let Carol and Margaret know what was happening.

Waldo thought that he should go and see Karen. He texted her to ask if it was alright to visit and she texted back immediately saying it would be good to see him.

Waldo made his way from North Street, across the docks, and up to where the 'knobs' lived in Clifton. Karen's house was in a beautiful Georgian terrace, with lovely views at the back, looking down on the fleshpots of Southville, where the peasants eke out a living.

He rang the doorbell. A young woman, probably in her early twenties, whom he suspected from her appearance was her daughter, opened the door. She was dressed in jeans and a top designed to reveal a fine cleavage.

"Hello, I am Waldo Wise. I believe I am expected," Waldo announced rather pompously.

"Not another one," she said disparagingly. "Though you're better looking than the last few she's had."

At the top of her voice she shouted, "Mum, a boyfriend to see you."

"No, no, no, you have the wrong idea," Waldo pleaded. "I am not her boyfriend; I am a work colleague. I work for The PI Shop in North Street. I need to see her about an urgent work issue."

"Oh, that's a new one. Do come in, work colleague, I am sure she will be pleased to see you."

Waldo followed her wiggling bottom into the drawing room and was invited to sit.

"Are you married; they usually are? They shag her and leave her, you know," she said sarcastically.

Waldo tried to ignore the fact that he was being teased mercilessly by this rather disturbed young person and played a straight bat.

"I am happily single," he said with dignity.

With that Karen came into the room.

"Mum, I have been entertaining your latest shag, though he denies it, of course. I must say he's better than your usual trash," and with that she left the room.

Karen apologised and explained that Miranda was going through one of those phases and was a total embarrassment at the moment.

"Waldo, I just don't know what to do with her. I'd appreciate any advice you can give me."

"It's no good asking me, Karen, I'm a hopeless case. Now, Jac might be more helpful."

They carried on the polite banter for some while, before Waldo decided they needed to talk seriously.

"Have the police been to see you yet?" he asked bluntly.

"Police, no, why, am I to expect them?"

"Alas, what I have to tell you is very shocking."

He proceeded to tell Karen the gory details of last night's events. He agreed to a whisky, even though it was still morning. Karen sat beside him on the sofa and they sipped and talked quietly. Karen was upset at James's death and shed a tear. Waldo thought it was good to see a doctor who cared, and he liked that about her. They then talked about what they might do to help Mrs Woodry.

"Well, I am still her GP, whether or not she is in custody. I am sure that means I can have access to her, if she wants to see me, of course."

"And she is still my client, so, presumably, I will be allowed to see her too," said Waldo, applying the same logic but with less confidence.

At that point Miranda reappeared, rather calmer than before.

"I've been searching the internet and found your website. I'm impressed."

"Well, thank you," Waldo said gratefully.

"Jac and I love what we do. Unfortunately, something tragic happened last night. I was just explaining to your mother. Two of her patients, and clients of ours, were involved in a very serious incident; a mother killed her schizophrenic son."

Miranda did not know what to say and clearly felt very foolish. Waldo decided to ease the tension for her.

"If you work in health or social care, it happens from time to time. You learn to live with it but, hopefully, one remains sensitive. Are you studying medicine?"

"No, after mummy's experience, I decided to read mathematics and philosophy."

"Which year are you in?"

"Oh, I've just completed my studies and I'm trying to decide what to do next."

"She got a first," Karen announced proudly.

"Oh mummy, don't be so middle class." There was then a pause before she added, "I am sorry about earlier, I had no idea."

"Don't worry. Strangely, I feel remarkably calm. Jac and I were discussing it this morning and she suggested that the adrenalin must kick in and enable one to cope with such horror."

"I'd like to meet Jac. She's a woman, isn't she?"

"Yes, my business partner and my best friend. Why don't you come to the office and meet her and the rest of the team? I'll find out when everyone's about."

"I'd love to come," she said with feeling.

"On second thoughts, Miranda, there are so many complications at the moment, I think we should delay your visit by a few weeks. I promise I won't forget. I will come back to you when life has settled down."

Miranda left the room, throwing a charming smile at Waldo. Karen shrugged he shoulders.

Karen and Waldo finished their meeting. They felt as though they were at the beginning of a friendship.

π

Margaret and Carol were busy dealing with press enquiries about Mrs Woodry when a tall and rather distinguished, middle-aged man walked into the office. He looked exceedingly solemn, and his face was drawn.

"Hello, my name is Woodfield, I wonder whether I could see either Dr Wise or Dr Beauley please; it concerns the Woodry case."

Margaret took control.

"I am sorry, they are both out at the moment. Were they expecting you?"

"No, I am sorry, I didn't make an appointment. You see, I am

James Woodry's father and the ex-husband of Mrs Joanna Woodry. You may know me better as Dunwoody. Because of my background, I now call myself Woodfield; Joanna and James chose Woodry."

"Yes, of course, Mr Woodfield, you signed the contract for us to carry out the work with Mrs Woodry and James. Can I see some form of identification, please? We have to be careful, because of all the reporters sniffing around."

"Of course, here is my driving licence, will that do?"

Margaret carefully checked the details on the licence and then disappeared to compare the signature with that on the contract.

"Mr Woodfield, I was so sorry to hear about your son. Please come with me to the interview room. Dr Beauley won't be long. Now, can I get you a tea or a coffee?"

"I'd love a coffee, if that is possible. White, no sugar, please."

Margaret returned having made a cup for Mr Woodfield and one for herself. She sat down with him and started chatting.

"We were all very upset. My son, Jem, and James liked each other, you know. Were you close to your son?"

"Well, it was difficult given the circumstances, but I loved him dearly. Tell, me Mrs uh, I am sorry I don't remember your name."

"Margaret, everyone calls me Margaret."

"You are probably unaware of my background, Margaret. I am—"

Before he could finish his sentence, Margaret interrupted.

"I know all about your conviction, Mr Woodfield. My son, who is autistic and a depressive, not a happy mix, I'm afraid, was the first one to make the connection between Mrs Woodry and yourself."

"So why are you treating me so kindly? Is it because I am paying your fees?"

"No, Mr Woodfield, it is not," she said firmly. "You have just experienced a terrible tragedy. Your son has been killed and your ex-wife has admitted to having killed him. I cannot imagine a worse scenario, especially on top of your own sad circumstances.

"Also, you see, we have a philosophy here, which guides the way we think and act and that we all sign up to. It is difficult to explain but it goes something like this. No matter what a person has done in life, there is always some good in them. Sometimes people do things which they are driven to do and which they cannot explain and do not understand. They often regret what they have done but cannot undo it. Sometimes, society, through the law, says that they should be punished for what they have done, and we do not disagree with that, providing they have a fair trial. But here we are not in the business of punishing people but of helping them, if we can.

"I know that you are a convicted paedophile. But you have served your sentence and, as far as I am concerned, and everyone in this office, the matter is over and done with and you should be given the chance to start again. Also, you have just lost your son, who you clearly loved. I lost one of my boys in the Falkland's war. I know what it is like."

"Thank you, Margaret, it is the first time that I have been spoken to in a kindly way since my arrest nearly six years ago."

Tears welled up in his eyes and he allowed himself to show his emotions.

"I am sorry, please forgive me."

Margaret was unsure whether he was weeping for his son or for himself, not that it mattered.

"There is nothing to forgive, Mr Woodfield. I take it as a compliment that you felt able to show your emotions in front of me."

Margaret heard the clang of the doorbell.

"I expect that is Jac."

She rose to go and allowed her hand to rest gently on his shoulder for a few seconds and they exchanged glances. He raised his hand and briefly touched Margaret's hand. The warmth of human contact and kindness surged through his body.

Margaret explained about Mr Woodfield and asked Jac to give him a few moments to gather his thoughts. Jac respected Margaret's wishes and sat quietly and reflected on what she might ask of him or he of her.

"Good morning Mr Woodfield, I am Jac Beauley. I am very pleased to meet you. I see Margaret has given you a coffee, would you like a fresh cup?"

"Do you know, I would," he said warmly.

He was beginning to enjoy his visit; not quite what he had expected.

Coffees organised, Jac sat down and was about to embark on her questions, when she was interrupted.

"Before we begin, Dr Beauley, I would just like to compliment you on your choice of receptionist. Margaret has treated me with great kindness and sensitivity and for someone with my background that is very rare indeed, in fact, it hasn't happened since my arrest. She explained your group's philosophy, admirable."

"Thank you, our values and philosophy are very important to us. Perhaps, I should correct your idea of our organisation though, we are not a group, in the business sense, we are just four people trying to provide a not-for-profit service, which sits somewhere between the statutory services and the commercial sector. We like it and it seems to be meeting a need. But who can tell what the future will hold?

"Now, I suggest I update you on the work we did for you and Mrs Woodry and then you tell me of anything that may affect the situation."

A nod from Mr Woodfield and Jac launched into her report about what they had done to gather evidence, their findings, and the results of the case conference. Mr Woodfield listened intently and gravely.

Jac concluded her report by commenting that, "It seems hard to believe that all this has happened in the last three weeks and here we are today. If only we had been able to act more quickly, this whole tragic event may never have happened."

"I don't think you should admonish yourself, Dr Beauley, it seems to me that you made very good progress. I think it unlikely, however, that Joanna would ever have agreed to relinquishing responsibility for James's care. I myself would have been keen to look after him but she would never agree to that either. I suggested it on a number of occasions but no luck, I'm afraid."

"I think that solution would have been good for James and, if I may be so bold, possibly for you too," Jac suggested.

"It would have been wonderful for me. It would have been marvellous therapy for me, and I think James would have enjoyed it. We get on very well you know, or rather, got on very well."

Mr Woodfield then went on to explain that he had seen Mrs Woodry in prison.

"She seems to have forgotten all about my problem and greeted me as though we were still together and that we had lost our son in a tragic accident. In many ways it was wonderful. You see, Dr Beauley, we are now both criminals, me a convicted paedophile and she a possible murderer awaiting trial. What better basis can there be for a love match."

He allowed himself a discreet smile.

"I jest, of course, but nevertheless, I would be happy to get together with Joanna, if she still felt the same way, on her release from prison."

"I take it that you don't hold her responsible for killing your son, then?"

"Well, there seems little doubt that she did it, but I don't blame her or hold her responsible. The poor girl was off her head. The same could not be said of me and my misdemeanour."

Jac decided to be bold.

"I have only the slimmest of professional reasons to justify my asking if we may talk about you and your problems. Would you mind if we discussed them?"

There was no sign of disagreement from Woodfield, so Jac continued.

"I have never come close to understanding how anyone could become a paedophile. I have read all the theories and I am sure that some of them touch on the truth, for some cases, but it is apparent to me that you are a very sensible, highly intelligent, and grounded individual. And your reputation was as a highly respected and dynamic head teacher, loved by students and parents alike. How could you be or become a paedophile?"

"I will try and explain, Dr Beauley. I was given the opportunity for therapy whilst in prison and I seized it with enthusiasm but what a waste of time. The sessions were carefully timed, a half hour each week, for six weeks. Even if we were about to make a breakthrough, the session closed precisely on the half hour. I finished all six sessions, because I was obliged to, but with no real progress having been made."

He then reflected for several minutes before speaking again.

"I had an exceptionally good deputy, Veronica Little. We worked very well together, and our talents were complementary. She was good with staff and students and understood their needs and enabled us to develop hugely effective responses to problems that arose in everyday school life. I was the strategist and politician and dealt with the Local Authority and the press and fronted the organisation. We were a formidable team and built a reputation for the school as the school to go to in Bristol. We were very proud.

"Veronica had one obsession and that was the fear that younger students were vulnerable to sexual abuse and exploitation by the older students. She did not distinguish between boys and girls; they were both vulnerable in her eyes. She had no concerns about possible staff abuse, which I thought much more concerning.

"She kept pressing me to take some kind of action to protect them from possible abuse. I remember a particular occasion, when I challenged her view, and asked her to explain what made her think that they were at risk. She said that older students watched pornography on the internet and had access to contraception and that most of the students were 'at it', as she put it, 'most of the time'. I had never watched pornography on the internet, so I had no idea why she felt so strongly about the matter. She explained that all I had to do was put in the word 'porn' and all would be revealed and it was disgusting.

"That evening, when I got home, I went straight to my study and entered 'porn' and sure enough the sites came up. I worried as to who would know I was accessing the sites, but I convinced myself that my professional duties overrode any thought of personal risk.

"The pornography blew my mind. I had never seen anything like it in my life, let alone experienced it. Apart from Joanna, I had had only one other sexual partner and we were very unadventurous, though it didn't seem so at the time. Joanna was also what you might call undemonstrative, and hence our sex life was …" he struggled for the right word and finally came out with, "… straightforward. I attempted oral sex with her once, but she asked me not to, and so I desisted. I have never received oral sex. The free porn sights showed me not only oral sex, in all its forms, but images the like of which I had never imagined in my wildest dreams. The problem was the impact it had on me. Dr Beauley, I was like a teenager, I went wild.

"As the weeks progressed, I became more adventurous and started to explore other sites and to pay for access to harder porn. Then, by accident, I entered a site which contained material of young people, not babies you understand, but children of about eight years upwards. This was my big mistake and the beginning of my downfall. If adult pornography excited me at the outset, these images drove me insane. Overnight, I became a sex maniac, and that is my description, not that of the newspapers or the court.

"I had the wit not to let it spill over into my public life or, indeed, to interfere with my marriage or family responsibilities. I am sure I appeared absolutely normal to those around me. At school, I even heeded Veronica's warnings about the impact of the older students on the younger students and together we planned how we might increase safeguards. My rational side said that, if pornography could have this impact on me, what effect must it be having on younger minds? I used to look at my young male students and think, 'Were they watching porn last night? Are they swapping stories about which sites to watch? Is it affecting the way they look at the girls in their class or, as Veronica would have it, the younger students in the school?' Though I kept my obsession contained, it affected my whole being.

"As time went on, I became more and more drawn into the world of pornography and, in particular, to images of young, pubescent girls; girls whose breasts were just forming and whose bodies were beginning to develop the first signs of pubic hair. For some reason, I became totally obsessive in my desire to view these images and, without putting too fine a point on it, I would stay up most of the night looking at these images.

"I then responded to an innocuous looking advertisement offering images for sale. It didn't mention young girls or children in any way, and I assumed they were of adults. Unwittingly, I became a member of a paedophile ring and though I did not produce any images, I bought them and I passed them on to others. If you like, even as a grown man, I was groomed by this set of people. Incidentally, they were of mixed gender. I had always assumed that sex offenders were all men, but this is not the case. They tried to persuade me to allow them to set up cameras, so that they could photograph my students and assured me it could be done without anyone finding out. Thankfully, I still had some moral strength left and I refused.

"I needn't explain the gory details of how the ring was discovered and what followed, for that is all public knowledge. Since then, of course, I have had many hours to reflect on my behaviour and to try and analyse why pornography and images of pubescent girls, in particular, had such a profound impact on me. I asked myself these questions. 'Was I genetically disposed towards obsessional behaviour?

Was I over-sexed? Was my upbringing repressed or misguided? Did my limited sexual experience, as a young man and in my marriage, lead me to repress my natural instincts? Was the focus on my career, to the exclusion of other pursuits, a contributory factor? Is there a fundamental flaw in my personality? Am I morally weak? Is pornography inherently evil and corrupting?' I concluded that none of these issues, of themselves, provided an overwhelming explanation for my behaviour. There were elements of truth in all of them, but they could not explain it. I suspect that, as with many things in life, there is not a simple reason or a single cause to explain what happened. But, when I look through the list of possible explanations, I do not find any of them, either singly or in combination, convincing as an explanation. I think that I must be missing something, and I do not know what it is.

"To be honest with you, Dr Beauley, I am no nearer providing myself or you with an answer, than I was when I set out on the quest. All I can say is that, once the floodgates opened, I had an overwhelming need to wallow in the filth of pornography and it gave me huge pleasure."

He raised his eyes to see Jac's reaction, but she remained impassive.

"I confess to you, Dr Beauley, that, if you asked me, 'Would I like to see naked images of young girls again?' I would have to say, 'Yes I would, very much'. As we speak, I can still see the images. They haunt me every moment of every day and every night. I remain uncured."

He bowed his head and wept quietly.

Jac left him, in order to make another coffee. On her return, he had managed to restore his equilibrium and apologised to her.

"Thank you for trying to explain it to me, Mr Woodfield, I

appreciate how painful it must be for you.

"Waldo and I have discussed the problem of trying to find explanations for such irrational behaviour, on many occasions, but we are still no nearer finding a satisfactory answer either. We all need closure about such matters, whether we are professionals in the business, the general public, the victims, or the perpetrators of such crimes; we need some explanation that will quieten our minds. For the moment, however, what is more worrying is that you still feel you would succumb to watching pornography, given the chance."

"That worries me a lot too. I wish I could do something about it," he said in a sullen, defeated voice.

"If one cannot resolve the problem, and it remains a threat, then I believe it is important to ensure that artificial controls are put in place. The individual must feel free to move within his or her psyche. I am sorry, Mr Woodfield, this is my favourite subject. I think you should resort to behavioural psychology to help you to contain your problem. You will not resolve it by this means but it will help you to control it. I am thinking of aversion therapy, which will help you develop a strong negative response, if you should ever be exposed to, or tempted to be exposed to, pornographic images. My colleague in London is an expert in the field. Would you like me to contact her for you?"

"I would appreciate any help you are able to give me. I am desperate, Dr Beauley. I need help."

Jac picked up the phone and immediately rang her friend Jo and arranged for Mr Woodfield to have an assessment within the next few weeks.

Seeing the colour return to Mr Woodfield's cheeks, Jac said very positively, "Now, what are we going to do in support of Mrs Woodry?"

CHAPTER 12

Waldo arrived at Polly's, a good bottle of red in hand, at seven thirty-five. Polly greeted him with apron askew, wet hands and dishevelled hair, and some flour on the tip of her nose. He thought of removing the flour but then thought better of it.

"Sorry Waldo, running a bit behind," she said breathlessly, "Bloody Council."

She presented her cheek for kissing. Waldo obliged and she turned her head for a second helping.

"Come into the kitchen and we'll chat there."

The kitchen resembled a battle scene. Pots and pans bubbled and spitted like geysers. The floor was awash with spillages. The surfaces were piled high with used dishes. Only her glass of red wine remained out of harm's way.

He handed over his very expensive wine with some trepidation and feared that he may never have the opportunity of enjoying it.

"Oh, thank you, dear, is this expensive, because my wine is crap?"

Waldo offered to open it, so they could carry out a tasting.

"Now, where did I put that bloody opener? Here it is. Will you do the honours?"

Waldo carefully opened the wine and looked around for glasses.

"In the dining room, in the cupboard, on the left," was the instruction.

There being no further directions, after a few false starts, Waldo found his way into the dining room. It was delightfully unspoilt and it had a very old-fashioned, Victorian feel to it and a gentle, relaxing atmosphere. One wall was lined with books, which he noticed contained a large poetry section, a section of women writers and a very large history section, all very well ordered. The rest was shambolic. The remaining walls were covered in paintings and etchings of the very finest quality. He took a particular fancy to a portrait of a young black woman, which was unsigned. Above the fireplace was a mirror of some elegance and in the recess on the left side, a built-in glass cupboard, clearly original to the house, which was full of wine glasses of various shapes and sizes, and glass bowls and antique plates. He helped himself to two clear, glass goblets; he preferred clear to cut glass, for he liked to look at the wine's depth of colour.

"Lovely dining room," he commented, as he walked back into the war zone. "I love that painting of the young black woman, who did that?"

"Thank you, a friend of mine. I wish he still painted. He's really talented but has virtually given up the idea of painting these days."

Waldo handed her a glass of wine. She stopped what she was doing, and they clinked glasses. Neither offered a toast, they decided just to taste the wine.

"Bloody hell, Waldo, this is wonderful, what is it?"

"It's a Carmenère, from Chile. It's not that expensive," he fibbed, "but it is lovely, isn't it?"

She took another sip and smiled.

It was another half an hour before they finally got around to eating but it was well worth the wait; a delightful fish soup, followed by duck. Neither of them had any room for cheese, so they just sat back, drank more wine, and talked.

Polly finally removed her apron and unveiled a cleavage of some consequence. Waldo recalled Vauxhall Bridge and their first meeting, when he had to fight to keep his eyes above chest height.

They talked about North Street and Southville, the bloody Council, the river, and even just a little about themselves. Polly had come from an upper-middle class family, somewhere in Surrey, with whom she had fallen out. She had been married but had no children and she had been divorced about twelve years. She had no intention of ever marrying again, 'Too bloody painful by half', was her verdict. She had devoted the last ten years of her life to researching local history and had written three books on the subject. She was also into fighting good causes and was particularly committed to furthering the cause of woman's rights.

Waldo gave an outline of his life but, as Polly had done, avoided getting too personal; just enough to whet the appetite. He decided to mention his time as a radio presenter. She had to know at some stage.

"I thought I recognised your name," Polly announced, rather too loudly. "You were called Ed Wise then, weren't you? I bet the Beeb and the Government were glad to see the back of you. You were nothing but trouble. Delightful I thought. I was sad when you disappeared from our radios. Well, I'm blessed," she concluded.

At eleven o'clock, Waldo made his excuses, as he had to be up first thing the following morning, but he suggested they both clear and wash up first. She wouldn't hear of it, as she would load the dishwasher and then leave the rest to Julie, who comes in on a Saturday morning. Waldo pondered as to whether employing a 'domestic' clashed with her claim to be an adamant supporter of women's rights but decided it was too early in their relationship and rather too late in the evening to risk opening up such a difficult discussion.

They gave each other a hug and polite kisses and Waldo agreed to host the next supper, in a fortnight.

He drifted off to sleep thinking how much he liked Polly and what a lovely body she had but he couldn't ever imagine them getting together.

π

The relationship between Waldo and Polly grew steadily but not spectacularly over the next few months. They e-mailed and texted regularly and met quite frequently for drinks and supper and, it must be said, sex. They grew fond of each other.

CHAPTER 13

It was a weekend to escape from the office and the closed world of their investigations.

Waldo had booked a room at an inn on Godney Moor, his favourite spot on the Somerset Levels. It was a romantic sort of place, simple but with a Georgian elegance and rural charm that for him worked better than any tranquilliser. It stood alone and near to where he wanted to observe the corncrake and to see if he could catch a glimpse of the cranes being re-introduced.

All week, he had been working on his bike, making it ready for his trip. He was very proud of his bike. A nineteen sixties Claude Butler, 'Nothing like it on the market today, look at the quality of that workmanship', he would proudly proclaim. Even Jac knew that it was a serious exaggeration but took no notice.

Waldo woke early on the Saturday morning and was up and showered before Jac had stirred. He was already dressed when he took her a cup of tea. She shuffled over to make room for him. They didn't say anything very much that morning but just sat and took occasional sips of their teas. They were probably the closest they had ever been.

Waldo had already prepared breakfast, so whilst he was waiting for Jac to get ready, he packed his saddle bags with a change of clothes and a few other essentials for the weekend and checked his tyres and brakes for the umpteenth time.

At breakfast, they shared the paper, Jac wafting vaguely through the Review in a sleepy sort of fashion and Waldo reading some serious article on child abuse. Jac said that she wasn't looking forward to the weekend, because it was bound to involve a tussle with Pat, though she couldn't wait to see her. She also confessed that she felt frustrated and that she had had extremely naughty dreams. He confessed to suffering similar frustrations.

By nine o'clock he was ready to go, so Jac went downstairs to see him off. Before he opened the front door, they hugged and Jac kissed him on the lips. Jac thought she saw tears in his eyes, but it may have been her looking through her own tears, she couldn't be sure. Then he kissed her again and wheeled out his bike. She held the door and blew him a kiss as he rode off. She watched him until he reached the bend in the road. He turned and saw her out of the corner of his eye and waved. She waved back and went indoors and had a quiet cry.

His journey took him about three hours, a bit longer than expected, because his fitness had slipped. He stopped in the village, before the final stretch of road leading up to the inn. He wanted to cool off and prepare himself for seeing Fiona, after a longer than usual break. He felt a bit nervous but also excited at the thought of seeing her.

As he approached the inn, he could just see its side profile and it looked smaller than he remembered; it happens sometimes. It also looked slightly less kempt than in the early spring. The wisteria had not been trimmed after blooming and was sending tendrils out in every direction. The pot plants had not been watered and many were dying. And the hedge was beginning to dominate rather than enclose. He wondered whether something was wrong.

As he turned into the parking area, Fiona ran out to greet him, shouting 'hello stranger', and did not wait until he had dismounted before giving him a hug. She looked bright and breezy and as sensuous as ever; what a mouth, he thought. They kissed, not worrying about being seen by others.

Fiona was the wife of George, the innkeeper. They jointly owned the establishment and were very proud of their achievement in building it into a successful business. They had gained a regional reputation.

Fiona and George no longer slept together but they were good friends and they liked running the inn together. George, as was his wont, was having a fling with the barmaid, who lived in a nearby village. Unfortunately, he had not been well over the past few months and had been unable to keep up with the garden. His normal job was to run the bar and restaurant and the hotel side of the business, tend the garden, and, of course, the latest barmaid. Fiona's role was cooking and housekeeping and, being a successful operation, it was a full-time and demanding job. George was just about coping; his inner ear problem had prevented him from doing the garden, but he had rustled up enough energy to look after the barmaid; there were priorities in life, he claimed.

Fiona showed Waldo up to his usual room, which looked out on to the reed beds and across the wetlands to the south. They had a quick kiss and cuddle, before she returned to the kitchen; lunch orders were still coming in and the under-chef was new. Anyway, Waldo himself was eager for lunch after his cycle ride. As she was leaving the room, she explained George's problem and why the garden was suffering. Waldo, being Waldo, immediately volunteered to help. 'Don't be daft, you're a guest,' did nothing to curb his enthusiasm. The only thing he had missed about his new life in Southville was his garden.

π

After lunch, he set about the garden with gusto and by late afternoon had brought it under control. Fiona, having finished in the kitchen, came out to admire his handiwork and to lure him up to their room; when Waldo was visiting, she always moved straight in, no questions asked. They showered together and spent the next two hours in rapturous love-making. They slept for a short while afterwards, before Fiona retreated to the kitchen and Waldo read, supping a glass of red wine. He felt very contented.

At seven thirty, precisely, he went down to dinner and it wasn't long before Fiona emerged. She asked which bit of her he would like for dinner. Ignoring her jape, he chose a simple green salad as a starter, and sea bream for his main, knowing it had been freshly delivered from Brixham that afternoon. He had brought down his bottle of Malbec, which was already half empty, and she poured him another glass. He had never liked white wine, even with fish, which he considered a serious flaw in his make-up but not quite as serious as not being able to drink a pint of beer. He was also careful not to order anything too filling, for he knew that they would be renewing the afternoon skirmish later that evening.

Whilst waiting for the salad, he took the opportunity to assess the other diners. An older man, probably in his early sixties, and on his own, was taking an active interest in him, so he was careful to avoid eye contact. A party of four, two couples, were thoroughly enjoying themselves and were getting rowdier by the minute. What their conversation lacked in intellectual content was made up for with ribald and hearty exchanges, all good fun. A young couple in the corner were resolving a personal conflict of some kind. She sat, red eyed, and with her head bowed. He moved to the chair beside her and put his arm around her. Waldo could not be bothered with their intensity, after all, this was his weekend off.

The salad prepared him nicely for his main course. He liked to start with a salad. At that moment, it must have been Jac's distaste of plain salads that reminded him of her. He ran upstairs and fetched his phone. He strongly disapproved of mobile phones in restaurants, so he made sure it was on silent. He then sent Jac a text.

'How's it going? Hope you and Pat are OK. Spent the pm gardening. Loved it. Love you lots. xxx'

π

Jac arrived in Langport at about ten thirty that morning. After fighting off Gladstone and Disraeli, their two Selium terriers, Pat and Jac wasted no time in spending the next few hours in bliss. Jac had known she was frustrated but hadn't appreciated quite how much. It was a no-holds-barred session. They both agreed it was one of their best.

Whilst Pat prepared dinner, Jac took the boys for a walk beside the river Parrot. The sun still had warmth in it and the river was in full flood, after recent rains. For the first time in weeks, Harmsworth and incest and Woodry and manslaughter, never entered her head. She breathed in huge gulps of warm air and her body and mind felt refreshed. Thoughts of moving to Bristol receded into the distance.

The cottage looked really good now. Over the past two years, they had gradually restored it to its former splendour, whilst trying to make it more environmentally friendly. The size of the cottage, its shape, the thickness of walls and the cosiness of the windows, all indicated that it was a medieval farmhouse. Local historians maintained it must have served the nearby abbey at Mulcheney. Unfortunately, in the sixties, the outside doors and the windows received a helping hand from the double-glazing merchants. The fireplaces were filled in and artificial log fires introduced. The internal doors were lovingly panelled and painted and the flamboyant wallpapers and yellow-painted wood gave the whole building a warm and interesting flavour. With the help of an architect, who lived next door, Pat and Jac had developed plans for its restoration. The last two years had been pretty disruptive but they both felt it had been worth it. Their dear home now oozed charm and was a pleasure to live in. Who would want to move to Bristol?

As Jac wiped the boys down – one of Jac's favourite expressions – she heard her phone bleep. It was Waldo's text message. She replied: 'Frustration ebbing away rapidly. Hopefully, lots more fulfilment to come!!! Gardening? Are they going to charge you for your stay? You must find yourself a woman soon. Gardening is not the answer. Love u. Love u. Love u. XX'

He replied to the effect that he had something important to tell her when they were back in Bristol and then signed off with his usual three, lower-case kisses – a strange but endearing parting gesture, presumably reflecting his French ancestry.

Jac replied that she was intrigued and couldn't wait. Then Pat called her for dinner. Fiona served Waldo his bream.

π

At eight thirty, after coffee, and when the sun was beginning to set, Waldo set off for his evening walk across the Levels, or that is what he told everyone. He kissed Fiona goodbye but said nothing; she was used to his weird ways.

He used the back door on these occasions, for no reason other than he had always done so. As he opened it, however, it squeaked noisily; he didn't like that. The air was quite chill, even though it was late summer. He took a deep breath.

There was no wind, not even a light breeze. The mist gathered on the reed beds and in the rhynes.

He knew exactly where he was going. He was heading for a very special place next to a lake. He walked up on to the road, turned left, and with long, silent strides made his way down the road for about a quarter of a mile. He then branched off on to a wide track, which bisected two large wetland areas. After walking for about ten minutes, he turned right on to a smaller track, which headed straight into the reed beds. The path skirted the trees. Thereafter, the path dwindled to nothing, but he knew the way across the scrub and bog and reeds to the lake. He had been many times. Human beings rarely ventured this far into the moor; it was the preserve of nature's citizens. On these occasions, he allowed himself to be one of them and they allowed him into their world.

He picked his way through the undergrowth, trying not to break twigs or crush delicate plants or disturb creatures. He headed towards a clump of low-lying willows, their roots resting in the dark, stagnant waters.

Then he came to his special friend, it was almost bent double, bowing to the waters. He loved this tree. He wasn't sure of its name, its human name that is, in fact, he was glad he didn't know. He went through his usual ritual of resting his hand gently on its bark and branches and he smoothed its lichen coat.

He lowered himself reverently into position underneath his tree-friend. He sat cross-legged with a straight back, like a yogi. In front of him, the mist hung above the water. There was no sound and no movement.

He maketh me to lie down in green pastures.

The top of Glastonbury Tor picked up the last of the light; a distant altar peeping through the greyness.

A butterfly landed on him, hoping to take in the fading warmth, but it was a forlorn hope. A vole clambered over a wood pile, stopped, looked around, waddled to the water's edge, and slipped silently and effortlessly into the water; each creature has its rightful place.

He leadeth me beside still waters.

Starlings stirred and fussed and squabbled and swished and swirled before gradually settling for the night.

A silver web joined him to his tree. They enjoyed a oneness.

He restoreth my soul.

Together they would lure flies and bees and wasps and dragonflies. But the tree and he were grateful to be joined, however short a time and whatever their purpose.

My cup runneth over.

He sat and watched and listened and sniffed the air: no binoculars; no chasing; no catching; no netting; no ringing; no collecting. He just sat and was himself and was at one with all that was about him; he belonged.

Goodness and mercy shall follow me.

Darkness enveloped him and daytime sounds were absorbed by the haunting sounds of night. He closed his eyes in prayer.

'Jac, why did I never tell you about Fiona? Yes, I remember, you'd just broken up with Anna but many chances since then, now it's betrayal, four years of betrayal, you have to be told, it has to be done.

'If Jac and Pat separate, they will both need all the help they can get over the next few months. Do I keep my friendship with Pat?

'Ian, you did the right thing, my friend, I hope I did what you wanted me to. We were good friends, weren't we? Miss you, old chap, miss you.

'New job, new people, lots of new people, how exciting. Carol, the lovely Carol. Ian, I have you to thank for bringing Carol into my life, our lives. I like her very much. I think we are going to be good friends, very attractive but too young for me, of course. Margaret, now there is a special person, I admire and like Margaret very much, I would like to know more about her, and her son Jem. And then there's James. I'm sorry I didn't have the chance to know you and help you. How good it was to see you and Jem working together. Mrs Woodry, now you do need help, though I'm not sure I like you very much. Robert, Mr Robert Harmsworth, what to make of Robert, committer of incest, yet not a paedophile, highly intelligent, cultured, thoughtful and sensitive but for some reason things don't ring quite true. Margaret likes him, he can't be all bad, I hope it will work out for him. Then there is Polly and Fiona, of course.

'No more, no more. Leave them behind now. Cast them away. Cast away your life's cast, Waldo Wise.

Still the mind. Cast them away.

Peace. Stillness.

Eyes tightly closed.

Stillness.

Darkness.

Steeped in darkness. Absorbed into the Black.

Practising for death.'

He opened his eyes and could still catch the outline of the nearby trees and the white mist edging the lake but the lake itself had gone. The distant high altar had gone. All around him was quiet.

He rose, mouthed his farewells, and then carefully picked his way back to the path. Before re-entering the human world, he sat and rested on a log and allowed everyday life and thoughts slowly to rise in him once more.

He believed that everyone has just one place in the world where they belong and where they need to practise for death. For him, it was one, small, patch of bog, beneath a deformed tree.

π

Jac's weekend took a turn for the worse.

On Sunday morning, after a short lie-in and a bit more love-making, they had a quick breakfast before taking the boys for a long walk. They headed for Mulcheney Abbey along the river Parrot.

All seemed peaceful enough and on reaching Mulcheney, Pat and Jac indulged in their favourite pastime of inspecting the monks' loos. The loos consisted of what appeared to be a row of ecclesiastical pews on the first floor of an outbuilding, a short distance from the abbey itself. Instead of kneeling at the pews, however, it was apparent that the monks would have hoisted up their habits, swept the heavy material into their arms, sat with their bottoms overhanging the gap at the rear of the seat, and given way to nature. Any emissions had a long drop to the rivulet passing below, which attempted to remove as much of the material as possible. Pat and Jac feared the consequences during dry weather. They giggled at the thought of the ecclesiastical bottoms heaving and straining and, in some cases, blasting their way to peace and satisfaction. The very thought of this frenzy of corporate activity always inspired Jac's stomach to cramp and she wanted to join in.

They thought that they would write to English Heritage and suggest that it might attract more visitors to this remote, ancient site, if they held an annual 'Defecation Day – free refreshments for participants, sightseers five pounds – wet weather permitting.'

They walked back using the cycle track, which enabled them to do a circular walk. They were about halfway back when Pat dropped her bombshell.

"I have met someone else. Don't get me wrong, we are not having a relationship. I would never do that to you, as you know. She lives in the village and has recently split from her partner."

Jac was frozen. She could not feel her body. It would not move. She had no option but to stand still and allow it to recover. She could not speak. She stood in silence. Pat continued.

"You know that I love you very much and I know you love me. But it is also clear to me that you have found a new life. It is very important to you, and I am not part of it. Sometimes, I have the feeling that you would rather be in Bristol and spend more time with Waldo and your wretched cases than be with me. I don't want to end up as the old woman at home, sitting waiting for 'wifey' to come in from work. I don't want to end up as a pain and someone you dread coming home to see. We always said we would call it day if that happened. I suppose I am acting now, before we get to that point. I don't want our relationship to eat itself up like a cancer. I am trying, albeit clumsily, to say that I think we should part, perhaps for a trial period, and then jointly decide if the idea is right or wrong. To be honest, I can't imagine my new friend will turn out to be my choice of long-term partner, but her friendship may help me bridge the gap."

Jac could not recall what she said in reply, if anything, or what else Pat might have said. She had no memory of the rest of the walk.

All she can remember was, that evening, she texted Waldo to tell him there had been developments. She had kissed Pat goodbye and had driven back to Bristol.

π

Waldo had left at lunchtime on the Sunday, so he was already at home when Jac arrived. He guessed from her text that she had broken it off with Pat, though he suspected that she would still be upset.

Jac ran up the stairs and fell into his arms. Waldo seized his moment to tell her about Fiona. As he told her the story, she stared at him in silence. He said he was sorry, he never meant to keep it from her. She wept. Timing was not one of Waldo's strengths.

Without warning, Jac started thumping him.

"How could you, Waldo Wise, you lying, fucking bastard. How could you not tell me? We have always told each other everything, everything important. We tell each other everything about who we are fancying and how we are feeling, and we share confidences, or I thought we did. This is a betrayal of our friendship and our love. I am not able to forgive you for betraying our love, you lying, fucking bastard.

"Yes, I am upset about splitting up with Pat, because I have always been in the lead and I never thought she'd have the strength to leave me. It was a shock but I know I would have been upset, even if I'd have left her, because I have loved her and shared my life with her. I still love her, and I think I always will. It's just that my feelings for her are less powerful now and I need to move on, but I love her and I am upset. But she never betrayed me. What you did, you bastard, was betray me. You betrayed our trust. Betrayed our love. I hate you, Waldo Wise. I hate you.

"The only other person to betray me in my life was my mother. She betrayed me when she realised I was lesbian. My own mother betrayed me. Can you believe that? I knew I was different from other girls; I was not like them. I used to sob silently in my bed. I did not want my parents to hear me, as I knew they would never understand.

I did not like dolls or pretend games about babies or dressing up in girly clothes or putting on make-up or skipping. I wanted to be a boy. I felt like a boy.

"My mother would say that I was a tomboy or I was going through a phase. A phase my arse. I knew differently. It was not a case of feeling differently. I was fundamentally different.

"At university I had a wonderful time away from my mother and I became a rampant lesbian and proud of it.

"When I went home at the end of my first year, I told my parents that I was a lesbian. My father said he had suspected that I was gay, and he was very understanding and loving and hugged me and said it was alright. But mother, well you'd have thought that I'd grown into a monster. She said that I was no longer welcome. She didn't exactly chuck me out, but I was not welcome. My father pleaded with her but to no avail. I felt unloved and betrayed. There is no greater punishment than a mother withdrawing her love from her child. I still haven't recovered from what she did.

"What you did, you rotten bastard, reminded me of the whole sorry affair. Perhaps now you can understand why I don't like betrayal, you unthinking, unfeeling bastard. I know that what you did was not in the same league, but it was betrayal. Can you understand that, you treacherous fucking prick?"

"That sounds like a reasonable contention," proffered the treacherous fucking prick.

And with that he received a fine uppercut to the jaw. He reeled backwards and in so doing rode the punch but pretended he had been badly hurt.

"Good, I hope you have broken something."

He then looked up and said, "Fancy a drink?"

At which she threw a second punch, which he anticipated and was able to let it pass harmlessly over his shoulder.

He grabbed hold of her to prevent any further attacks and apologised and said that he loved her more than anyone in the world and he did not know how he had managed to get himself into such a tangle. He then said he would like to tell her a bit more about his visits and his true purpose in going to the Levels and his special place.

They held each other tightly, as he told her the story, and he explained that he hadn't told her about the special place because he was embarrassed about it, and that no one else knew. He finished by saying that he would like to show her the place, if she would like to see it, and she could also meet Fiona, providing she didn't steal her from him. This was the final straw and she wrestled him to the ground and sat on him and bounced up and down on him and declared herself the winner.

Between gulps of air he managed to utter, "Now, do you fancy a drink?"

"I haven't forgiven you yet, you fucking monster."

In calmer tones, ignoring her protestations, he managed his usual sensible approach.

"I don't think that we should get squiffy tonight, I don't think that would be wise. But let's just have one drink and then go to bed."

As always, Jac took him by surprise.

"I think I'll give alcohol a miss tonight. May I have a cup of tea?"

Even Jac could see the funny side of her remark and they collapsed helplessly into each other's arms.

CHAPTER 14

After several weeks delay, Jac was finally able to see Robert Harmsworth's youngest, Lucy. They met for the first time on Lucy's doorstep, where the women eyed each other suspiciously. They were both very unsure of the encounter and what would emerge.

"Hello, I am very pleased to meet you. I am Jac Beauley."

Lucy invited her in by gesture. Lucy was not in the best of humours.

"Thank you for agreeing to see me," Jac added in a tentative and rather high voice. Jac felt a bit foolish and weak.

She was shown into the kitchen, which Jac took as positive. It seemed to her that many women did their serious thinking and talking there.

"Would you like a coffee; I've just made some?" Lucy said heavily.

"That would be good. Black, no sugar, if I may." Jac avoided sounding too chirpy.

"Ah, the same as daddy," Lucy observed.

"Yes, I've recently changed. I used to like a touch of cold milk, but I've adopted your father's choice in recent days. Indeed, the more I get to know him, the more I realise we have the same tastes in a lot of things. I admire your father. I suppose that might not be the right thing to say in these circumstances, but it is true."

"I love my father very much. It is just that I think he is making a serious mistake in pursuing this matter. I don't have a problem with what happened, so why should he? Surely, it is for me to decide whether or not it should be exposed?"

Jac decided to get stuck into the interview. No point in wasting time on niceties.

"As I understand it, you were the victim of sexual abuse for about nine years, is that correct?"

"My father and I had a close and loving relationship, which included beautiful sex, from when I was twelve years of age, until my last year at uni."

"So, you don't consider it to have been abusive?" Jac challenged her.

"No, I do not. I was a willing partner; indeed, I started the whole thing. I expect you have heard all about that from daddy?"

"He didn't go into details, but I got the gist."

"I went into his bedroom and, well, you can guess the rest. It was a wonderful beginning to a wonderful relationship, the best relationship of my life. Nothing that has followed has come anywhere near it."

Lucy paused.

"If we are going to discuss such intimate details of my life, I would like to think we can talk frankly and be a bit less formal. Perhaps we could start by using our first names. Please call me Lucy. Can I call you Jac?"

"Oh, please do. I must confess, I was not looking forward to this discussion. I don't think I have ever talked this openly to another adult woman about a sexual relationship, not even with my partner."

"No, I'm the same," said Lucy reassuringly. "I love doing it but talking about it is a different matter. I am going to find it embarrassing."

Lucy wanted to know what sort of detail Jac was looking for. Jac was unsure.

"I don't know yet. I need to know enough to understand why you and your father had a sexual relationship and why it lasted so long. It would also help me to understand the degree to which you felt any psychological or physical obligation to continue, and it would help enormously if I knew whether it has had a lasting impact on the quality of your life and your ability to form healthy relationships. These are the crucial issues, if I am to capture the essence of what the court will need."

"I wish I could persuade him to change his mind. Does he not realise the affect it is going to have on my marriage, not that it isn't already suffering, and the affect it will have on my relationship with my son and my sisters, let alone my friends and neighbours? I can see the looks on people's faces, when they hear that daddy is a child molester and is on the sex offenders' register and I was the victim of his abuse."

After a brief interlude and having refreshed their coffees, Jac managed to get Lucy back on track and to explain what happened on that first night. Her description was of a beautiful and life-changing experience. As she drew to the conclusion of her tale, the two women reached out to one another and Jac clasped Lucy's hands. Lucy cried quietly. Jac felt very moved but held back her tears. They sat in silence.

Lucy broke the silence.

"Did you enjoy losing your virginity, Jac, or were you like some of my friends, scared and traumatised by the experience?"

"I am a lesbian, so I suppose it was not quite as traumatic for me. My girlfriend, at the time, was much older than me and was very gentle and caring. I don't remember it being of any great consequence, it all seemed so easy and natural. Perhaps I had a very weak hymen," Jac added feebly. They both laughed.

Lucy asked if Jac would like some lunch. "I was only going to have a tuna salad. Would you like to join me?"

"That would be kind. Next time, if you agree to see me again, that is, perhaps I could take you out to lunch. I know a fantastic little place in Redland and it's possible to find a discreet corner, where we can talk quietly."

In conspiratorial tones Lucy whispered, "It would be great if people thought that we we're lovers having a clandestine meeting."

Returning to her normal voice she added, "I'd like that a lot, lunch that is. To be honest, mostly, I don't care what people think."

With that, they settled down to enjoy lunch and talk of politics and people and nothing in particular. It was clear to them both, that if circumstances were different, they would very quickly become friends. They agreed to meet in a couple of days time and for Jac to pick up Lucy from her Clifton home and for them to walk the mile or so to Redland.

π

Waldo was anxious to learn how Jac had got on with Lucy, so he grabbed her as soon as she returned to the office. Margaret and Carol had already gone home, so they sat on the sofa in the front office and Jac told him the full story, including how much she liked Lucy.

"I think there is something fundamentally flawed in our makeups," Waldo observed. "I like my clients very much too. Did I tell you that, once the Cam case is resolved, I'm thinking of joining the chess club with him? I really like him. You and Lucy are probably going to become bosom buddies too and, before you know it, you'll be inviting her round for supper.

"On a more serious note, though, it does not look good for Robert. It reinforces his role in the early part of the relationship. Even at seventy-six, and with his daughter's support, he will be lucky to escape a prison sentence."

Jac agreed and, anxious to make a record of her findings, left Waldo in order to set about writing it up and preparing the ground for their next encounter. She also took the precaution of ringing the pub in Redland and reserving the table just inside the main door, which was partitioned from its neighbours by a high wooden screen.

π

On Friday morning, Jac was looking forward to seeing Lucy again. She realised that she would have to keep her distance, in case matters didn't develop in the way anticipated but, with this reservation, she had high hopes of their lunch together. Lucy too was full of smiles when she answered the door to Jac and was clearly anticipating an enjoyable girls' day out. They chatted amicably as they made their way across town.

Whilst they perused the menu, they both sipped on a gin and tonic. Jac decided on moules et frites and Lucy on a chicken liver salad. Jac ordered a bottle of New Zealand sauvignon blanc, much to Lucy's delight. The ordering business completed, they settled into their discussion.

"So, where do you want me to begin?" Lucy asked.

"Well, I don't think we need to explore how your relationship with your father developed but perhaps you could clarify one or two points for me. Did you ever have boyfriends during those years?"

"Yes, I did, but they were always a disappointment. They seemed so immature and so sexually and emotionally clumsy. My father encouraged me to have boyfriends and was always trying to end our relationship, because he said it wasn't healthy. But I wasn't having any of it. For me it was everything. I was so happy. My girlfriends couldn't understand why I wasn't interested in boys. I knew I was very attractive to boys and was physically mature for my years. I did have one boyfriend, who lasted about six months, but we were friends more than lovers. He was an old-fashioned lad, who did not believe in sex before marriage. If only he'd have known what I was up to."

"So, your father did attempt to end it?"

"Many times, and for short periods, he succeeded. But I would never let it last for very long. I was in love with him and everything else seemed insignificant in comparison. I know he was in love with me too. In a weak moment, he once told me that, though he loved my mother, he had never experienced such joy and happiness with her as he did with me. We were in love and that is all there was to it."

"Your relationship finally came to an end towards the end of your time at university. How did that come about?"

"As I say, daddy tried many times to end it, but never had the strength to overcome my overwhelming love and commitment. The end came when I brought my new boyfriend, Michael, home with me from uni. He and daddy got on like a house on fire. They went to rugby together and came home from the pub a bit tiddly on numerous occasions. It was lovely to see. Daddy could see that I was very fond of him, and he took the opportunity to tell me that he was not going to sleep with me again. He was very firm this time. 'It has to stop', he said emphatically. This was a very different daddy and a very different approach to anything I had experienced before. I suppose I thought he was right and that it was time I flew the nest. We never made love again and, to be honest with you, Jac, I still miss it. Even though he is seventy-six, I still want to make love to him. That sounds awful, doesn't it?"

"Human emotions are strange and wonderful things and, as far as I am concerned, whatever you feel is right for you, is OK with me. Alas, the law is less forgiving. I am sure a judge would say that your father should have shown that level of firmness from the outset; it was his parental duty to do so."

"I know you are right, but the law cannot legislate for every circumstance. I loved my father and loved the sex we had together. I do not blame him at all and feel not one ounce of guilt myself about what happened. I wish it could have gone on for the rest of our lives."

Lunch arrived and they broke from their serious conversation and gossiped about the barman, who seemed to be trying to seduce one of his customers, who had had too much to drink. Then Lucy turned the tables on Jac and asked her about her relationship with Pat.

"Well, until very recently, when we broke up, we had been together for over three years and were very much in love. We had, no still have, a lovely medieval cottage in Langport, on the Somerset Levels.

"I suppose some of the spark had been seeping away from our relationship for some time, but this happens in most relationships, don't you think? And, of course, I was devoting more and more time to the business with Waldo. It meant that I was away from home a lot more and it finally pushed Pat over the edge, just as I was preparing to say similar things. I am still very sad about the whole business, but I know what has happened is right."

"My relationship with John is rocky. It has sort of run out of steam. No, it hasn't, he is pissed off with my behaviour, that's the truth."

Lucy left this hanging in the air, knowing very well that Jac was bound to pick it up. Jac decided not to say anything but just looked at Lucy and raised her eyebrows. They smiled at each other.

"The truth is, Jac, that I love sex. I just can't get enough of it. Don't get me wrong, John is a good lover, and he too enjoys sex, a lot. But having just one guy isn't enough for me. I need lots of sex and lots of variety, men and women. We are part of a circle of friends who like to do the same and that helps enormously. But John tells me that, even within the group, I have a reputation for being wild. Mind you, not in comparison with 'C'."

"'C'?" said Jac, raising her eyebrows."

"I think that 'C' stands for clitoris," Lucy replied.

This made Jac laugh.

"The group can be quite good fun," Lucy added. "This is not exactly an adult version of a Torremolinos night club, it is very middle class; there are lawyers, accountants, academics, and a doctor; this is posh, exotic sex."

Lucy needed to go to the loo, so broke off the conversation. As she slid out of her seat, her dress rode up and exposed two beautifully toned and tanned legs. Instead of squeezing passed Jac, or asking her to move, she took a huge stride over Jac's legs in a very seductive manner.

"Pardon my bottom," she said mischievously.

Jac smiled and made light of it but then couldn't resist watching her bottom jiggle under her dress as she marched to the other end of the bar and out to the loo. There was no doubt, in Jac's mind, that Lucy was a very attractive and sexy woman and, if Jac wasn't mistaken, was probably naked under that dress. Jac muttered to herself, 'Oh my God, I hope she isn't intending to seduce me? I'd better be on my guard.'

Lucy returned all smiles and ready to resume her story.

"That guy over there is gagging for me. The truth is, Jac, that if you weren't here, I'd probably end up spending the afternoon with him; I just can't resist it. I prefer your company, of course, though it is a pity we have to waste our time talking about sex and not doing it. Still, where was I?"

"You were just about to tell me about 'C' and your reputation with the group."

"Well, we meet once a month in one of our houses and we all bring wine and something to eat. In many ways, it's just like a group of friends meeting for a supper party. At some point in the evening, a couple slopes off and the shenanigans begin."

"That's strange, your father used the same word, 'shenanigans', recently," Jac recalled.

"I have my usual people I warm up with and then I tend to join a small group who enjoy a bit of S & M, nothing too serious, but it can be good fun, especially if you are on the receiving end of everyone's attention. But, lingering in the back of my mind, throughout the evening, is my pending encounter with 'C'. Most people avoid her like the plague, especially the men, they find her truly scary and apparently lose their appetites."

She laughed outrageously at this thought.

"Lots of the women put up with her because her husband is very well blessed and, whilst not the sharpest knife in the drawer, has the energy and stamina of an ox; sex with an animal without its unseemly implications, you might say. But even though I find 'C' very scary, she satisfies my needs like no one else can."

Seamlessly, she moved into a new frame of mind.

"Do you mind if I have a pudding? I am fancying that chocolate gateau; it looks absolutely delicious."

Jac opted for cheese and they both had coffees to try and bring some semblance of decorum to proceedings, the wine having taken its toll.

Over coffee, Lucy spent a little time talking about the state of her marriage and whether it was going to survive the rigours of her sexual adventures. She concluded that it was unlikely to survive, especially since John seemed to have taken a particular liking to one of the group. The big problem for Lucy, however, was not the marriage, as much as what would happen to their son; she feared he would opt to go with John, and she didn't know how she would cope with that. Jac didn't push Lucy as to the reasons why he may choose his father.

"Tell me about 'C' and why she lingers in your mind throughout the evening."

Jac was numb with disbelief at her description of their antics together but tried to retain her composure, as she could see that Lucy was starting to get emotional and was near to tears.

"I know you are thinking that I am a disgrace. How can anyone sink as low as me? You think that I am sick, and I need help. I suppose you are right. All I know is that after experiencing one of those evenings, I feel a hundred percent better and I can live through the following weeks quite happily and, for a while, I don't need to screw blokes I don't fancy and I can concentrate on John and his needs. Do you think I should seek help, Jac, or will I grow out of it?" she jested.

"I really don't feel qualified to answer that, Lucy. Would you like help?"

"No, not really, but I don't like what I do either and the sooner it ends the better."

"I suppose what concerns me is that the prosecution will have a field day with this. They will claim that your behaviour is a result of your father abusing you, when you were young. You still feel guilty about what you did and blame yourself and hence have to punish and humiliate yourself, in order to rid yourself of these feelings. I am not sure that wouldn't be far short of the truth. What do you think?"

"No, I don't feel like that. I certainly get up to all sorts, because I am not satisfied sexually and emotionally. The truth is that I wish, all those years ago, I had not let my father persuade me that we should part. I would be very happy to have spent the rest of my life with him. I believe that I would not have got into this sort of thing had I done so. I could be wrong, of course, but that is what I believe."

"Unfortunately, I don't think it is the interpretation that the court would put on your behaviour. Whatever you say, they will impose their own logic and the accepted behaviours of our society in judging your father."

"I could lie."

"No, that would not be wise. You will both end up in jail if you do. There are clearly a lot of people who know about how you behave, many of them professionals, and to save their own skins, they will tell the 'truth, the whole truth' about you but not, of course, about themselves."

"Could you adjust the report and pretend we haven't had this conversation?"

"Lucy, can you imagine me deceiving the court, by omitting your testimony? It is not my way and I had hoped you would have made that judgement about me. I like you very much and one day, perhaps, we can be good friends, when all this is over. But I will not lie, not to save you or your father."

"Sorry, I did not mean to offend you. I just don't want daddy to go down and it is my testimony that is likely to seal his fate. You can understand why I feel so desperate now."

"Do you think that over the next few months you could curb your behaviour and cease going to the evening sessions?"

"Yes, of course. John will be relieved, and it might help save our marriage, if it isn't already too late."

"Would you like me to fix an appointment with a friend of mine; she's an excellent psychologist and I am sure she can help you?"

"No thank you, Jac, though I know what I would like. I would like you to facilitate a meeting between daddy and me, so that we could discuss the implications of his exposing this matter."

"You could, of course, just meet him without me there. You are still very close, why don't you do that?"

"Very simply, because I don't think he would listen to me. He has taken this decision to proceed without consulting me and it will take a lot to dissuade him. You being there, at least, will give me the opportunity to air my views and to argue my case."

"If I agree to do this, you must understand that I will not influence him in any way. He has employed us to help him put the case together and avoid the worst repercussions of a police investigation. We cannot avoid all of them, of course, but by presenting a full, honest, and well-researched report, all they will have to do is confirm our findings."

Jac paid the bill and together they walked back to Lucy's place, chatting amicably. Lucy invited Jac in for coffee, but she declined. They kissed fondly and Jac made her way back to the office.

$$\pi$$

Waldo agreed to meet Cam at the Bedminster cafe, where they had first met. In many ways, he was now a local and much more confident in dealing with the cafe staff. They didn't single him out or take any special interest in him and yet all the ingredients appeared to be exactly the same as his first visit. He arrived five minutes earlier than the agreed time, in order to give himself the opportunity to settle and get into the right frame of mind.

When Cam arrived, he came straight up to Waldo and greeted him warmly. Waldo took his hand in both of his hands and grasped him tightly. Waldo was not sure why he did this, perhaps something to do with giving him reassurance.

This, of course, was the big meeting. This was the meeting when Cam had to decide what to do next. The meeting when he had to determine how he was going to react to the confirmation of Hugo's misdemeanours. The meeting when he had to decide if and when Hugo would be told. Waldo's role was to guide him through the decision-making process.

The first question lacked serious challenge.

"Tea or coffee, Cam?" Waldo asked, plunging his hand into his pocket to dig out change.

"Coffee please, Waldo, just a little cold milk, if I may. You know my usual."

They were already fairly familiar with each other's habits and likes and dislikes.

With coffees before them, Waldo opened proceedings.

"What I suggest, Cam, is that I start by updating you as to the outcomes of my research. You react how you see fit. Then we will determine what to do next. Does that sound reasonable?" Cam just nodded. He had obviously prepared himself for the worst.

"Well, in essence, I have nothing new to report. I can confirm that Hugo attends the parlour each week, at the same time, and receives a massage from the same guy. It lasts about an hour and Hugo looks pretty tired and rough when he emerges. The masseur has a reputation for being at the hard-end of the gay massage business."

To balance matters, he then explained that there was no evidence that he was having an affair or, in any other way, misbehaving or being unfaithful.

He continued to try and put a positive spin on Hugo's behaviour.

"There are some very good messages in this, Cam. At the outset, you thought he may be seeing someone else. I think what has emerged is evidence that he has a very strong need for a particular sexual practice, which you find difficult, even unnatural, to provide. So, he has sought another solution, which enables him to remain faithful to you."

At this point Waldo stopped to let Cam reflect on what he had said. There was a long gap before he responded.

"I hear what you say, Waldo, but I am still devastated by what he is doing. If only he'd have said there was a problem, we could have discussed it and come to an agreement as to how to overcome it."

"I expect, when we come to share this with him, he will say that he tried to tell you and to discuss the issue, but you were unable to pick up the nuances of what he was saying. It is not easy to tell your partner that they are not meeting your needs."

"He knows how hard I find it to inflict or receive physical pain. I am a total wimp when it comes to those things."

"Cam, it is important that you don't blame yourself for what has happened. I am sure that there are very few relationships, however long-lasting and delightful, that don't have their flaws and their difficulties. Whilst things seem very difficult to manage, at the moment, in the longer term, I expect you will come to look on this as a minor hiccup in your relationship and no more.

"Let's move on for a minute. We can always come back and discuss the implications in more detail later. The next critical question is, do you want to tell him that you know?"

"You mean, I could just ignore it and accept it."

"Yes, or not accept it, of course; you could walk away. That is always an option."

"No, I would like our relationship to continue. I am fully committed to him, if only he were fully committed to me."

"I think he is fully committed to you, why else would he pay for a solution and not just have an affair? So, one option is that you allow matters to carry on as they are, knowing where he is and what he is doing but you don't let him know that you know. I am not recommending this as an option, merely saying this is one way of dealing with it."

"I don't think I could pretend that it never happened."

"OK, so he needs to know that you know. This sounds a bit like

Donald Rumsfeld on a good day."

Even Cam had to giggle at that one.

"Are you going to allow him to continue to have the massages or are you going to require him to stop?"

"I had assumed he would stop, but I suppose that is not necessarily so. My God, am I going to have to live with him carrying on in this way?"

"There is a possibility that he would want or need to continue. Are you going to suggest a suitable alternative for his needs? From what you have said you are not willing or able to satisfy them."

At this point Cam became rather melodramatic and despairing and Waldo took some time to bring him back to some semblance of normality.

"Cam, I am just trying to enable you to face the possible outcomes of sharing the news with Hugo. It is far better that you face your feelings now, than find yourself struggling later. Can I suggest, that we leave here, I don't think this place is right for a conversation of this nature. I know you thought it would be, but I think you should come back to the office with me. We have a private room there where no one will disturb us, with an endless supply of coffee, and we can send out for food if we need it. Come on, the air will do us good."

Cam accepted the suggestion meekly and they left the cafe and strolled back to the office. As they did so, Cam loosened up a little and even managed a passing comment about the street.

"I rarely come to this end of North Street. It has gone up in the world; it used to be hellish rough."

Carol greeted them when they arrived at the office and offered to make coffee. She judged that Cam was not feeling too robust, so did not indulge in light banter.

The two men went straight into the interview room and occupied two seats next to one another.

"As I read it, Cam, you are very keen to continue your relationship with Hugo, and you do not want this situation to cause a break-up between you. You believe it important that Hugo is made aware that you know of his behaviour, though at this stage you are still undecided about whether you could face him continuing to attend for a massage. We'll come back to that one, that's a tricky one. Let's talk about how we are going to tell him. Will you tell him?"

"Oh heavens, I don't think I could. I would have to confess that I employed you to help me."

"He will have to know about me at some point, I didn't just appear out of thin air. I suggest that I meet him at your flat, when you are out. We contrive a situation, when you are out for the evening or, at least, for a couple of hours, and I tell him and discuss matters with him and then I send you a signal, when it's appropriate for you to return. Then I stay and facilitate a discussion between you."

"Oh, that sounds wonderful, Waldo, would you really do that?"

"Of course, but you have to realise that the discussion may not go well. One very clear and possible outcome is that he will just walk out and that will be the end of your relationship. You understand that it is a possibility?"

"Yes, I suppose you are right, but if I want him to know, and I do, then I have to be prepared for that. Oh God, this is awful."

They continued to think through the implications of it all for the next few hours. Carol knocked from time to time to see if they needed refreshments but on each occasion they refused. It was gone four o'clock when they emerged and asked if it was possible for them to have coffee and sandwiches. Carol, being Carol, had anticipated this moment and produced the goods within minutes.

"Do you gentlemen want something a little stronger or will fruit juice and coffee suffice?"

Cam looked up and shocked them with, "Is there any chance of a nice glass of wine; Sauvignon Blanc or something really dry?" and then immediately apologised for his extravagance.

Waldo explained that he thought that there may be a bottle in the fridge left over from a birthday celebration. Carol raised her eyebrows and allowed herself a light grin, nothing very noticeable, just a suggestion, which Waldo couldn't fail to notice but that passed Cam by.

As they ate their sandwiches and Cam supped his wine carefully, Waldo summed up what they had agreed.

"I'll just put on the recorder, if it is alright with you, Cam, whilst I try and capture what we have said. Firstly, next Thursday evening, you will leave the flat at six thirty p.m., as though you are going to the chess club. You will stay out until I give you the signal to come home. You will not prepare Hugo in any way for my visit. I will visit Hugo at your home at six forty, introduce myself as your colleague and friend, and explain that I need to talk to him about your relationship. I will persuade him to let me in, by proving my credentials, yet to be decided, but it will be something that only you and he will know. Once in, I will then tell him that I know about his visits to the masseur and that you also know. I will explain that you are very anxious for the relationship to continue and want to be open about things and try and find the right solution for you both. The rest you will have to leave to me to work out and to respond according to his reaction at the time. Is that a fair summary of what we have said?"

"I would just add, Waldo, please reassure him that I love him very much and that I only brought you in because I was worried about him."

"Of course, Cam. He is going to need all the reassurance he can get."

As he was leaving, Waldo gave Cam a hug and whispered, "Stay strong, Cam, stay calm. We can resolve this."

π

At six forty precisely, Waldo knocked on the door. Hugo answered and gave him a quizzical look.

"Hello Hugo, I am a colleague and friend of Cam."

"Oh, I am sorry, he is out this evening."

"Yes, I know, we arranged it that way. You see, I have agreed with Cam that I will talk to you about a matter which greatly concerns him. It is about your relationship, and he thought it would be better coming from me; that may or may not prove to be right. I'd be most grateful if we could talk for half an hour. Can I come in?"

Hugo looked very uncomfortable but, after eyeing Waldo up and down a few times, decided he looked and sounded OK.

"How do I know you are who you say you are?"

"I have asked Cam to text you at exactly six forty-five. The text should confirm that he has asked me to visit, and it should ask if you would listen to my story. Could you check your phone for me, Hugo, please? I will stay here until you have checked."

A few minutes later, Hugo invited him in. He turned off the television and he invited him to sit in an armchair, which was clearly

Cam's perch.

"So, what's this all about?"

"About a month ago, Cam came to me very upset and worried about you. He thought that over the past few months, you had become very introspective and had changed in some way. You seemed remote, though he thought that you still loved him. He is certainly still deeply in love with you. He asked my advice as to what he could do. I agreed to research matters to see if I could find a possible cause. To cut a long story short, I know about your visits to the masseur and I have shared these with Cam. I have reassured Cam that there is no one else involved, but you seem to have a need to visit Paul, who is on the harder edge of the gay scene. Can you confirm that this is right?"

Hugo nodded gravely but did not say anything. He was breathing heavily.

"Obviously, Cam is disappointed that you did not share this with him, perhaps disturbed might be a better word, but appreciates that he is not capable of providing you with S & M to meet your needs. He is relieved that there is no one else involved and hopes that you still love him. He hopes that you and he will remain partners."

Waldo stopped there to let the information sink in and Hugo's emotions to catch up.

"Are you some kind of social worker or private detective?"

"I am a private investigator, but our agency is different, in that we specialise in resolving injustices and personal issues that people cannot resolve themselves. Both Jac and I have professional backgrounds and bring our experience in medicine and psychology to bear on our work."

THE PI SHOP: OPEN FOR BUSINESS

"Good God. How did Cam find you?"

"He came across our website when looking for help and, of course, we are based just down the road in North Street."

"I will be frank with you, sorry, what did you say your name was?"

"Waldo, Waldo Wise."

"I will be frank with you, Mr Wise, I need what Paul gives me. And Cam, love him as I do, finds it impossible to do the things I need; it is alien to his whole being. I am not sure I can do without it. I just get very down when I cannot get it and then start bickering with Cam. I don't like that."

"Cam thought you would be furious with him for hiring me."

"Well, I have been caught fair and square. I did deceive him but with the best of intentions."

"Let me call Cam and let us talk this whole thing over together. Better still, why don't you call him, so that he knows that you are willing to talk and that you still love him; he needs all the reassurance you can give him."

It could not have gone better. Cam and Hugo made it up, and the last Waldo heard, Hugo was continuing to attend the massage parlour and Cam sits and has a drink in the pub, just like Waldo used to do.

When Waldo spoke to Cam last week, he asked if he could join them for a drink in the pub. He was thinking he might introduce Cam to Jean Pierre and encourage him to have a massage with the gentle giant. He thought that would be a neat little ending to his first case.

Waldo was feeling pretty smug.

π

Jac set the scene.

"Thank you both for coming this morning. As you know, this meeting is taking place at your request, Lucy, and the main purpose is to enable you to explain to your father the reasons why you feel that he is wrong to proceed with this matter, given the implications to you and your family. I suggest we start with listening to your analysis of the problem, and I don't think we should interrupt you whilst you make your case. Perhaps you could then explain the situation from your perspective, Mr Harmsworth, or may I call you Robert?"

"Oh Robert, please Jac, I'd like that."

"Good, thank you Robert. After your presentations, I suggest that you both have an opportunity of clarifying with each other any areas of confusion or misunderstanding. We'll finish by seeing if we can find any common ground and a way through, which will meet both your needs."

"That seems unlikely, I must say, as we hold opposite views on the matter," added Robert, unhelpfully.

"I never worry about that," Jac commented optimistically. "I have seen sworn enemies find common ground after an hour or two of discussion and you have the great advantage of being a father and daughter, who love each other deeply. Let's be optimistic. Lucy, over to you."

Lucy made a tentative start but after a few minutes settled into her stride. She made a powerful case as to why her father should not confess his sins. She started by acknowledging her father's point of view, namely that she understood how he had seriously offended the norms and laws of society and he needed to reconcile his conscience, before it was too late to do so. To counter this position, however, she made two main points. The first was that the initiative should be hers and not his or, at least, they should have a joint approach, for any other way ignored her needs and wishes. She also stressed that, in law, she was the injured party. The second was that he was completely ignoring the implications of his actions on her relationship with her husband and son and her sisters and their children. She explained that the confession was likely to cause major rifts in the family, which would never be healed. She described what he was trying to do as overwhelmingly selfish.

Jac admired the way Lucy presented her case. She was concise and made Robert's decision look like an act of self-indulgence.

Robert took his time before responding. He accepted that he should be acting in concert with her and not in splendid isolation and he would like that to change. He hoped that as a result of today's meeting, Lucy would join him and help him make the case. He did not accept, however, her analysis of the implications. He believed that Lucy was exaggerating these and that, in fact, people would turn their venom on him and sympathise with Lucy's situation. Lucy tried to interrupt at one point, but Jac intervened and asked her to let her father finish, before coming back. He went on to make a strong case for her relationship improving with the rest of the family, as a result of his confession, and believed that one of the issues between her and her sisters had been her special relationship with him; her sisters could sense that she was the favourite.

He put his case well, but Jac was unconvinced by his arguments and, if she was not convinced, she was pretty sure that Lucy would feel the same way.

"Before we proceed any further, I would like you to ask questions of clarity. Robert, is there anything in Lucy's presentation that you did not understand, or which has left you confused?"

"No, I don't think so. I suppose I was a little confused how you think my confession would affect your relationship with John, Lucy. Surely, it would help explain some of your unresolved issues and would enable John to help you come to terms with them. Why do you think he would react adversely?"

Lucy lowered her head and thought deeply before responding.

"If we present the situation as though you assaulted and raped me, and I was the injured party, then I think you would be right in your supposition. But that is not the truth. I was totally compliant, and, in some ways, I was the leader and certainly argued forcefully for it to continue. There was never one point, in the whole of the time that we were together, that I wished it had never started or I wished it would end. I was deeply in love with you and I still am. Indeed, I wish it had never ended. Given that perspective on matters, of course, John will react badly."

"But we have no need to present it like that, nor would it make any sense to people if we did. I am your father, and I should not have allowed it to start. Remember, you were just twelve years of age and still in your formative years. However strongly you felt towards me, I should have re-directed your feelings into more positive and healthy pursuits. I should also have had the strength to bring it to an end earlier. We were lovers for twelve years and my attempts to end it, during those years, were feeble and self-serving. There is no other way of looking at it. And my belief is, if we were to present the case jointly, on the basis that we were equally guilty, it is likely to result in even more severe punishment for me, than if I had accepted full responsibility. No, that approach is a non-starter."

Lucy's response was robust.

"Well, I am sorry, I cannot view this other than a joint issue. You make the mistake many people make, in assuming that children, even at the age of twelve, are incapable of making sensible and mature judgements, just because they are inexperienced in life. I believe children are very often more sensible than adults, for they have not been tainted by life's pressures and twisted by the prejudices of religious beliefs or social norms. You are also forgetting that we were still lovers, even when I was in my twenties and at university. Are you claiming that I was still incapable of making decisions for myself? I was the one who insisted that we continued and you the one who was constantly trying to bring it to an end. I had boyfriends and had sex with them, as you know, and you encouraged me, but nothing came near to the joy and delight that our relationship offered me, and, I hope, you too. Indeed, that has remained the story of my life. I love John but not in the way that I love you."

No one moved or said a word. Jac let the exchange find its place.

"Lucy, do you have anything that you wish to ask Robert?"

"No, I understand what daddy is trying to achieve and why. But he is wrong, and I will not allow him to convince people that he was totally to blame for what happened. Indeed, I am of the view that no one is to blame. What happened between was beautiful and wonderful. How can anyone be punished for that?"

"Do you wish to say anything further, Robert? Any general comments?"

"No, I think I need to let what Lucy has said sink in and to reflect further on matters but, at this point, I have nothing further to say."

"Do you wish to make any further comments, Lucy? No, then I will leave you both to reflect over the next few days on what you have said and heard this morning, and then I will visit you separately, and discuss how you are feeling and what you think the next steps should be. Don't be disheartened by what has happened; this is not unusual or unexpected. What has come out of today has been a sharing of how you both feel and that can only be positive. The difficult challenge will be deciding how you reconcile your views with one another and it may not be possible. I suspect, however, that something will emerge from this process, which will bring you together. I suggest we leave it there."

Robert and Lucy kissed and hugged each other, and Lucy rushed out in tears. Robert had tears in his eyes and was clearly shaken by the experience. He shook Jac's hand and left without saying another word.

Despite her positive presentation to Robert and Lucy, Jac was dejected by the outcome of the meeting and was feeling very low. She did not feel as though things had gone well. Carol sat beside her on the sofa and cradled her in her arms. The two women sat quietly together, Carol gently rocking Jac and soothing her, as though she were a child. Jac made her jumper wet with tears.

$$\pi$$

Jac made several attempts over the next few weeks to make contact with Robert and Lucy but neither answered phone calls or emails. Robert sent a text message to say that he was still reflecting on matters, but Lucy seemed to have gone into hiding. Jac and Waldo talked it over at great length and decided that it was Robert's call, as he had employed them to help him, and whilst they might have a view as to what he should do, it was not their role to interfere. Jac waited patiently.

CHAPTER 15

Eventually, Lucy made contact and Jac arranged to meet her for lunch in the Redland pub, where they had met previously. She thought it would do Lucy good to get out. Lucy readily agreed.

Jac thought that Lucy was still looking a bit rough.

"The truth is I'm pissed off with my father not listening to me, the silly old buffoon. If he carries on like this, it will be a disaster for him, for me, and my sisters."

Jac changed the subject and asked how her marriage was fairing. It was not good news. Her husband had arranged to see a solicitor and was advising her to do the same. He had decided to sue for a divorce on the grounds of her unreasonable behaviour. He was citing 'C'.

They enjoyed lunch and each other's company and talked of clothes, politics, men, and other women. The only serious note came when Lucy talked of her son, who she thought was still likely to choose her husband in the event of divorce.

"I will be devastated if he does. But you know boys of thirteen and fourteen, they prefer their fathers at that age, and let's face it, the old bugger has been a very good father to him."

Jac and Lucy arranged to meet every Friday for lunch and Lucy agreed to think of somewhere they could meet by next week and to text Jac. They parted with a hug and kiss.

π

They met in Clifton at one of Lucy's favourite restaurants in the Galleries. There were no sticky moments; no silences; no talk of the case; no talk of the divorce or the boy; no talk of Robert; no talk of misdemeanours; just two very good friends, enjoying each other and building a good and lasting relationship.

π

Their next lunchtime meeting was on the docks. Jac was seriously thinking of moving into a barge as her next home, and she wanted to show Lucy. Once Jac had confessed her motive, Lucy couldn't wait to go and see it. She peppered Jac with questions about where it was, what colour it was, how big it was, so many questions and so few answers, because Jac had only seen it online. Jac explained that she had arranged for them to meet the estate agent at two. So, they had an hour to enjoy themselves and, as they didn't have far to go, they needn't rush their meal.

The estate agent turned out to be a tall and elegant young woman, wearing a dress low enough to reveal a substantial cleavage and short enough to expose powerful thighs. Jac and Lucy exchanged knowing glances and Lucy told Jac to sod off, as she was first in line.

The estate agent's high heels were entirely unsuitable for the quayside cobbles and the nautical task that lay ahead of her. Jac, being gallant, jumped into the boat and gave her a helping hand down on to the deck. Lucy rejected Jac's assistance and called Jac a tart, as she brushed by her.

Thereafter, all eyes were focussed on the boat: the size and practicality of the rooms; the colours; the workings of the loo and shower; the heating arrangements; the stove; and the general challenges of living aboard. They were both swept away with the fantasy of a life, if not on the ocean waves, then on the rippling waters of the dock. They were particularly taken with the double bunk and Lucy let herself down by suggesting that perhaps they could try it for size. Jac chastised her and gave her smack on the bottom. The estate agent asked if this was going to be a joint rental.

Lucy congratulated Jac on having had such a brilliant idea. She gave her a special hug and told her not to have any doubts and to 'just do it'.

By the time they met the following week, all the arrangements were in place and Jac moved in on the following Saturday.

$$\pi$$

Jac had decided the time had come to take firm action with Robert. She decided to visit Robert's home, just as she had done with Lucy.

Robert answered the door but looked old and unwell.

"Please, may I come in, Robert? I do not want to pressure you. I just want us to talk, so that I know exactly what you want us to do for you."

He waved Jac in.

"Would you like a coffee?" he enquired.

She said she would and asked if he would like her to make it. He thought that a good idea.

They sat at the kitchen table. Jac thought that Robert looked depressed and asked him if he had been to the doctor, as he didn't look well.

"As a matter of fact, Jac, I have been thinking I must do something. It isn't like me, but I hardly have the energy to get out of bed these days. I think I must have cancer or something."

"That doesn't follow at all, Robert, and you know it. But you must look after yourself, otherwise, at your age, you will go downhill very quickly and no one wants that."

She didn't think that this was a wise thing to have said but, for some reason, it had the desired effect and he perked up after that. Jac thought it was probably just having company that helped him stir his bones.

"When did you last have company, Robert?" Jac asked.

"I can't remember to be honest with you. I think I saw my grandchildren about five weeks ago, but I have made my excuses since then."

Jac spoke sternly to him.

"That is not good enough, Robert. You are just punishing yourself. What I suggest is that you go and tidy yourself up, have a shave for a start, and then we'll go to the riverside cafe for lunch."

"I haven't been spoken to like that since I was a child. You sound exactly like my mother."

He paused.

"It will take me about half an hour, may be longer, is that alright?"

"That's fine," Jac agreed. "Do you mind if I play the piano. I'm out of practice but it looks so attractive standing there."

"No one has played it since Lucy went to university. I'm afraid it needs tuning, but you're welcome to have a go."

With that, Robert went off to do his ablutions and Jac found sheet music for 'Bewitched, bothered and bewildered', and tried to make sense of it, after years of not playing.

When Robert finally appeared, he looked more like himself, still a little pale, but he was no longer bowed but standing bolt upright and was clean and tidy. He even had a glint in his eye.

"Would you play it for me one more time please, Jac, it was Susie's favourite."

Jac was really a little bored with playing the same piece over and over again, but she thought it would give her a chance to get closer to Robert, so did her best to produce a faultless performance. At one stage, he even started to hum along, though he didn't risk giving it full voice. He smiled quietly to himself at an intimate memory, which he did not share.

Outside the house, he took a deep breath and knew that Jac had rescued him from himself. He thanked her.

They made their way slowly down to the quayside and across the bridge to the riverside restaurant. They were early enough to get a window seat so that they could watch the boats go to and fro.

"Well Robert, do you still feel the same way? Do you feel that you must press on with the case? If that is what you want, then that is not a problem for us. You have employed us to support you and we will do that whatever you want."

Ignoring Jac, he asked his own question.

"How is Lucy? Is she still upset with me?"

Ignoring Robert's direct question, Jac answered in a way she felt more reflected what he needed to know.

"Lucy's love for you is unwavering and she will stand by you, whatever decision you make, you must know that. She is a little ragged at the moment and a bit down, like you, but she is OK. She believes that what you are proposing is harmful to you, to her, and to the whole family. Essentially, she thinks that after all these years, it is an unnecessary and fruitless act of contrition."

"Oh dear, I think that you and Waldo think so too. Am I right in saying that?"

"I know that, in my previous life, it would have been deemed to be unprofessional of me to express a view on the subject, but it is one of the reasons why Waldo and I changed tack and why we are doing the job we are doing now."

She checked with Robert that he wished to hear her view. He nodded.

"At the beginning, when you came to see us, I admired your stance and believed that you were doing the right thing. Now that I understand the wider context, namely, the implications to your family and Lucy, in particular, I am no longer so sure."

She hesitated to give herself a chance to determine the most appropriate way forward.

"I believe the decision, whatever it is, should be a joint decision between you and Lucy. I am absolutely sure you can reach agreement on this. I am convinced that when two people love each other, as deeply as you and Lucy, you can always reach agreement. All you need do is spend time with one another.

"My suggestion is that we take a leaf from the Quaker way of doing things. They do not talk of agreement, for agreement is the end result of negotiation and in negotiation one party is always the winner. They believe the same to be true of compromise. Quakers talk of discernment leading to the right path. It is a slow and quiet process. One party expresses how they feel and then both reflect in silence on this. The other party then expresses their point of view but cannot criticise the other, ideally, they will link the ideas in some way. Both parties again reflect in silence. This process of discernment continues until the right path emerges or it is shelved for another occasion."

Robert asked a number of questions to try and understand what Jac was saying, at the end of which, Robert agreed to give it a try.

"I will have to see if Lucy is happy too. By the way, I think I should only be at the first meeting, just to ensure that you have both understood the process, after that I think that it should be a private meeting between the two of you."

Lucy also liked the idea and within a few days all three came together in Robert's house.

They were in the sitting room. There were no teas or coffees, no distractions. Jac started the session with all three sitting in silence. She thought this necessary, in order to bring peace and calm to the process. The quiet within the house was a great help. After three or four minutes, she invited Robert to say how he felt about the issue and to explain why he had opted to bring the matter out into the open. He took just a few minutes to express his view, as by now it was quite well rehearsed. There was just a faint trace of sadness in his voice but, apart from that, he delivered his view without emotion and almost in a whisper. They all three sat in silence and reflected on what Robert had said. Jac allowed ten minutes to pass, before she asked Lucy to say what she felt. Like her father, Lucy took only a few minutes to explain her thinking. She shed a tear at the end, and they all sat in silence again. Jac then explained that either of them could say whatever they wished, providing it wasn't critical of the other.

There was a fairly lengthy silence, before Lucy said that she wanted her father to be reconciled with his problem and, she understood why he was doing it, but thought there must be a better way, which did not impact so seriously on the family. Jac stopped Robert from replying, which was his instinct, and asked that they all reflect on what Lucy had said.

After a suitable interval, Jac nodded to Robert that he could respond. Robert said that he understood Lucy's concerns, but he couldn't think of a way of facing his problem without doing what he had proposed but he would like to think of an alternative.

After a further period of reflection, Jac brought proceedings to a close.

Before they broke up, she asked if they both felt comfortable with the process. They both said they had found it very calming and whilst they were not convinced it would help them find a solution, they were happy that it had brought them back together. Jac asked that they reconvene each day and they repeat the process, allowing a suitable time for reflection between each contribution.

CHAPTER 16

It was Friday and time for a working lunch and their weekly business meeting. Carol, with her Business Manager hat on, had produced an agenda and, whilst they tucked into their sandwiches, she launched into topic number one, the accounts. She didn't want to trouble them with the detail, so she pulled out a few salient points for their attention. In effect, they were doing pretty well, and the business was prospering. Her only concern was the increasing amount of funds going on expenses. She pointed out that these had risen from one hundred pounds a month in the early days, to well over three hundred at the present time. Jac shrugged noncommittally and Waldo took another bite of his sandwich.

Margaret did not approve of their attitude.

"I think you should take this matter seriously. I know you don't want to trouble them, Carol, but I think it is important. Businesses fail because these matters are allowed to get out of hand. I know you are helping people who would otherwise be in trouble, and that is very commendable. But you also have a responsibility to make sure the business continues to thrive."

Waldo and Jac shuffled in their seats and sat up, acknowledged the validity of her argument, and thanked her for reminding them. Margaret had become their conscience and they appreciated it.

Carol then went on to identify a number of instances where expenditure seemed high, and they attempted to justify their expenses. How the world moves on. Waldo and Jac exchanged smiles, knowing that they had chosen their colleagues well.

Whilst Carol and Margaret tucked into the sandwiches, Waldo and Jac gave an update of their current cases. There was nothing particularly exciting to report but they still found it useful as a sounding board for ideas and as a check to make sure they weren't doing anything too crazy.

What Carol had to say next, however, changed the rest of the day, in some ways, changed what they did and said in the forthcoming weeks and months.

"We are being targeted by a hacker. I thought something was rather odd on Monday but ignored it and put it down to the vagaries of computer systems. On Wednesday, I knew something very strange was happening. I decided to bring in outside help and, sure enough, he confirmed that our files had been searched and one or two copied. Now, as you know, when I set up the systems, we agreed to operate two entirely discrete systems, one for contact with the outside world and an internal one, in which we could exchange confidences about our clients and store all our confidential information. Hence, our intruder has not managed to access any of our confidential files, as far as I am aware, but they have copies of our out-going and incoming emails, including one or two from clients."

Carol then went on to ask Waldo and Jac if they had broken the rules of the game and stored any files on their laptops, instead of on memory sticks or used the main system for case work. All three turned to Waldo, who was the most likely to ignore the rules.

"Why are you looking at me? I have been assiduous, I assure you. But," he added cautiously, "we'd better check just in case."

Jac agreed that Carol should do the same with hers for the sake of equality.

Though their immediate concern was to make sure their systems were secure, their main interest centred on trying to determine who might be targeting them. It was suggested that it could be an agency wanting to copy their modus operandi or someone they had offended in the course of their work or a reporter looking for a juicy story. They then spent some time examining each of their current cases to see if they might tempt anyone but concluded that none of them lent themselves to this sort of extreme measure.

Carol then asked if any of them had received phone calls or emails in the past few days, which they had found strange in any way. She stressed that, at the time, they may have just shrugged off the matter as a bit odd but, in the light of developments, it might be worth re-examining. To Waldo and Jac, Carol sounded like a real detective, not like them.

"I had a phone call this morning," Margaret ventured in a tentative voice. "It was from someone interested in finding out whether we could help her. She said it was a very personal matter and she would need to be re-assured that our systems were secure and there was no way anyone could find out about her personal business. I reassured her and explained that our client files were kept on a separate system from our day-to-day communications; not that I understand exactly but that is what I have heard you all say. I was right about that, wasn't I?"

There were nods all round.

"I offered her an appointment, free of charge, but she said she would be back in touch soon and immediately put the phone down. I did the right thing, didn't I?"

They all gave Margaret their full support and reassurance that she had acted properly and that they would have done the same.

"The problem was that she didn't sound like one of our normal clients," added Margaret. "She wasn't distressed, though she sounded nervy. She seemed very well-rehearsed, almost as though she was reading from a script. Normally, when I offer people an appointment and say it won't cost them anything, they jump at the chance."

Carol thought the matter too much of a coincidence to let it pass and that the enquiry was suspicious. The caller had left no contact number, indeed, had rung off the moment that Margaret started to show an interest. The contact log showed the caller had withheld her number.

They quizzed Margaret about the caller's voice to see if she could remember anything significant, which might give them a clue. According to Margaret, she sounded quite young, probably in her thirties but she couldn't say for sure. She was quite posh, not 'la-di-da' like the queen but well-educated, a bit like callers from universities.

Jac suggested that it was pointless to speculate further and recommended they concentrate on making their systems hacker-proof. The next half an hour was taken up with determining what that meant. Carol was the strong leader of the discussion and agreed that she would be taking all of the necessary actions. She turned to Waldo and Jac, however, to make sure that they were going to play ball.

"I will need the two of you to be very careful in everything that you do from here on. You are on the frontline and the most vulnerable targets."

She then turned specifically to Waldo. "Waldo, you are particularly vulnerable."

Everyone knew this wasn't really true and giggled. Carol decided to sharpen her criticism of Waldo.

"You are not as disciplined as Jac. You tend to be a bit lax when it comes to files and records, don't you agree?"

"Moi, lax, this is a gross calumny," he retorted, knowing perfectly well that he was not well-behaved when it came to such matters.

"But, under the circumstances, I promise to be extremely careful and to follow whatever rules and procedures you think necessary. I don't think I have done anything untoward, thus far," he added apologetically.

With that they moved on.

Jac asked Waldo what he was up at the weekend. He brightened up considerably.

"I am walking the Mendip Way or, at least, the bulk of it, about forty miles. I have booked myself into a hotel in Wells tonight and start first thing tomorrow morning. I've booked into my favourite B & B at the halfway point and then should reach Weston-Super-Mare by four-ish on Sunday afternoon. Even the weather forecast is favourable. What are you up to, Jac?"

"I am doing some tiling and grouting to improve the shower on the barge. I've been promising myself to do it for weeks and I am finally getting around to it."

Margaret asked about colours and Jac explained her plan to make the barge more homely. Margaret was duly impressed and asked if she could come and see it when it was all done. Jac invited everyone to dinner.

Jac was pleased to hear that Margaret was still seeing Robert and the two of them were going to a concert on Saturday night, to see the

Birmingham Philharmonic.

"It's my first real concert, I'm so excited."

Waldo asked after Robert and was pleased he was still well.

Then, Carol, in front of the rest of the team, asked if she could join Waldo on his walk.

"That would be wonderful," responded Waldo. "Do you have the gear, walking boots etc? Are you fit enough for such a strenuous walk?"

He knew very well that that Carol was a Tai Chi expert and a fitness fanatic. Carol gave him a look.

"I was only asking. I don't know what you get up to in your spare time. You could just lie around watching the tele and drinking beer, how would I know?"

This was one step too far and resulted in Carol getting up from her seat and pretending to throttle him. They all decided to join in, and he claimed sexual harassment. It was a great way of releasing the tensions that had built up during the hacking discussion.

As soon as they had stopped harassing Waldo, he got on the phone to see if he could arrange accommodation for Carol. The B & B was fine for the second evening, but he had to arrange for her to stay at a sister hotel in Well's High Street, on the first evening. They had never spent any leisure time together before, though they often worked quite closely, so this was an opportunity for them to get to know each other better.

π

They set off from the centre of Wells at eight o'clock the next morning. Waldo knew his way quite well, having done the walk a number of times before. He loved the views from the top of the

Mendips down on to his beloved Levels.

Waldo led the way through the narrow streets of Wells and then, by a well-trodden path, up to the foot of the Mendips.

Waldo was keen to get the heavy trek to the top of the hills over early, whilst it was still quite cool, so he set off at a brisk pace. They both concentrated on the walk and said very little to one another. As they neared the summit, the mist still lingered over the Levels and the whole scene took on a magical effect. Carol was overwhelmed by its beauty. They decided on a brief sit and stare, but their stay lasted more than half an hour. They watched as the mist slowly thinned. It revealed a cross-patch of fields. The mist clung to the river courses and the rhynes, giving an other-worldly appearance.

They had a wonderful day's walking. By five o'clock, they had dropped down off the Mendips and had reached their overnight stay. They went their separate ways to shower and change, ready for dinner. They met at seven in the tiny bar in the lounge of the B & B and ordered a bottle of merlot. Mein host explained the evening menu to them, which they both accepted with alacrity; herb and tomato soup for starters; venison casserole for the main; sticky toffee pudding for dessert – all homemade and organic and just the ticket when you've been on the hills all day.

There was just one other couple in for the evening meal and they seemed keen to get the meal over and retire to their room.

After pudding, Waldo ordered a coffee, but Carol preferred a brandy. If Waldo had known what was about to be unleashed, he might have gone for brandy too.

"I would like to put a proposition to you, Waldo."

"That sounds a bit frightening. But, if you absolutely insist, I suppose I could let you enjoy the delights of my body, this once."

She ignored his comment.

"I want to have a baby and I would like you to be the father. I am not asking you to be my lover or partner or to take the role of a father or to support the child financially. All I am asking of you is that you father the child. I am very fond of you. I like the way you have treated me, encouraged me, and nurtured me since I first joined the team. I also admire your intelligence hugely." After a pause she added. "I thought about using a donor agency but why would I, when my friend would make a perfect donor. What do you think?"

Needless to say, Waldo was dumbfounded and struggled to know how to respond.

"Well, this is a huge shock. I am very flattered, of course, but when you say that all you want me to do is father the child, that in itself is huge."

In his usual style, when cornered, he turned to humour.

"Have you thought that, at my age, my sperm may not be quite as vigorous as they were? This, of course, would mean that we would have the onerous task of having to make love many, many times and for many, many months before success would be realised, if at all; just think, all that effort and it may be in vain."

"I think I could live with that, if you could."

"That was not the answer I was looking for. Let me ask first, why you don't find yourself a partner? Have you tried internet dating? One or two of my friends have found really good relationships that way."

"For the past twelve months, I have tried every known method of catching a fellah. I have met one or two OK blokes but none I wanted to spend the rest of my life with or, indeed, did they want to spend the rest of their lives with me. There was one close call but, in the end, we decided it just wasn't going to work. It would have been a relationship stuck together by the glue of two very needy people and, try as I might, I could not fancy or love him enough. The rest, to be honest, were just selfish shits."

Waldo sympathised. "Jac keeps encouraging me to find someone. I am having a good relationship with Polly, but I can't really see us getting it together long term. Also, nowadays, I enjoy my independence and my ways of doing things, far too much to sacrifice them, for what, sex and company and a fuller social life. The truth is I am no longer looking for a partner.

"So, I do understand your position on that score. As you know, by asking the question, I was really just buying time, whilst I thought through the consequences of your proposition. I am asking myself, can I just father a child with you? Am I likely to find that I am unable to divorce myself from my feelings for you and the child and from wanting to play a more profound role in your lives? You are someone whom I greatly admire, respect, and find hugely attractive. Obviously, I am not in your league in respect of looks but, as Margaret would say, 'I brush-up-well' on a good day. Wouldn't it be better if you asked someone you didn't know quite as well? Someone you were not associated with day to day, perhaps, someone at the university? If my memory serves me well, they are always up for a good shag."

"Waldo, I have been weighing up what to do for the past three months. Believe you me, I have considered all the options. But I couldn't bear the thought of my child having a father whom I did not know well. I have decided that I would rather not have a child than put it through the indignity of having a father who is no more than a passing sperm."

"Nice image," Waldo commented.

They suddenly realised that during this conversation, their signing hands had interlocked and they were holding on tightly to each other, as though saving themselves from sliding into an abyss.

"Let me sleep on it, Carol. It has come as a huge shock and I need to reflect on what it means to me, to us and, of course, to the baby. It would be a great honour but one that maybe I am not up to fulfilling."

With that, they hugged and they went to bed without saying another word.

$$\pi$$

A full English breakfast set them up for the morning's walk. By eight o'clock they were on their way, ascending to the top of the Mendips once more. It was cloudier than the previous day but still fine. It was ideal for walking, and they made good progress. Not a word was mentioned of the previous evening's discussion. It was typically British, almost as though nothing had happened between them. In truth, they both knew the right moment would come and there was no rush. They had to get this right.

The B & B had prepared a sandwich lunch for them and by half eleven they were both starving. On principle, however, which principle they couldn't determine, they decided to suffer until at least twelve noon. Noon coincided with a particularly unsuitable bit of land for a picnic, so they carried on for another quarter of an hour, when they were only a mile short of Crook Peak; an ideal spot with magnificent views.

Carol took charge of unpacking the lunch and spreading out the goodies, whilst Waldo planned the next bit of the route. He knew this was going to be the tricky bit, as there were several different routes they could take. He decided on the one that avoided most of the traffic and went alongside the river.

Carol had spread the lunch to make it look like a feast and they both tucked in with enthusiasm.

"The problem is, Carol, that I think I would find the experience of bringing a child into the world terribly irksome. Despite my better judgement, I seem to burden myself with responsibilities."

"You do the same at work to some extent," she added. "I believe I may suffer from the same complaint. Is it catching?"

"It's probably a STD, a sexually transmitted disease," Waldo spelled out in full, in case Carol was not aware of its meaning.

"I know what a STD is, silly."

She thought that sometimes he was a bit like a schoolteacher.

"No, it can't be a STD, I haven't had sex with anyone for so long, I can't remember when. Oh, yes, I can. It wasn't too bad either. He was a prick, but he knew how to make love. Sorry, I distracted you from your point."

"Yes, the enormous responsibility of bringing up children. You know that line in the Anglican creed, which says, 'the burden of these sins is intolerable,' or, at least, it used to. They have probably found less challenging wording by now. We need a parent's creed that spells out the truth for those thinking about bringing little ones into this world – 'the burden of childrearing is intolerable.'"

"I know what you mean but I don't feel quite as burdened by the prospect as you. I would certainly take it seriously and would feel a heavy weight of responsibility. But I know that I would enjoy it."

"Your proposition provoked me into re-examining what I am doing and how I am shaping my life. It looks as though I have decided to stay single and to bury myself in my work and my favourite cultural and leisure pursuits."

He seemed to be building to making a formal pronouncement.

"But your proposition left me asking myself the question, 'Is what I do now, what I want out of life?' 'Is it enough?' 'Am I just being cowardly?' You have presented me with the chance to change tack, not a complete change, for once again, I am being offered the opportunity to avoid responsibility. You have said, father me a child and then turn away and leave the rest to me. As a young man, I would have revelled in the idea. As an older man, however, the decision is not as straightforward. Do I have the strength or the desire to be released from the sense of responsibility which seems to keep me together as a person? I don't know the answer to this."

Carol responded immediately and with strength.

"I too have been reflecting on last night's conversation. For me, last evening's discussion was a wonderful experience, for a reason that would not have occurred to you, I am sure. Apart from conversations with other deaf people and professionals working in the field, this was the first time in my life that I have had a serious conversation with a hearing person, who used my first language, signing. Did you notice that, for the most part, we spoke by signing to one another? When I first joined, you went out of your way to learn lip-reading and signing without my asking and without an ulterior motive. In the early days, because I was aware that you knew of my behaviour with Ian, I thought you may just have been after sex and that sooner or later you would make a pass. But this never happened and there has never been the slightest hint that it may; I am so grateful. My life has been peppered with men trying to take advantage of me but with no serious intention of a relationship. You will never know how bad it is for women who are vulnerable.

"You say that I am stunningly beautiful, I suspect that you may be somewhat biased. Even if I am as beautiful as you say, I have a moderate to severe hearing problem and many people find this disability hard to handle. My voice is also very unpleasant to most hearing people, I understand. My beauty seems to dissipate for them once I open my mouth and they hear the harshness of the sounds I utter. I have had training to try and change the timbre and pitch of my voice, but I just cannot change it. I suspect that even if I had normal hearing, my voice would be awful.

"So, I suppose what I am saying is that, in many ways, we are equal or, at least, our strengths and weaknesses balance each other out, when you take everything into consideration. But, more importantly, we share so much. We have a similar philosophy of life. We are good and trusting people. Our intellectual and cultural interests are compatible, and we communicate so well."

"Is this an argument for us getting together or me fathering the child? It sounds more like the former?" Waldo asked, assertively.

"I had not envisaged us getting together. But I had hoped that once the baby was born, we would remain close friends, you would visit regularly, and the baby would know you were her father. I had not gone further than that. Would you prefer us to live together?"

"I wasn't saying that; it was just that your explanation conveyed that impression."

He broke off the discussion whilst he gathered his thoughts.

"I will be honest with you, Carol, it was my intention this morning to say, 'No, I don't think I could do it, nor do I think it would work'. The reason was going to be because of my feelings and vulnerabilities and not because of you or the baby. But you are convincing me that what you are proposing makes sense. Obviously, I will need more time to reflect. It isn't the fathering bit, I can't wait for that, it is the drawing back and leaving you and the baby to get on with things. I suppose what I find most convincing is what you have just said about us being close friends, and me visiting regularly, and the baby knowing I am the father. That is very powerful and gives me the space to accommodate and deal with my issues."

They agreed to leave their discussion there and, with that, they packed up their lunch things and set off for Weston.

π

A fortnight later, they were ready to tell Margaret and Jac. They had decided to use the Friday meeting to make the formal announcement. Naturally, Waldo wanted to tell Jac privately beforehand.

Waldo texted Jac on the night before the meeting and asked if he could come over; he had something important he wanted to tell her. Unfortunately, Jac was in the middle of a heavy discussion with her ex and did not want to be disturbed. Waldo then tried to get hold of Carol to explain but she was out with her girlfriend and not responding to her mobile.

By the next morning, Waldo was in a bit of a panic, not wanting the news to be revealed before he had chance to share it with Jac.

Unusually, Jac was late getting to the office, after a heavy evening on the wine and the emotions. They were already in the interview room, ready to start the meeting, when Jac strolled in; she was looking somewhat worse for wear. Waldo asked to see her, but she waved him away saying, 'Don't be silly, you can say anything you have to say to me in front of the others. His protestations were insufficient to convince her.

The first hour was devoted to the hacking problem and the fear that the hacker's inability to access their files might result in someone trying to break-in. Reluctantly, Jac went along with the others and agreed to the installation of cameras and better security and to ask Jem to install them.

Waldo looked more and more pale as the meeting progressed. When the business items were out of the way, he asked again if he could have a 'quick conflab' with Jac. Again, because she was suffering from a hangover and still reeling from the previous night's discussions, she brushed his concerns aside. Carol decided not to hesitate any longer and launched in.

"I have been trying to find a suitable partner for the past year but without success. I won't trouble you with the detail, except to say, most men are shits; please excuse my language, Margaret."

Carol judged that the others would have used the same language and didn't deserve an apology. Margaret looked disapprovingly at Carol but did not say a word.

"Despite this failure," Jac could tell that something very important was about to be said; it was going to be one of Carol's corkers. Because of Waldo's plea to speak with her, she jumped to the conclusion that the two of them were going out together. She felt rather numb and disoriented by the prospect and began to sober up rapidly. "… despite my failure to find a suitable partner, I would like to have a baby."

Carol glance towards Margaret, for some kind of hint from her that she was going to disapprove. Margaret was stoic and did not reveal anything. Carol pressed on.

"There are many different ways in which this can be achieved nowadays and, to be honest, I do not like the idea of an anonymous sperm donor and my child not knowing who the father is."

The penny suddenly dropped with Jac. 'Of course, Waldo, oh dear, why was I so insensitive this morning.' Going through her head was her apology to Waldo, 'Oh, why did I not listen to you, my darling man, I am so sorry'.

Margaret nodded her approval in response to Carol's point.

"To cut a long story short, Waldo has agreed to be the father. We will not live together but we will be close friends and he will visit us regularly. The child will know he is the father and will call him daddy, or whatever Waldo and the child decide. Do you want to add anything, Waldo?"

"No, you explained that very well," he said with head bowed, trying to avoid Jac's eyes.

Margaret rose and kissed them both and said she thought it was wonderful news. She would have preferred them to marry or co-habit, but she realised that the world had moved on and things were different nowadays. Carol was hugely relieved.

Waldo was waiting for Jac's reaction. Jac was so happy for Carol and hugged and kissed her with great joy. She then turned to Waldo and kissed him.

"I love you so much and I think this is just right."

She then whispered in his ear.

"I am so pleased you managed to shrug off your desire to live with Carol. It must have been so difficult for you and I'm sure it wouldn't have been right. I am sorry I was so naughty this morning. I had no idea it was anything quite as significant. I was so insensitive. Please forgive me."

Then publicly, Jac announced, "Congratulations to you both."

This resulted in a spontaneous round of applause from everyone, including the mother and father-to-be, and there was much laughter and whooping.

CHAPTER 17

Carol, with Margaret's permission and Jem's foreknowledge, visited Jem in his attic lair. It was not the most savoury of rooms, for Jem usually kept the curtains closed to prevent light ruining his screen images. He had three computers and there were files and papers and books and gadgets everywhere. Carol thought the room clean but unkempt, a bit like the occupant.

She explained the nature of the problem and asked Jem if he would install cameras and an alarm system to try and prevent the office from being broken into and from confidential files being stolen.

Jem suggested that they use the cameras he had installed in the Woodry's house, as they wouldn't be needed anymore. Carol thought it a good idea and made a note to get permission from the police to remove the cameras.

Jem and Carol then searched the internet for value-for-money alarm systems and honed in on two possibilities. Jem thought the cheaper option good enough for the task and so Carol ordered it there and then.

Carol felt a little uncomfortable in Jem's presence but not in any way threatened; she certainly found keeping up a conversation hard going. She was about to thank him for his help and say her farewells, when Jem asked if he could do anything to help with the hacking. He volunteered to examine the computers and try and trace the source of the problem, but he would need access to the office computers, perhaps overnight, when they were not in use. Carol welcomed the suggestion but said she would have to clear it with the others.

Before she left, Jem asked about her deafness and whether or not she used sign language. Carol explained that her first language was signing, and that lip reading was a helpful part of the process. He nodded and said nothing more.

Carol was relieved to get back to the office and discuss matters with Jac. Jac thought it a good idea to involve Jem in the hacking business and said she would clear it with Waldo.

It took the police a few days before agreeing to the cameras being removed from the Woodry's house.

$$\pi$$

Waldo and Polly were having supper together at Waldo's place. He had excelled himself with a very fine clam starter, a main course of sweet mutton, and a chocolate pudding of huge delight. They were both feeling full to dolly's wax, to use one of Polly's favourite expressions, and, at some point during the evening, had clearly made a mutual decision, without discussion, to forgo sex and give full vent to their other appetites.

Waldo refreshed their glasses as they moved from the table into the sitting room. They sat side by side on the sofa and leaned into one another.

They sat silently, as they were both preoccupied with their own thoughts. Polly had been considering suggesting to Waldo that they moved their relationship on but did not want to run the risk of ruining what they had. Waldo was preparing to tell Polly about Carol and the baby.

Whilst Waldo was still hesitating, Polly decided to give it a go.

"Waldo, please don't get agitated with me, you may not like what I am going to say. You should understand that I am not sure that what I am going to say is a good idea."

"This sounds ominous, are you sure this is the right moment?" Waldo cautioned.

"No, I am not, but if it doesn't strike a chord, don't worry. We'll just dismiss the idea."

She took a long pause before making her proposal.

"I love you very much and I have been contemplating ways in which we may be able to take our relationship forward without compromising our beliefs and without ruining what we have, both of which are very precious to me."

"I have been doing the same but have failed to come up with anything," Waldo commented supportively.

"My suggestion is that we move into the same house. We have separate bedrooms, bathrooms, and studies and these would be our own private rooms and could not be violated by the other person without permission. We would physically share the kitchen/dining area, the sitting room, and the utility room. Hopefully we would have sufficient space for a guest bedroom. We would be free to shag in mutual territories or in our individual spaces with permission. We would look after our own finances but share the cost of running the house. There, what do you think?"

Waldo did not rush into a response. He had learnt, long ago, always to give a measured response when something life-changing was happening. He considered some of Karl Popper's criteria for problem solving; Karl being his favourite philosopher. Change things incrementally, which this did, for it built on what they had developed over the months. Show boldness of imagination in determining a solution, which this also did but it pushed their beliefs to the limit of acceptability. Apply emotional as well as intellectual investment in determining the solution, and he could not question that it must have taken a lot for Polly to suggest this. And then, of course, there is Karl's idea that, at no point, can one prove, beyond reasonable doubt, that a solution is true or, in this case, is the right solution. Only time would prove its veracity.

He took a deep breath and completely ignored his analysis.

"I think it is wonderful idea. I cannot imagine anything I would like more."

Polly was flabbergasted. She could not believe her ears. She sat forward on the sofa and looked at him to check that he wasn't teasing.

"You are serious, aren't you?" she checked.

"I am, indeed."

Waldo did not want to lose the opportunity to explain the issue that had been troubling him, so in his best, quiet, calm, doctor voice, he explained that Carol had asked if he would father her a child and that after much reflection, he had agreed.

To say that the revelation took the edge of the excitement of the earlier discussion would be an understatement, but Waldo realised he could not hide the issue any longer.

There followed a long and deep discussion, after which Polly accepted the idea but she was profoundly shocked, and Waldo knew that it would take her some time to come to terms with the idea. He was glad to have the house sharing to fall back on.

"Let's return to your idea. How do we do it, Polly? How do we progress our sharing? You must have given it some thought."

Polly wasn't sure she was ready to return to her topic but a lifetime of disappointments and fighting for her rights had made her able to cover up her hurt. She took a deep breath and managed it.

"Well, please do not think I assumed your agreement," she stated sharply, pointing out that Waldo had not discussed the issue of him becoming a father with her at all. He had just told her what he was going to do.

"That would be far from the truth. In fact, I assumed you would turn it down. But, on the remote chance that you would agree, I tested out the idea by looking over one of the big houses for sale in Greville Road. I think it would work perfectly. The house is in a bit of a bad way at the moment and would require a lot of work and money to restore it to a standard that we would both find acceptable and would give us the space we need. But it has many of the original Edwardian features and has huge potential. Would you like to see it?"

$$\pi$$

The next day, after they had made love and reassured one another of their commitment to each other, they inspected the house. They both fell in love with it. In broad principle, they agreed their respective areas; Waldo in the attic rooms, Polly on the first floor, the ground floor being common.

Polly confessed that she had quite a bit of money tucked away, which would enable them to bridge the selling of her house and Waldo's flat and the completion of the renovation work. Waldo confessed that he had quite a bit of money tucked away for, well he wasn't sure what for, but he was sure it would come in handy and help them achieve their objective. They were very excited.

Waldo was anxious to tell Jac. He didn't want her to think that he had been planning things without her knowing.

π

Two days after meeting Carol, Jem moved into the office, as soon as his mother and Carol had left for the evening. He was welcomed by Waldo and Jac, who, after ensuring that he had all that he wanted, withdrew upstairs. He only had to ring if he wanted drinks or a bite to eat or assistance, though the latter seemed highly unlikely from two such technological innocents.

Jem arrived with a bag in which he carried a number of electronic items, which neither Waldo nor Jac recognised as being of this world. He spent the next seven hours examining the files and working through the systems and taking things apart and putting them back together again. He did not make any notes or make any requests of upstairs.

At two o'clock in the morning, he rang to say he had finished and was leaving but there was no response. He closed the door after him, ensuring the mortise locks were secured, as Waldo had asked. No one would have known he had ever been there.

π

Jac heard nothing from Robert or Lucy and was worried about them. She tried phoning but to no avail. Then, after three weeks, Lucy texted and suggested that she and Jac had lunch together. They agreed to meet at the riverside cafe.

Jac was relieved when Lucy greeted her warmly; they gave each other a big hug.

They sat at the same table that Jac and Robert had occupied some two months earlier, but, unlike her previous visit, it was a wet and rather miserable day.

After ordering drinks and lunch, Lucy explained that she had moved back in with her father and was sleeping, once again, in her old room.

"It feels really good, Jac, I can't tell you how good it feels. I should never have left all those years ago. I should never have married and had a baby. These things were not for me. Don't get me wrong, Dad and I are not living as lovers, we are just father and daughter, living in the same space and thoroughly enjoying each other. We are so natural together; it is such a lovely feeling."

She broke off, as the drinks were being brought to table. Jac smiled a 'thank you' at the waitress, who seemed to understand that the conversation was intimate and confidential and placed the drinks down quietly and withdrew respectfully.

Lucy continued her story.

"We have been having our meetings, as you suggested, but we have stopped meeting daily and just get together twice a week, as we didn't appear to be making much progress. We still find the meetings helpful though."

Jac had not wanted to put pressure on them to reach a decision and, whilst Lucy and her father were still talking, there was always a chance that they would find a way between them. She thought the news that Lucy had moved back in with her father a very hopeful sign.

The serious business out of the way, they got on to other things and chatted and laughed as usual.

Jac explained about life on the barge and the strange guy who was her neighbour and how, though he was no trouble, he was very eccentric and practised yoga every morning at five, on the end of the walkway overlooking the main expanse of water.

"He probably thinks it's the Ganges," Lucy commented. "Thinking about it, the Ganges is probably a very similar colour."

Lucy then went on to explain how she had cleared the back garden of the worst of the weeds and had ordered stone and withies from the Somerset Levels, so that she could start her sculpture again.

"Sculpture, I never knew you were a sculptor," said Jac, very surprised.

"I abandoned it some years ago, but it is still in my blood. I found my old tools in the garden shed and have replaced some, as they were a bit worse for wear. I have been practising on a small off-cut of stone, but I have placed an order of sufficient size for me to do a full-sized piece. It arrives next Thursday. Oh, I can't wait, Jac." By way of an afterthought, she added, "The withies will have to wait till the new season's harvest."

The conversation continued in this fashion for several hours. Every now and then, they couldn't resist reaching out and holding each other's hands. Jac could see no harm in this. It was clear that they were becoming extremely fond of each other.

Jac encouraged Lucy to carry on the meetings with Robert and to let her know if there was anything she could do. She sent her love to Robert. The two women kissed and hugged each other firmly and said their goodbyes.

"Keep in touch, Lucy," Jac shouted, as they went their separate ways.

π

The police granted permission for the cameras to be removed from the Woodry's house and, within three days, they were installed in the office, together with a new alarm system. Carol reimbursed Mr

Woodfield's account accordingly.

Meanwhile, Jem had also been pursuing the matter of the hacker. He had been in touch with his fellow 'Angels' – an underground group of hackers across the UK, who work quietly for the good of society – and they had started to unravel something very suspicious.

Jem asked Carol if they could visit a site of particular interest to his investigation. He was unsure whether it was an industrial or domestic site, but it was on the outskirts of the City.

Carol decided to involve Waldo and Jac before taking matters further. It was agreed that Jac would take the lead on the case, though it wasn't a case in the usual sense, for they were both client and detective. They agreed that there was a possibility that it could get messy and, if they were not careful, they could stray into illegal territory; not that either of them understood what was or was not legal, in terms of IT.

Jac, Carol, and Jem set out to visit the site that Jem had identified as a possible source of the hacking. Jac had recently joined the City Car Club, in preparation for doing away with her old jalopy, and decided to use one of their cars, partly as Jem was a big lad and there was no way he could have sat comfortably in the back seat and partly because she did not want the vehicle to look out of place. She needn't have worried. It was an ordinary street, in a rundown area of the city.

The entrance to the site was situated between the end of a terrace of houses and a small car park belonging to a local shop. The entrance was undistinguished, except for two black metal gates, which were open. Inside the gates was a barrier, similar to the bar at a level crossing, and a small guard box with a security guard inside, who appeared to be reading a newspaper. The gates and the fencing between the houses and the shops were topped with barbed wire; on close examination it looked more like a prison camp then a commercial unit. A small sign on the upright of the gate indicated that the company was part of the 'Informatica Group'. Other than its name, however, it provided no further information.

There was clearly no way of entering the premises without revealing their identities. The two women turned in their seats and looked to Jem for advice as what to do. At that moment, a large silver van emerged from the site with a circular antenna on its roof.

"Follow that van," was the clear and forceful instruction from Jem. "But don't get too close."

Jem's voice was authoritative, and he clearly understood the importance of the sighting, which was more than could be said for the women. From here on Jem was definitely in charge.

The van drove to Avonmouth, the modern port of Bristol on the banks of the River Severn. The van stopped near the offices of a large chemical works. Jac pulled up some fifty metres behind the van and switched off the engine. Jem put his finger to his lips and signalled that they should not talk.

"It's a listening unit," he whispered. "They may well be planning to listen to a conversation inside the building. I don't want them to pick up our conversation and become suspicious."

The three sat patiently and waited. Jac passed round a bag of wine gums and told Carol to suck quietly.

After about fifteen minutes, a convoy of three, large, black limousines arrived and delivered seven besuited businessmen. There was no discussion or warm welcome. They were ushered into the building without ceremony.

For the next few hours, the temptation to speak and the tedium was almost too much for the women, so they walked down to Ellie's Cafe, a road-side van that sold every fry-up imaginable. They arrived back at the car with three bacon baps and three cups of tea. Jem reinforced the necessity for quiet.

At two thirty precisely, the seven black suits emerged, got into their black limousines, and left. At three o'clock precisely, the silver van drew away and they followed it back to the 'Informatica' site.

Jem asked if they could stay a little longer to see the people leave at the end of the working day, as that would give them a better idea as to what was going on inside. Jac and Carol agreed that it was a good idea.

From four thirty, for about an hour, a steady stream of people left the complex. They counted fifty staff in all; this was not a small enterprise. For the most part they were casually dressed and many, perhaps half, were cyclists. Jem announced that most of them were techies; the women concluded that it took one to know one.

Jem agreed to do some more research and then write up his findings so that Carol could make a presentation at the following Friday's meeting. Jem agreed to attend.

$$\pi$$

It was Jem's first team meeting and he sat beside Carol with his head bowed. Jac was chairing the meeting and welcomed everyone but did not make any special announcement about Jem, lest it cause him anxiety. After a few general matters of business, Carol was asked to present their findings in relation to the hacking. For the next thirty minutes, Waldo and Margaret sat in silent disbelief at what Jem and Carol had achieved. Jac knew most of what they had uncovered but not all.

Carol began by giving an everyman's guide to the world of

hacking, which Jem had explained to her.

"Jem is one of ten people across the UK who belong to a group known as The Angels. They hack but only with a view to stopping corruption and preventing criminal activity; they are the goodies. There are other groups, like Jem's, who specialise in particular areas, such as banking, who are known as The Specs, the specialists. There are many other groups that are less philanthropic, however, most notable among them are The Devils, who hack with the specific intention of disrupting national and international systems, like power stations, and who generally set out to cause havoc in society. They have little to do with individual punters, this is left to smaller fry in the hacking chain. Obviously, The Angels and The Devils are sworn enemies. You must understand, we are talking electronic enemies here. None of the Angels have ever met nor have they met any of the Devils, that is how the cyber world works. Then there are the Pros, who hack for money and the Ams, who do it for sheer pleasure. These often work alone and generally target individuals but, as we shall see, some Pros are employees of companies and work in hacking teams."

Carol turned to Jem to make sure that she hadn't said anything untoward. He nodded his approval and then he launched into a stream of signing, which left Waldo struggling to follow and caught Carol unawares; she had no idea he had learnt to sign. Carol signed in response and thanked him but said she thought that any further detail would only leave the team struggling to understand. Jem, with a puzzled look on his face, shrugged his shoulders. Waldo was able to follow Carol's signing, but Jem's was far too fast.

"Jac, Jem, and I visited a site on the outskirts of Bristol, which Jem had identified as a possible source of our hacking problem."

Carol then told them the story of the fortified business unit, the pursuit of the 'listening' van and its trip to Avonmouth, the seven dark suits and the return to the factory and their observation of staff leaving the premises; she omitted to tell them of the bacon baps and tea.

"Since then, Jem has been beavering away with his fellow Angels. They have discovered that all the major cities in the UK have an 'Informatica' site, where security is at a premium. Fortunately, the Manchester Angel has a friendly Pro, who works in one of the centres. He works at a fairly low level and, therefore, is not aware of all the innermost goings-on. What he has managed to discern, however, is that the workforce is composed of teams which uncover information which is then sold on to other organisations. In Manchester there are sound technicians, who listen in to conversations through the listening van. There are photographers and cameramen. There is an IT research team, of which our Manchester friend is a part, which hacks organisations and celebrities looking for 'juicy nuggets', and perhaps that's what they were hoping to get from us. There are plants, people that is, not horticultural specimens, who operate in large corporations, local government, and presumably in UK Government offices as well, who gather intelligence and hard evidence, wherever possible, and who knows what else."

Carol turned once more to Jem to see if she was still on course. He nodded.

"The Angels decided to track the information from the meeting in Avonmouth in the hope of piecing together its progress down the information chain. What they found was that the meeting was about fixing the price of fuel at the pumps for the next three months. The Angels were anxious not to be detected and, therefore, could not go too deeply into the systems and hence are not certain that what they have found is accurate. They give their results a confidence level of about 70%.

"In order to increase their level of confidence, they then traced other likely juicy stories from their own areas. Whatever the source, all information seemed to flow into a central hub in Oxford. The problem was that everything came to a halt at that point. There was no further transmission of information to other sources. This was hugely puzzling to the Angels, and they did not know how to proceed.

Jac very kindly agreed to take us to Oxford, so that we could see matters for ourselves."

Waldo cast a critical glance at Jac, who pretended not to notice.

"We discovered a similar set-up to Bristol 'Informatica': entrance gates topped with barbed wire; a guard in the guard box; an inner white vehicle barrier; and cameras scanning every inch of the property; impenetrable. 'Informatica' was next door to a seventy's office block of a particularly undistinguished nature. Its brass plate announced that it was the 'Oxford Distribution Centre', so we assumed it was to do with food distribution to supermarkets or something of that ilk.

"We decided that the only way we could get a better look at 'Informatica' was to ask permission to go into the university block, which backed on to the 'Informatica' building. Jac rang the bursar's office and asked permission for her and her friends to take a sentimental journey round the old block. The bursar agreed and arranged with the front office to give us passes.

"When we got to the third floor of the university block, it was possible to map out the buildings and, to our surprise, there was a link corridor between 'Informatica' and next door, with a great deal of human traffic passing between the two buildings. We decided it would be unwise to stand and stare too long at this phenomenon, in case we were seen. Jem took a few photographs and we left hurriedly."

Jem passed the photographs around for everyone to see but made no comment.

"Following this visit, the Angels concentrated their efforts on the 'Oxford Distribution Centre' and unearthed a huge flow of information to all major newspapers and magazines in the UK and across the pond. A well-known broadsheet published the story of price fixing at the pumps within a few days of our observations in Avonmouth.

"Since then, we have been trying to trace the owners of 'Informatica' and the 'Oxford Distribution Centre' but neither is listed on the stock exchange. They appear to be in private ownership and registered offshore. At this time, we have no idea who owns the organisations."

Carol, having finished her statement, looked towards Jem and thought she detected a slight smile but perhaps not.

Waldo gave a huge sigh as an opener to his comments.

"Good God," was all he managed, initially, and then he decided to check what they were implying through their statement.

"Are you saying that there is an organisation which has been set up to uncover intelligence, using both legal and illegal means, which feeds the media of this and other countries?"

Carol replied with a single word, "Yes."

"Are you of the opinion that this enables the press and other media to work within the law, and avoid accusations of illegal operation and intrusions of privacy?"

Carol repeated the word, "Yes."

Much to Margaret's disgust, Waldo resorted to a favourite combination of male expletives favoured in these circumstances.

They all sat in silence.

Jac explained that, in discussion with Carol and Jem, she had weighed the advantages and disadvantages of The PI Shop going public on the hacking issue and spelled out the implications for the team's consideration. She concluded by saying that all three of them considered the advantages of going public far outweighed the disadvantages.

Jac then proposed that the 'Informatica' report should be carefully edited to ensure its anonymity, in terms of The PI Shop and the Angels, so as to avoid prosecution and any comeback from the 'Informatica Group'. She then suggested that hard copies, not electronic ones, be sent to the local Chief Constable, the local MP, the Chief Executive of the local Council, the BBC, ITV, Channel 4, and the Chair of the Press Complaints Committee, despite its reputation for inaction; she believed that hard copies would be more difficult to trace than electronic ones. She recommended that the names of all recipients should be enclosed with the copies, so as organisations could see the breadth of the circulation and hence reduce the likelihood of a cover-up. She had thought of enclosing a letter explaining what would happen if no action was taken, but thought it was better left unsaid, in order to keep the recipients guessing. There was unanimous support for Jac's proposal.

There followed a brief discussion about how to make the tracing of the documents more difficult. Everyone bowed to Jem's suggestions of using paper and envelopes from a different source from the office's normal stocks, paid for in cash, gloves worn throughout the production and posting process, for the documents to be weighed and the correct stamps added, without using a post office and for them to be posted in a central Bristol Post Office. This was Jem's first spoken contribution, and everyone was very pleased to see that he was becoming a fully participating member of the team. Margaret, however, was shocked at her son's insight into the criminal mind.

CHAPTER 18

Lucy's silence was broken by a simple text message. 'Robert and I look forward to seeing Jac and Waldo for afternoon tea on Wednesday 6th January, if that is convenient to you both. Lots of love, Lucy xx'.

By text, Jac tried to persuade Lucy to tell her more about the purpose of the meeting, but she would say nothing.

Jac and Waldo discussed what afternoon tea might bring, in addition to some very fine scones, strawberry jam and Cornish clotted cream. Jac suggested that they may have reached an understanding and they might want to share that with them, but it seemed unlikely, given Lucy's report some weeks earlier. So, after identifying the various scenarios, so as to avoid being caught unawares, Jac agreed to put the finishing touches to the report and send one posh copy in the post to Robert and take another with her on the big day. She also prepared notes, in case she was called on to make a brief, informal presentation.

They both felt rather unsure of themselves. It had gone on a long time, and they had rather lost control of things.

π

Waldo and Lucy took the scenic route to Robert's house, so that they could gather their thoughts and prepare themselves mentally. When they reached the street in which Robert and Lucy lived, it brought back memories of the early morning raid and Robert's reaction when

THE PI SHOP: OPEN FOR BUSINESS

Jac had knocked on the door all those months ago.

Lucy was standing on the doorstep waving to them. She had clearly been looking out for them. She appeared rather anxious.

She hugged and kissed them both.

"Well, here goes," she said. "What is he going to reveal? I have no more idea than you. Fingers crossed."

She led them into the kitchen, where the table was already laid for tea and a plate of scones had been placed in the middle, some fruit, and some cheese. Pots of strawberry jam and clotted cream and a butter dish finished off the offerings.

"This is what daddy asked me to prepare. I hope you two have good appetites."

At this moment, Robert entered the kitchen and gave Jac a kiss on the cheek and shook Waldo's hand warmly. Jac thought he was looking a bit better, though his shoulders and neck were still bowed; it happens to some tall men as they get older, she thought.

Underneath her arm, Jac had tucked her posh copy of the report and inside the cover had placed a copy of her notes, in case she was invited to provide a summary.

Underneath Robert's arm was a transparent, pink folder, which contained a few sheets of paper with his hand-written notes. He had planned what he was going to say very carefully.

"Let's enjoy a scone and tea before we get down to business. I like to have one fruit scone with jam and cream, followed by one cheese scone with butter. Waldo, coming from Devon, you might prefer to have butter with your fruit scone as well, am I right about that?" Robert asked.

"You are, indeed, Robert. I am not sure how widespread the

tradition is but, as children, we would spread the butter on the fruit scone first, then the strawberry jam, and only after that, add the clotted cream. It was a careful balancing act to get it into the mouth without spillages."

The women expressed alarm at the cholesterol damage they must have done to themselves.

It all helped break the ice and everyone started to relax. Robert seemed to be in fine form and was even enjoying himself. Lucy remained on edge. She clearly had no idea what he was going to say.

Robert suggested they remain in the kitchen to make it a little less formal and so that they could help themselves to tea. It also gave him the opportunity to sit close to his darling girl.

He could see that everyone was looking rather anxious, but he quite liked that, and he knew that what he had to say would be welcomed by everyone, or he thought it would. He was in confident mood.

"OK, shall we get started? Firstly, I would like to thank you, Jac, and you, Waldo, of course, for the report. I have read it very carefully and it is an exceptional piece of work, both in terms of its detail, its accuracy, and in providing a clear foundation on which the police and lawyers could develop their cases. It is just what I asked for; indeed, it exceeds my expectations by a large measure. Thank you both.

"Alas, having done all this work and produced such a fine document, I am going to ask you to destroy it and to destroy any associated computer records that you hold and which are likely to lead to its discovery, long after my death. I would be grateful if you would take all the hard copies that you have produced and shred them immediately, including our copies. I don't know what other records you have but please destroy them immediately, following this meeting.

Does anyone have a problem with what I have just said?"

He waited a few moments, but everyone was taken aback by his sudden change of heart and the strength of his statement.

"Good. I am very glad about that and somewhat relieved. You will have surmised from this that I have come to the conclusion that, by revealing all, the impact on Lucy and the rest of the family would be too great."

Suddenly, Lucy started to hug and kiss him. She then held his arm in both of hers and pressed herself against him. He loved her being that close and he could feel her breasts pressing into his arm. He thought her breasts still felt as firm as when she was a young girl. He turned and looked into her eyes. He loved her so. He knew he must return quickly to his script otherwise Jac and Waldo would realise what was going through his mind.

"What you advised, Jac, in terms of Lucy and I meeting in silence worked like a dream. I believe you said it was akin to how Quakers resolve their issues. Well, all I can say is it is no wonder they are such a peace-loving sect. Thank you for advising us to adopt the approach, it was an inspired thought.

"When we came together in that first meeting, I had no intention of changing my mind. I was absolutely convinced that I was right and Lucy was wrong. Over time, and in a quiet atmosphere, and feeling and hearing Lucy's hurt and despair, I gradually came to understand that my approach was selfish. I was just interested in putting matters right for me, regardless of the consequences for others. The longer we sat in silence and contemplated issues and shared the occasional thought, the more my understanding evolved and, it seemed to me, the more our thoughts coalesced."

Robert paused to gather his thoughts for the next revelation.

"I find what I am going to say now quite disturbing, so please excuse me if I do not express myself well.

"During our sessions together, slowly, inexorably, I began to lose the sense of shame that had haunted me over the years or, at least, it began to lessen. Slowly but surely the hollow where my shame had nestled and squirmed so painfully, was being filled by my overwhelming love for Lucy, the same love I had felt all those years ago and which I had denied myself.

"Then I began to realise that when I had asked Lucy to leave home and encouraged her to marry, I had been wrong. I left us both bereaved. I cannot be sure how much of this is rationalisation to ameliorate my feelings of guilt and how much is a true reflection of my feelings and beliefs. The whole thing has become too confused for me to unravel. What I can be sure of is that I love Lucy now, even more than I did in those early days, and my love is beyond comparison with anything else I have experienced in my life.

"That is not to say that I believe we should make love now. I find it rather repulsive to think of an old, misshapen body like mine making love to a body as lithe and beautiful as my darling Lucy's."

Turning to Lucy, he addressed her directly.

"I suppose what I am saying is that I would like to live out the rest of my days, without sounding too morbid about it, with you, my darling, but, of course, this should not inhibit you from enjoying relationships at any time with whomsoever you wish. But I hope you will continue to live with me and to love me, as you have been doing these past few weeks."

He took a deep breath and announced, "And that, ladies and gentlemen, is the case for the defence. Shall we have some fresh tea and some more of Lucy's delicious cheese scones, whilst you consider what I have said?"

Everyone sat quite still, quietly reflecting. They found it difficult to react. So, Robert decided to set the visitors a challenge.

"I cannot quite believe that you two accept what I say without a word of disagreement. How can you support an old man who has abused his daughter? You are ethical and moral people, surely you cannot condone what I did. I appreciate that, had I abused other children or, if Lucy had not expressed the views she has, you would have been obliged to inform the police. But the simple truth is that I did abuse her, and it must have had a detrimental effect on her well-being."

Jac responded.

"Given that the abuse was confined to one person, namely Lucy, we have based our judgement on the views that she has expressed. She did not view it as abuse, when she was a minor or later as a young adult or, indeed, today, so many years later. You both seem to see yourselves as the victims of an overwhelming love. We cannot, of course, condone what you did, Robert, but we understand."

Robert smiled and shook his head in disbelief.

"Well, I thought you would struggle with it and argue that you had no alternative but to report the matter to the police."

Gaining in confidence, he asked if anyone wanted more tea and then thought better of it.

"This calls for a celebration. Let's open a bottle of fizz? I have a really nice champagne, which I'm sure we'd enjoy.

Lucy fetched and opened the champagne.

"Let's toast a successful outcome to your investigations and to Lucy and I getting back together," Robert announced with joy in his voice.

Everyone raised their glasses and drank to success.

$$\pi$$

The next morning, Lucy made breakfast and waited in the kitchen for her father to appear. She knew that he would come down at eight-thirty, precisely, as he had done for many years. By eight-forty she was becoming concerned. She poured him a cup of tea, before it became stewed, and took it up to his room. The door was closed. She knocked, politely. There was no answer. She opened the door quietly and called out, "Daddy, are you awake?" There was no answer. She put the tea on the sideboard and went over to the window and drew back the curtains. Even the light did not disturb him. She crept over to the bed. Robert was lying on his back with his mouth wide open. He made no noise, and he did not move. He had clearly been dead for some time. She sank to her knees and said a prayer, her elbows resting on the bed. She rose and kissed him on the cheek. Her tears fell upon his face.

CHAPTER 19

Margaret, Waldo, and Jac attended Robert's funeral together. Lucy was with her sisters and their families in the main funeral cortège. Naturally, Lucy was very upset but the grandchildren helped keep her together

The service was held in St Mary Redcliffe. According to Queen Elizabeth I, it was 'the fairest church in all the land'. Despite the grand surroundings, the service was short and modest. The mourners then made their way to the Victorian cemetery at Arnos Vale, where Robert Harmsworth's remains were interred.

The mourners took a stroll around the grounds and chatted quietly in small groups. After a suitable interval, Lucy gave the signal and everyone went back to Robert's house, where she had prepared tea and nibbles, including a selection of some of Robert's favourite scones.

Most people opted for tea but the more adventurous accepted a glass of something stronger. It was almost a jolly time with the children rushing in and out of the garden and people exchanging stories about Robert and his eccentric ways.

Both sisters asked if Lucy would like to go back and stay with them, but she said she was fine and would rather be alone. After a suitable interval, the sisters and other family and friends left. Only Lucy, Jac, Waldo, and Margaret remained.

Jac seized her moment and asked Lucy to come back with her to the barge. Without hesitation she agreed.

"Oh yes please Jac, just for a few nights, until I decide what to do next. It has all happened so suddenly, I haven't had time to think."

Waldo and Margaret volunteered to tidy up everything and told the other two to carry on; they would lock up.

CHAPTER 20

Jac and Lucy had finished supper and were doing the washing up. Jac could see that Lucy wanted to say something but was struggling to find the words. She decided to ask if she had reached any conclusions about her future.

"Oh dear," exclaimed Lucy, "have I outstayed my welcome?"

"Of course not, you idiot, you can stay as long as you like, you know that."

And, with wet hands, Jac held Lucy's face and kissed her lovingly.

Lucy summoned up her courage.

"You are right, of course. I think I am ready to move on and I think I have decided what I want to do. It's just that I feel safe here with you."

There was a short break as she gathered her thoughts. She hadn't really said out loud to herself what she was thinking, so she was looking forward to hearing what might emerge.

"I want to sell daddy's house, with Audrey's and Linda's agreement, of course, and then move to Frome. I like it there and it's become a centre for the arts, perhaps crafts might be more accurate. You see, I want to take up sculpture as a career. I think I'm pretty good at it, even if I say so myself, and I also find it very therapeutic. I will try and make a living at it by placing my pieces in the local galleries. I would also like to get my boy back but, if not, he could come and stay at weekends or whenever suits him.

"There, I have said it. Yes, that is what I think. Would you help me, Jac? Can I stay one more night, so that I can start to put things in place?"

Jac gave her a big hug and a big kiss and suggested they went to the local to celebrate.

Lucy stayed another week.

π

Waldo was in his sitting room supping a glass of red wine. He was glad to be alone and in the quiet. The room was lit only by a small lamp in the corner; the room's gloominess reflected his own.

For the first time, he was wearing Robert's old slippers. Lucy had offered them to him, and he hadn't liked to refuse. He thought that they were very comfortable and rather fetching; it was a pity about the stain.

He had convinced himself that he was trying to make a decision but, in reality, he had skipped the decision and was already wrestling with the knotty problem of how to tell Polly. He set down his glass slowly and quietly on the table beside him and placed his wine guard over it.

The guard consisted of a square of silk, weighted on the edges by sequins and tiny baubles of every hue – a delicate and colourful version of an Australian cork hat. Its task was to protect the wine from attack by wine flies. Harriet had given him the guard some time ago, following one of their riotous drinking sessions. Despite her inebriation, Harriet couldn't help noticing the vigorous way in which Waldo defended his wine from attack by the fly, punching the air in taekwondo fashion, in an attempt to snatch the fly before it alighted on his glass, or worse, touched his precious wine. Jac had become so used to the flashing arm that she didn't see it anymore and just instinctively ducked when it shot in her direction.

Looking at the wine guard, Waldo smiled to himself and rose from his chair to read once again the card that had come with the gift. He had framed it and put it on the mantelpiece.

'Danger: Wine Flies

Small, silent, deadly – one touch, and your wine is vinegar – the wine fly.

Who has not felt the menace of the wine fly? Our only protection until today has been the lightning reaction of our bare hands, but even the greatest vigilance must sometimes relax. Until now. We are proud to bring you the No-fly Fine-Mesh Wine Guard, the ONLY protection against this age-old enemy (especially effective against the virulent Bristol strain of this global pest).

At last you can relax! Open the bottle and sup with peace of mind!

All you need to enjoy maximum protection is simply to place the No-fly Fine-Mesh Wine Guard over your filled glass. Ensure no gaps exist, and remove and drink, replacing immediately after each sip.

WARNING: Some customers have been tempted to cut a small hole in their No-fly Fine-Mesh Wine Guard, in order to insert a straw and so avoid the constant on-off motion of the protective mechanism. DON'T! The latest research shows that wine flies have trained themselves to fly down the straw to gain access to your vintage. Remember, that used properly and carefully, the No-fly Fine-Mesh Wine Guard will ensure many years of safe enjoyment of your wine. (Hand wash. Dry flat.)'

It cheered him hugely.

Somehow, it convinced him that the deed should be accomplished without further ado. He took another sip of his wine and carefully replaced the wine guard; an act accomplished with the delicacy of a priest replacing a paten on a chalice of consecrated wine.

He put on his coat and walked slowly to Polly's house. He knocked on the door. Polly opened it to find her friend on the doorstep looking exceedingly grave.

"I am sorry, Polly, but I cannot go through with our idea. I am very sorry," Waldo announced slowly and solemnly.

Polly did not show any reaction. Her emotions missed out temper and went directly to numbness. She shut the door quietly without saying a word.

Oh, how he had soured matters. He thought of himself as a wine fly.

Back home, he slumped into the chair and felt truly dispirited. He sipped his wine and quietly shed a tear. He wanted his relationship with Polly to continue but he just did not want to live with her. He was not optimistic.

His phone rang and he decided not to answer it, but he couldn't resist looking at who had the impertinence to ring when he was feeling so distraught. It was his beloved Jac. Despite his resolve, he answered it. Before he could say anything, Jac blurted out, "Fancy a drink? Lucy has moved to Frome and I'm feeling a bit low."

"We must be telepathic. I have just told Polly that I can't go through with our plan. Do you want me to come down to the open seas or would you prefer to come up here?" Waldo asked.

"I am outside your front door, but I didn't like to disturb you. I can't see a light on."

They gave each other a very long and special hug. No words, just a hug.

It was some time before Waldo ventured a few words.

"If I can't get it together with Polly, then I will never be able to get it together with anyone, that is quite clear to me. I love her and she is a very fine person, whom I admire immensely. But the thought of moving in with her and sharing our lives together, even with our own spaces, is one step too far. It is not what I want. Perhaps the only person I could ever spend my life with is you and we both know that that wouldn't work, for obvious reasons."

"I feel the same way about Lucy. I have never liked and loved someone quite as much as I do Lucy. But the idea of spending the rest of our lives together, no, no, no way. Oh, how selfish that sounds and I suppose it is, but I don't think I want to share my life with anyone, at least, not yet. You, of course, may be an exception to that, because we don't encroach on each other and we don't consider each other as potential sexual partners."

"I have been thinking about that," he said mischievously, brightening a little.

She smiled and changed the subject.

"How's Carol? She looks stunning at the moment. Do you wish you were still lovers?" Jac enquired.

"We were never lovers, Jac. It was all rather clinical and business-like and didn't last many weeks. There was little or no foreplay, well, just sufficient to get things moving and matters were brought to a swift conclusion, without much ado. She was much more mature and considered about everything than I could ever have been. I think she is very special. She will be off for six months, of course, but will then want to come back, if all is well. We'll need to think about how we cover her maternity leave."

As usual, Jac had already thought matters through and had a plan.

"Harriet is going to start training as a Maths teacher from next September. She has asked if she could cover Carol's maternity leave. Now, I realise that there may be tensions between Margaret and Harriet, but it would be a temporary measure. We know we can trust her, at least in respect of business matters, and I'm sure Margaret would love to have the opportunity of reforming Harriet. What do you think?"

"I think it is an excellent idea but let's raise it at next Friday's meeting and see what reaction we get from Margaret. Any news on the Informatica front?" Waldo asked.

"Well, it is still headline news on the tele and Channel 4 is having a field day. It's just wonderful. And the good news is that they haven't managed to trace it back to us. Jem, of course, closed down The Angels before the report went out, so that they would not be implicated. So far, we all seem to have escaped, which is more than can be said for Informatica and the price fixers."

They then turned their attention back on to their own lives. Waldo began.

"I have been thinking that I would like to sell the flat, not the office, of course, and I would like to rent somewhere. I want the freedom of not owning and preferably not doing very much domestically. I thought I might rent one of those serviced apartments in town."

"A bit soulless but I see where you're coming from," Jac muttered.

Waldo then played an important card.

"I would like to make short films, or film shorts, as they seem to call them nowadays. Why change the words around, Jac? Do you understand why they do that? I don't want it to interfere with our business, but I have a real hankering to become a film director."

Jac nodded wisely. She had been wondering whether to say anything about her ambition and Waldo's confession gave her the opening she needed.

"Waldo, I do not want you to misinterpret what I am going to say now, for I am still committed to our venture."

Oh, here we go, Waldo thought. She is beginning to suffer from our old illness, 'early onset boredom', for which there is no known cure. He thought she might have interpreted his film director proposal in that light but probably waived it pending her own revelation.

"I would like to go back to seeing clients again, just for one day a week, as long as you don't think it would affect the business."

She looked anxiously at him, in an attempt to judge his reaction.

He lifted his head very slowly, mainly for dramatic effect.

"Good," he said, "I'm surprised you haven't suggested it before. I think you need that in your mix of work, just as I need to develop as a film director. It is the way we are. It is about having the right mix and the right degree of ambiguity in our lives. I think it is really good."

Jac rose from her chair and, leaning over him, kissed him. They smiled lovingly at each other. Tired and a little drunk, they went to their beds.

They had no inkling where life or work would take them next.

ABOUT THE AUTHOR

Isaac French spent his early career in education and training before moving into senior roles in public service, mostly the NHS. He very much enjoyed his work but was pleased to retire; in fact, he made a habit of it and retired on three occasions but only managed two retirement parties.

Upon retirement, he tried four activities.

Mathematics – He never managed to recapture the excitement and joy that mathematics had given him in his younger days.

Saxophone – Not a talented saxophonist. His embouchure was weak.

Sculpture – He enjoyed sculpture, but he did not love it.

Writing – He soon realized he was a natural storyteller, but it wasn't until his close friend Vicky wrote to say that she was bored with her job and could they become private investigators that his imagination was liberated and the Waldo Wise series was born.

The first two books in the series centre on The PI Shop in Bristol and Waldo's and Jac's experience as private investigators. The third is a set of short stories based on the characters from Books 1 and 2 and include the PI Shop team and some of their clients. Jean Pierre, from the gay massage parlour, features in the first short story. In the second part of the series, Waldo accidently becomes a spy, working for, well he isn't sure, but for the sake of simplicity, he settles on MI6. The stories take place in Nice and Monte Carlo in the South of France, Alonissos in the Sporades, Greece, and Book 6, which is nearing completion, in Paris and northern France.

Isaac French spent most of his working years in Bristol and Bath, in the Southwest of England, but upon retirement relocated to Cornwall with his wife, Liz, and their whippet, Cassius. He is what is known locally as a 'West Country Boy'. Writing remains his chief occupation, but walking, croquet, and beekeeping are important parts of his life.

Printed in Great Britain
by Amazon